TIGER

WILLIAM RICHTER

An Imprint of Penguin Group (USA) Inc.

Tiger: A Dark Eyes Novel

RAZORBILL

Published by the Penguin Group
Penguin Group (USA) Inc., 375 Hudson Street, New York, New York 10014, USA
Penguin Group (Canada), 90 Eglinton Avenue East, Suite 700, Toronto, Ontario M4P 2Y3, Canada (a division of Pearson Penguin Canada Inc.)
Penguin Books Ltd, 80 Strand, London WC2R 0RL, England
Penguin Ireland, 25 St Stephen's Green, Dublin 2, Ireland (a division of Penguin Books Ltd)
Penguin Group (Australia), 707 Collins St., Melbourne, Victoria 3008, Australia (a division of Pearson Australia Group Pty Ltd)
Penguin Books India Pvt Ltd, 11 Community Centre, Panchsheel Park, New Delhi–110 017, India
Penguin Group (NZ), 67 Apollo Drive, Rosedale, Auckland 0632, New Zealand (a division of Pearson New Zealand Ltd)
Penguin Books, Rosebank Office Park, 181 Jan Smuts Avenue, Parktown North 2193, South Africa
Penguin China, B7 Jaiming Center, 27 East Third Ring Road North, Chaoyang District, Beijing 100020, China

Penguin Books Ltd, Registered Offices: 80 Strand, London WC2R 0RL, England

ISBN: 978-1-59514-458-4

Published simultaneously in Canada

Library of Congress Cataloging-in-Publication Data is available

Printed in the United States of America

10 9 8 7 6 5 4 3 2 1

This is a work of fiction. Names, characters, places, and incidents either are the product of the author's imagination or are used fictitiously, and any resemblance to actual persons, living or dead, businesses, companies, events, or locales is entirely coincidental.

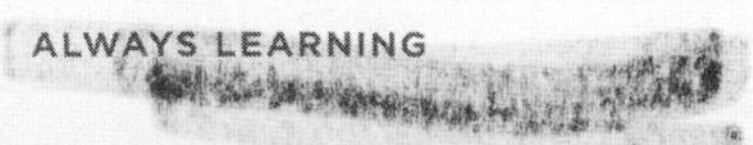

PEARSON

For the Richters—
Ann, Harlan, Laura, and Sarah.

THE NIGHTMARES WOKE WALLY, AGAIN.

Shelter Island. The hush of the forest at first light, the touch of snowflakes landing delicately on Wally's cheek and melting there. The acrid scent of gunfire hanging in the air.

The weight of her mother's body in Wally's arms as the life drained out of her.

"My babies," Claire whispered with her last breath, looking up at Wally and her brother, Tiger, together for the first time.

And then she was gone. The sound of sirens—dozens of them—descended upon the scene, shattering the peace.

"Run," Wally said to Tiger. And he did.

It had all taken place in November, five months earlier, but the memory played fresh in Wally's mind—in her dreams and in her waking hours—as if no time had passed at all.

The sky outside Wally's window was still dark. The time on her cell phone read 5:22, at least half an hour to go before sunrise. She tried to get back to sleep, but it was no use. Wally slid out of bed and into her workout clothes, heading out of her apartment and south on Nassau Avenue toward Orson Dojo. Along the way, she resisted the rich, seductive aroma of coffee and pastries from the corner café where her neighbors, January and Bea, were already working the early shift.

"Well, well," Orson said when she walked through the door. "Look who's turning into a morning person."

"Not by choice," Wally said.

Orson Mbaha was a chiseled and powerful black man originally from Namibia, a full six-and-a-half feet tall with brilliant amber eyes. He had quit his Mixed Martial Arts fighting career at the age of thirty-six, and now enjoyed inflicting daily agony upon his clients in Greenpoint. His studio was sparse—pure function and no frills. Every inch of the floor was covered in mats, one wall mirrored from floor to ceiling.

There were eight or nine other students joining Wally for the class, and Orson led them through a sadistic, twenty-minute routine of core exercises that left them gasping for breath and sweating buckets in the hot, humid air. They finished off the session with six minutes of military leg lifts, Orson walking the line and hurling an eight-pound medicine ball to each of them in turn, challenging their balance and intensifying the misery. It was impossible to think about anything but the pain. Wally's adrenaline gave her a warm, buzzy feeling of tranquility.

"Go to pairs, everyone," Orson said. "Live target."

He matched Wally up with a young guy, muscled but a

little heavy, maybe a former college athlete who still worked out but was overindulging on New York nightlife. He had six inches and at least seventy pounds on Wally.

"Ladies first," the guy said with a slightly condescending tone.

He slipped into a protective target outfit: headgear, target vest, full leg padding, and target mitts on his hands. There were orange target circles all up and down the outfit, from his knees to his thighs, kidneys, ribs, solar plexus. He held out the mitts, up high, and crouched into his ready position.

"Go," he said.

Wally began slowly, holding back on the force and speed until her muscle memory could take over and establish a rhythm. Crosses to the mitts, *whap-whap*, right and left, six times each. Then down to the kidneys, *whap-whap*, crouching and rotating her entire body to deliver the blows, four times each.

And now down to the thighs, the first kicks of her assault. People outside the discipline had little understanding of the importance of these blows—of the devastating, debilitating effect the kick could have on thigh muscles. Enough clean strikes and the opponent would lose all ability to balance or launch a counter-attack. Wally delivered the kicks cleanly, driving hard off her back foot and into the guy's upper thigh. She heard her partner exhale with each blow and knew he felt the force of the attack even through his pads.

Wally started to feel the heat and rhythm and adrenaline coursing through her well-toned physique. She renewed her assault on the mitts, now picking up the pace and force, driving hard with each crisp blow. *Whap-whap, whap-whap.* She could hear the force of her shots echoing against the walls louder than all the other fighters in the dojo. Mitts, abdomen, thighs, and back up again. Her target's exhalations became grunts as he received the increasingly powerful strikes. He crouched lower in an attempt to keep his balance.

But then the images came again, uninvited.

Her mother, Claire, and Tevin, her best friend, gunned down in front of her by Alexei Klesko, her father: a psychopath who killed without hesitation or regret. Every morning in the mirror Wally saw Klesko's eyes in her own reflection, a fathomless, merciless gray.

Ochee chornya. Dark eyes.

Klesko had left her only one thing of value: a brother, Tiger.

Wally had said "run" and Tiger had obeyed, turning away from her and disappearing into the woods of Shelter Island without once looking back. He'd been lost to her since that moment.

Where was he?

Wally tried to keep her focus on the elegant, ferocious

rhythm of the attack. Her strikes continued, coming faster and harder now. *Whap-whap! Whap-whap!* She felt the delicious ache and burn of her muscles as the assault became one continuous blur of violence, the individual strikes flying too fast to count, anger and frustration rising closer to the surface with every blow. Something powerful and unnamed took hold of her.

Wally heard a loud *snap!* and froze, cutting short her attack. She looked to the floor and was surprised to see her training partner lying on his back, fear and outrage covering his face as blood gushed from his mangled nose and spilled out onto the floor.

His thickly padded headgear had not protected him.

Wally looked at her right glove and saw the smear of blood on the leather. She had no memory of the strike. It was as if some dark corner of her soul had reached out on its own. When she glanced to the mirrored wall and looked into her own eyes, Wally caught sight of the violent stranger within.

1.

WALLY EMERGED FROM THE SUBWAY STATION AMID the swarm of morning commuters and hurried up Lexington, headed to work. Her day had gotten off to an early start, but a long, harsh lecture from Orson—her sensei—had held her up for almost half an hour, compounded by a maddening wait for the G train. She'd be at least forty minutes late and stressed out by the time she reached the Ursula Society office in Manhattan.

Not that it mattered much—it wasn't as if she'd become an indispensable part of the team. She'd been doing her internship with Lewis Jordan at the Society for nearly four months, and so far she hadn't even come close to taking on a case of her own.

It was starting to piss her off.

Wally spent her time at the Society tidying up the office, brewing oolong tea for Lewis, and, of course, digitizing all the Society's case files, which was a massive undertaking. The Ursula Society was dedicated to reuniting family members who had been separated for various reasons, specializing in complicated adoption cases in which clients had tried all the standard methods and come up empty. The file room in the back of the office contained the paperwork for almost three thousand cases, some reaching back for decades. Wally had been assigned the Herculean task of entering all of them into a new digital, searchable database.

"You're messing with me, right?" was her response to Lewis that first day in January, the two of them standing together inside the musty, unheated file room, the air in there so cold they could see their breath. "You want me to build a database for *all* these? There must be thousands of them."

"Better get started then," Lewis said, without sympathy. "And as a gesture of my endless appreciation, I will brew the oolong this morning."

Once she had begun the grueling task, Wally calculated that it would take her nearly a year to finish. She'd stomped into Lewis's office to object, and he'd looked up at her through his reading glasses, his eyes bulging at her through the thick lenses.

"This is bullshit, Lewis. It's too much."

"I'm sorry to hear that you're so easily discouraged," he answered in a measured voice that she found maddening. "The work we do requires a great deal of patience and optimism. Instead of being daunted by the size of the task, you could be focusing on the wealth of opportunity."

"What opportunity are you talking about?"

"I mean that when the job is done, you will know more about the history and casework of the Ursula Society than anyone in the world, myself included. My memory isn't quite what it used to be."

The two of them had a complicated relationship—Lewis had unintentionally played a role in the devastating loss of her mother, Claire, just five months earlier—but when it came to the mission of the Ursula Society, Wally and Lewis shared a genuine passion rooted in their own experiences of loss. Wally's commitment to the Society, of course, was just four months old, while Lewis had worked tirelessly at it for almost seventy years.

Seventy years. A frighteningly high number. For Wally, almost beyond imagining.

She had swallowed her objections and gotten back to work, determined to finish the job ahead of schedule. After four months, she had entered over a thousand cases into the database and hoped to finish the entire job by early the next fall.

Lewis had been right, of course, about the benefits of the job: Wally's sixteen-year-old brain had absorbed tons of new information, including the research strategies used by Ursula Society caseworkers and some of the shadowy resources that were available to them. Many clients whom Lewis had helped over the years worked security-sensitive jobs—in law enforcement, government, the military, technology—and they often put themselves at risk, showing their gratitude by helping solve the Society's cases.

Wally had recently digitized a case from the early nineties, when Lewis had reunited a young guy with his father, who had been classified as "Missing In Action" during the war in Vietnam. It turned out that the U.S. Army knew all along that the soldier had gone AWOL and had been hiding in Canada for almost twenty years.

"How did we get this information?" she asked Lewis, interrupting some research he was doing at his desk. He set aside his work and peered thoughtfully at Wally over his reading glasses for a moment before answering.

"A former client of ours works in the Pentagon," he answered simply.

"Okay," Wally said, considering this for a moment. "But this information would probably be classified, wouldn't it?"

"Certainly." Lewis kept his eyes on her, giving her a chance to puzzle the situation out.

"Then our source gave us classified military information. So that's very illegal. And illegal in the military means treason. Right?"

Lewis's nonresponse was her answer.

"And the penalty for treason is very harsh," she went on. "Sometimes even death. Why would our source risk that?"

"Because we helped her with her own search some years ago," Lewis replied. "Free of charge, when no one else was willing to take on her case. We provided her with the outcome she needed to get on with her life."

"So she's returning the good deed by feeding us classified information."

"Because it was something she wanted to do," Lewis said, wanting to be clear. "Not because we compelled her."

Wally thought some more. "And if government people came in here with a warrant or something, they might go through these files and discover clues to the identity of our source, and what she had done for us."

"Maybe," Lewis said, considering her point. "I've been careful to avoid leaving details in the files that might be traced that way, but I suppose it's always a danger."

"Okay then," she said, after thinking the problem through. "Since I'm digitizing everything anyway, maybe I should encrypt the database as well."

"Good thinking," was all Lewis said, and returned to his work. He was not huge on handing out compliments, so *good thinking* qualified as a major pat on the back.

Wally stopped for a couple of chocolate-glazed doughnuts in the shop downstairs from the Society offices, then punched in the security code to enter the building. She climbed the stairs to the second floor and was fishing through her messenger bag for her keys when she became aware that there was someone else in the quiet hallway: a young guy around Wally's age was seated on the floor at the very end of the hall, right outside the dark doorway of the Ursula Society. He was leaning forward with his head resting on his folded arms, and Wally had the impression that he had been there for some time.

The guy stood up—a little stiffly, she noticed. He was tall at around six foot one, with a lean and athletic build. He wore jeans, expensive high-tops, and a faded blue polo shirt under a brown canvas work jacket. He combed his fingers through his longish dark hair in an apparent attempt at looking presentable. Behind his bangs were warm blue eyes that were swollen and bloodshot—had he just woken up, or had he been crying? Wally also noticed a mark on the left side of his face, above his jaw: a fresh bruise.

"Can I help you?" she asked. Wally could tell the guy was a little puzzled at the sight of her—he probably wasn't expecting someone so close to his own age.

"Uh … yeah. Are you with the Ursula Society? That's what I'm here for."

"How'd you get into the building?" she asked.

He gave a little shrug. "I was here really early and no one answered the buzzer. I typed in the building address as the security code and it worked, so…anyway. Maybe you should get your super to change that."

"Technically, that's probably breaking and entering," Wally said, making a casual observation. The guy gave another shrug but didn't offer a response.

"Okay," Wally said, unlocking both bolts on the door of the Society. "Come on in. I'm Wally."

"I'm Kyle."

Wally sat down behind Lewis's desk and invited Kyle to take the visitor's chair across from her. He folded his arms tightly across his chest and began casting his eyes randomly around the room. Wally opened the bag from the doughnut shop and pushed it toward him, but he just shook his head.

Wally grabbed one of the doughnuts and took a bite. It was partly a stall tactic—she had a decision to make. Wally was all alone in the office, and here was a new walk-in client roughly her own age. It seemed like a perfect opportunity for her to take on a case of her own. Would Lewis sign off on it? Probably not.

"You don't seem old enough," Kyle said.

"I'm actually still an intern here," she said. "You'll need to talk to one of our caseworkers. Someone should be here soon, if you can hang..."

"Uh, okay." Kyle checked his cell phone for the time. "I guess so. This place...you help people find their biological parents and stuff? Kids who have been adopted?"

"That's one of the things we do, yeah. We bring people back together who have been separated for all sorts of reasons."

Kyle just nodded, keeping his eyes on the floor. Apparently, he was in the right place.

Wally checked the time on the wall—10:20 A.M.—and guessed that Lewis wouldn't be in for a half hour. Both of the other caseworkers, Carmen Black and Peter Maduro, were out in the field, not due back until the end of the week.

Wally turned on her computer and started her usual slog of data entry, but the silence quickly became awkward. There was no harm in having a regular conversation with the guy.

"I'm guessing we're about the same age," she said. "You go to school in the city?"

"Sexton," he said, "since I was five. I'm a junior. But I haven't been in a week and I'm not going back."

The sudden force of Kyle's declaration took Wally by surprise, and she studied him for a moment. The Sexton Academy was a private school on the Upper West Side, and Wally could see that Kyle—a more together version of Kyle than he was right now, anyway—would naturally fit in there. She pictured him in the dark blue blazer, colorfully striped school tie, and light khakis that made up the uniform, a Sexton insignia on the breast pocket of the blazer, of course.

Wally herself grew up in that privileged part of town, and she remembered the Sexton boys making the two-block trek from the school to the athletic-practice fields in Central Park, wearing their full sports gear. Wally could picture Kyle in that scenario too, a lacrosse stick slung over his shoulder with helmet and gloves hanging off the end, striding easily along the city streets with his Prep friends, a mob of handsome, born-to-rule guys with endless wealth and success in their future. Oftentimes, girls from nearby sister schools would linger on Central Park

West to flirt with the boys as they ambled by.

Wally wondered what secrets those girls knew about Kyle.

"What about you?" he asked.

"I'm currently reevaluating my educational options."

"Cool. Me too."

Another silence fell, but Kyle seemed restless and eager to keep talking.

"My mom, her name was Laura," he said, clearing his throat. "She died two years ago, a car accident on the Parkway. October sixteenth."

"Oh...that's awful. I'm really sorry, Kyle." He was being unexpectedly candid, intriguing Wally but also making her feel a little cautious.

"My father, he's...I'm sorry, he's a total fucking prick, like a weapons-grade asshole. And he's probably..." Kyle hesitated, as if nervous about a leap he was about to take. "Not even *probably*, he's *definitely* a dangerous person. So now he tells me that he's going to marry this new woman. Deandra. Whatever. Some art dealer or something—I met her once for like two minutes. So my dad and I got into it. I mean, I don't really give a shit who he wants to marry...."

The words were spilling out of Kyle now, a stream of anger and sadness. His lower lip trembled and his face flushed red in embarrassment. Wally suddenly realized that Kyle wasn't about to wait for Lewis to arrive—he was plowing forward and laying out his story right now...for her. It crossed Wally's mind that she could stop him, but she didn't want to.

"It's like he got over my mother so fast," Kyle went on. "Really fast, like in days. So we had this fight, and he tells me how I idealized my mom too much and that, by the way, she's not even really my mother. Then he says he was with another woman before my mom, but she went psycho and took off right after she gave birth to me."

"That's a lot for you to hear, all at once," she said.

"I mean, my old man is a total liar, and I don't believe anything he said about my birth mother. I want to find out who she is. And meet her, you know? But my father…he'll never let go of me. I know things—about who he is, about things he's done."

"What do you mean? What has your father done?"

Kyle just shook his head and looked away, suddenly evasive. Wally began to wonder if Kyle's situation was more than she could handle. Had she made a mistake by letting him get started?

"You know, Kyle, my boss will be in really soon. Maybe the best thing—"

"How long would it usually take you to find someone?" he asked.

"Uh…well, that depends," she stammered a little, realizing that in his current state of mind, Kyle wasn't going to be happy with the answer. "Finding your birth mother could be difficult or it could be easy, but there are other issues to work out first—"

"What issues do you mean?" Kyle asked. "You'll find her for me, right?"

Wally hesitated, and Kyle saw it.

"If your mother can be found, we'll find her," Wally assured him, but she heard a twinge of hesitation in her own voice.

Kyle heard it too, and shot her a distrustful look.

"You said that's what you do here."

"Yes, but there's a process to it. The idea is to bring people together in the right way, when they're ready for it to happen."

More than half of the reunions between separated family members ended badly, even in the best of circumstances. From what Wally could tell, Kyle's circumstances were complicated, maybe even explosive.

"But I *am* ready," Kyle said as if she were accusing him of something.

"You're in a rough place right now," Wally said. "I get that. But you need to understand something: finding your birth mother won't solve the problems you're having at home. Things are going badly with your father, and you're reaching out for something that feels like a solution. I get that, but you have some steps to take first—"

"What are you talking about?" Kyle cut her off.

"There's a therapist we refer a lot of clients to, and she's really good. There are ways to get you into a safer living situation, also." She could see that Kyle was struggling to understand what she was saying. "We have strong connections at Social Services, plus some private groups that help out in these situations. A friend of mine is with the NYPD, so we can—"

"A cop? Why?"

"To start with, I think that bruise on your face was made by a closed fist. You've described your father as dangerous and violent."

Kyle was silent for a moment, his jaw clenched in anger.

"This was a mistake," he said, rising quickly to his feet. "I'm sorry I wasted your time."

He headed for the door.

Wally felt a stab of panic—she stood and went after him.

"Please don't go," Wally said. "This is my fault. My boss will be here soon. . . ." She reached out and tried to hold Kyle by the arm, but he shrugged her off.

"Forget everything I told you."

Kyle rushed out of the office. Wally ran after him as he made his way down the hall.

"I promise we can help you, Kyle!" she called out, feeling desperate now.

But Kyle never looked back. Wally watched helplessly as he hurried down the main stairs and disappeared from view. *Shit!*

2.

LEWIS DIDN'T ARRIVE UNTIL ALMOST NOON.

"Hello, Wallis," he said as he entered, his faint Australian accent lending him a jaunty, gentlemanly air. He hung his fedora and overcoat on the hat rack by the door. For a man somewhere in his late eighties—he refused to verify his exact age—Lewis was still strong and sharp. His taste in clothes had frozen in limbo somewhere in the early fifties; he always dressed like a detective in an old black-and-white Humphrey Bogart film.

Wally could almost feel herself radiating an aura of guilt.

"Uh oh," Lewis said when he turned to face her. "How bad is it?"

"Pretty bad," she said, anxiously flicking the corner of the musty old case file she was working on.

Lewis sighed, and turned to retrieve his hat and coat from the rack.

"Come along. Everything goes down better with dumplings."

There was a Mandarin place with pretty good dim sum on Second Avenue that Lewis loved. The place was loud and steamy and already crowded when they arrived, but the staff treated

Lewis with deference—he and Wally were given a table immediately, and a quick nod to his favorite waitress was all it took to order two lunch specials.

"Tell me," Lewis said as soon as their order was placed.

"We had a walk-in this morning," she began, already dreading his reaction. "Carmen wasn't in yet, and the guy was in rough shape. More than anything, I think he needed someone to talk to."

"Wallis," Lewis gave her an exasperated look, "please tell me you didn't do the interview."

"No!" she exclaimed. "Not intentionally. But we were sitting there waiting, and he just started talking."

Lewis sighed. "And what happened?"

Wally described the entire session with Kyle. She kept checking Lewis for his reaction, but his expression revealed nothing. Lewis had heard a million tragic stories in his years with the Society. It took a lot to impress him.

"I see," he said evenly, when she was done.

His calm demeanor only made Wally more anxious about what he was thinking. She caught herself holding her breath in anticipation and let it out.

"And how would you grade your performance?" he finally said.

"Well, the session ended with him running out on me. I never had him fill out a bio sheet, so I don't know his full name or any other specifics that would help us follow up," Wally said, feeling even more ashamed as she heard herself listing her failures. "He was upset when we started, but worse when he left. He might actually be in danger, and now there's nothing I can do to change that."

"Rough morning," Lewis said. "And a little bizarre, don't you think?"

"I guess," Wally said, though she hadn't seen it that way, before. "Yeah, he was a little 'out there.' Whatever's going on has got him incredibly stressed. But that was no reason for me to fumble it so badly. I think I'd give myself an F."

"I think that's about right," said Lewis. "On the bright side, you now have a better appreciation for how fragile the process can be."

"Lucky me."

Their food arrived, and they began eating in silence. Wally, however, soon lost her appetite. After slowly consuming half his plate of dumplings, Lewis dabbed his mouth with his napkin and studied her for a moment.

"So," he said, "your failures are obvious. Tell me what you did right."

"Uh..." Wally tried to think, but she was still too upset to dissect the situation objectively.

"Very well," Lewis said. "Allow me. First, you showed confidence in your ability to do this job. That's something to build on, even if that confidence was premature. Second, from what you've said about Kyle, you made a correct assessment of his state of mind. The turmoil in his life would make him a bad candidate for our process at this point, and you were right to be direct with him about that."

"Okay," Wally said, grateful that Lewis was being generous with her.

"What you're doing right now is a bigger mistake than all the rest," Lewis added.

"What do you mean?"

"You're beating yourself up. You think you broke this young man, but in fact he was already a train wreck when he walked through the door. Do you understand?"

"Maybe. But I still feel like I let him down." Wally wasn't willing to let herself off so easily.

"I understand, but there must be boundaries. Kyle's well-being is not your own personal responsibility. We have to maintain a certain distance, the way a good surgeon might with a patient he finds on his operating table. It's why doctors aren't supposed to practice medicine on people they have a personal relationship with—because their emotions might compromise their ability to do their job. Doesn't that make sense?"

"Yeah, I guess so. . . ."

"And this is a philosophy you can apply in your personal life, as well."

"What do you mean?"

"I'm referring to Tiger."

The mention of her Russian brother caught Wally by

surprise. On her own time, she had used some of the Society's resources in an effort to find him, wherever in the world he was. So far she hadn't had any luck, but she would never stop looking.

"Lewis—"

"I know you're preoccupied with the idea of finding your brother, and you've been using some of the Society's assets in an effort to locate him."

"I should have told you—"

He held up his hand to stop her. "I don't object. I hope you find him, of course."

"Thank you," Wally said.

"Your brother is on your mind a great deal."

"All the time," Wally said.

Lewis knew more details about Wally's life—her *entire* life—than anyone else in the world. He was the one person she could talk to frankly about everything.

"Lewis," she continued, "I think a lot about how luck plays such a huge role in how our lives turn out, and we have no control over that. Tiger and I are brother and sister—same genes, same parents—but I grew up on the Upper West Side, with every imaginable advantage in life. Tiger basically raised himself on the street—"

"You were on the street also, Wally."

"By choice," she said adamantly. "That's the difference. He became a hard, violent person because that was the only way he could survive. It isn't fair."

"You want to find him and help him."

"I want to find him. I don't know if he would accept help from anyone, least of all me. If I had the chance, though, I think I could even things out a little. Maybe tip the scales back in his favor."

"And what else?"

What else did Wally want? She wanted to turn back time. She wanted her mother, Claire, to be alive again. She wanted Shelter Island never to have happened.

She wanted the nightmares to stop.

"I don't know what I want," she said.

"All right. But as you try to figure that out, I want you to remember something. This applies to Kyle, and even to your own brother: however pure your intentions are, no one can fix another person, not really."

3.

WALLY GRABBED THE SUBWAY BACK TO GREENPOINT and dragged her exhausted self the two blocks from the station to her address near McCarren Park. It was a renovated three-story industrial building, a beehive of former sweatshops converted into a dozen small lofts. Wally's one-bedroom unit was on the roof. It had the smallest square footage of all the spaces but the luxury of an airy rooftop that was hers alone.

A sweet, mossy aroma emanated from the turtle tank, greeting her as soon as she walked through the door. She needed to feed Tevin, a baby snapping turtle that had already grown two inches since she'd bought him on impulse from the pet store a month earlier. The smell of the tank had gotten stronger over the past few weeks. Wally would have to clean out the habitat soon, before it went completely native with algae and other disgusting things.

She grabbed a chunk of frozen fish from the freezer and set it on the rock island at the center of the large tank, but Tevin remained motionless, floating on the surface of the water and ignoring the food. He kept his cold, inscrutable gaze fixed on Wally, and she imagined he was more interested in eating one of her fingers—or even her nose—than what he'd been offered. With jaws as powerful as a pit bull's, young Tevin was fully capable of harvesting one of Wally's body parts.

"You're welcome, beast," Wally said.

Wally threw off her work clothes and pulled on stretchy black yoga pants, an oversized green sweatshirt, and sheepskin boots, happy to be comfortable and warm after a difficult day. She made a cup of hot chocolate and opened the sliding door onto the rooftop deck, where she sat down at the used set of wrought-iron patio furniture that she had bought—along with most of the loft's furniture—from a local thrift shop.

Like the rest of the loft space, the deck seemed only halfway put together—Wally had signed the lease only three months earlier, once she had finally admitted to herself that she could not live in the fancy Upper West Side apartment she'd inherited after her mother's death. There were painful memories that came with that place, of course, but it was more than that—her mother's old apartment was very upscale and luxurious, and Wally felt she hadn't done anything to deserve that kind of lifestyle.

Along the perimeter of the roof were half a dozen new planter boxes with big, unopened bags of fresh potting soil waiting beside them. A local nursery had delivered it all for her, but nothing was planted in them yet. When it had come time to choose, Wally stood before the massive, confusing display of seeds at the nursery, paralyzed by indecision. Was she a flower person, a vegetable person, an herb person, or what? All three?

Each packet of seeds came with a chart of its particular seasonal planting schedule, and the information overload had forced Wally's brain to shut down.

Her only other addition to the outdoor area had been a few strings of white Christmas lights around the perimeter, giving off just enough light to illuminate the space with a warm glow. Wally left the lights off for now, though, content to sit in the cool, quiet darkness of the early evening, watching the last traces of sunlight fade away behind the Manhattan skyline.

She enjoyed the peace for all of two minutes before there was a knock at her door.

"NYPD. Open up."

Damn it, Wally thought, spilling her cocoa a little as she jumped up from her chair, pissed off. *Again with this shit.*

Wally tended to inspire protective instincts in older men—except for her actual father, ironically—and one of those men was Detective Atley Greer of the 20th Precinct in Manhattan, the neighborhood where she had grown up. Greer was friends with the local precinct captain in Greenpoint, and he'd arranged for the foot patrols to keep an eye on Wally. At least once a week they came up with excuses to sniff around her apartment, and tonight she was in no mood.

Wally opened the door to find two very young cops whom she hadn't seen before. She knew the minimum age for a probie cop in the NYPD was twenty-one, but these two looked barely out of high school. One was tallish and thin and maybe of Indian descent and the other was white and a little stockier, with curly blond hair that was kind of cute but would definitely *not* help him intimidate perps on the street. Wally thought that if she ever saw these two in civilian clothes, she would figure them for chess-club dweebs.

"I don't even want to hear it," Wally began before either officer could speak. "Leave me alone. Now and forever."

The cops were obviously thrown a little by her attitude, but eventually the curly cop spoke. His nametag read GARTH.

"We, uh…we got a call about a domestic disturbance—"

"No you didn't, Garth," Wally snapped. "I know your captain told you to check up on me."

"Uh, that's absolutely not true, ma'am," said the taller cop, a terrible liar. His tag read SHAHI. "When we receive a call on a domestic, we're obligated to—"

"You're calling me *ma'am*?" Wally objected. "Really? I'm at least four years younger than you, and you guys barely look old enough to shave."

The situation was interrupted, thankfully, by January and Bea—Wally's neighbors from downstairs—who arrived at her door, looming behind the cops. The appearance of Wally's "protection detail" had become so routine that the girls were completely unconcerned.

"Uh oh," January said, checking out the cops. "Are you headed for the slammer, Wally, or can you come out with us tonight?"

"These Eagle Scouts were just leaving," Wally said.

The rookie cops gave each other looks and turned on their heels, both eager to move on.

"Don't be strangers," January called after them in a flirty tone.

January was a very tall, curvy redhead, nineteen years old with the cockiness of a strong, competitive athlete. She played volleyball for a local junior college in the hopes of landing a scholarship for a Division 1 school and worked at the coffeehouse on the corner, with Bea, to pay her way. Bea was a first-generation Cuban-American, smaller and not as aggressively outgoing as January. She still got plenty of attention because of her fine, sensuous features—her long dark hair and huge brown eyes were guy magnets.

These college girls were different kinds of friends for Wally—they seemed completely carefree, blessed with an optimism about the world that she had never felt. They were also rule breakers, in a way that Wally appreciated—she'd first met them when they had scaled the fire escape up to her apartment, unannounced, and offered her free cable TV. Apparently, Bea was good with mechanical things, and she'd pirated the feed for the entire building.

For Wally, hanging out with January and Bea was always like a little vacation from her life, and in the few months she'd known them Wally had come to appreciate their influence.

"We're going dancing later," said Bea. "At Cielo, in the city. That DJ Louise is spinning Latin electronica tonight."

"Thanks, but I'm not really in the mood."

"We reject your antisocial funk, Stoneman," January said. "Dance or die."

"No, seriously—"

"We'll be back for you at eleven," said Bea.

Once the girls were gone, Wally retreated into her apartment and picked up her cell phone. She dialed Detective Atley Greer.

"Make them stop, Greer," she told him as soon as she heard him pick up the line.

"Who are we talking about?"

"Your junior narc squad. It's too much."

"Speaking hypothetically," he answered, "if I *had* arranged for a low-profile police presence at your location, what would be the harm?"

"I'm trying to fit in around here. That's gonna be tough with your uniformed probies busting in on me every other day."

"Wallis—"

"I'm doing fine, Greer. Really."

There was a pause on the other end of the line.

"It's okay to acknowledge that the world can be a difficult and frightening place," Greer said. "Don't forget, kid … I was there, too."

"I remember."

Shelter Island. Wally's father, Alexei Klesko, had shot

Greer in the shoulder, and the cop had endured months of rehab just to get back on the job. The role he'd played in her survival that day had cultivated in him a sort of fatherly preoccupation with her well-being. Wally owed him something for what he had done, but the interference in her daily life was unacceptable.

"You go through something like that," Greer said, "you come away with scars. No one is immune. It's too much to carry by yourself. Let me help."

"I'm dealing," Wally insisted.

"If you say so. But when friends offer help, think about accepting it."

"I will, Greer, if you start thinking about boundaries."

Greer was pathologically annoying, but Wally also knew that he wasn't necessarily wrong. She was glad when January and Bea showed up at her door at eleven—right on schedule—both dressed in black skinny jeans and loose, layered tank tops, their beautiful faces made up just enough to give them an edgy club vibe. Wally was dressed down a little—in a fitted black T-shirt with jeans and flats—but the girls were excited just to find her ready and waiting.

"Nice," said January, giving Wally the once-over.

They took the subway to the Lower East Side, reaching the club before midnight. They joined up with a group of January and Bea's other friends from the city—six party girls, all fired up and ready for the night. Wally did her best to relax and avoid thinking about how different she felt from the carefree, uncomplicated party girls.

The massive bouncer had bulging arms and an intimidating scowl on his face, but he raised the rope for the girls without hesitation, not even bothering to check their fake IDs. Being young and pretty in Manhattan definitely had its advantages.

The inside of Cielo felt a little claustrophobic, totally packed with dancing twentysomethings and teenagers with fake IDs. A DJ named Louise something was spinning some really loud Latin electronica, the synth percussion mixed so heavily that Wally could feel each electronic drumbeat like a little punch in the chest, right at her heart. She had an immediate and primal reaction to the music, and she felt it pulling her—irresistibly—onto the dance floor.

January, Bea, and most of their friends peeled off toward the ladies' room to score drugs—they were mostly into coke these days. Wally was about to object, but she figured there was no point—they had already heard her argument against dope and shrugged it off. Wally remembered Lewis's words—*you can't save another person, not really*—and instead she went on ahead and joined the swirling, throbbing ocean of young people already dancing.

The massed bodies were packed in close, their motions in sync with the synthesized Latin drumbeats. The air was thick with the heat and moisture of the sweating bodies, and Wally closed her eyes as she began to move with them. Almost no one was dancing in couples—they all moved in a collective mob—and Wally released herself into it, eager for the moment when she wouldn't feel like a separate person at all but just one element of the whole, throbbing tribe.

As she heated up, other bodies touched hers, their skin hot and wet. January and Bea suddenly appeared in front of her, euphoric smiles on their faces. Their drugs were already kicking in, and Wally realized that she must have lost track of time, which felt good. Her friends wrapped her up in sloppy, doped-up hugs and hung for a moment around her neck.

"We love you, Wally," Bea said.

Wally knew it was the drugs talking—X-induced affection—but she didn't mind. It was a nice thing to hear, so what was the harm? The three of them danced facing each other for a long time, the continuous music track never letting up but veering off on different paths, momentary explorations into parallel universes of tweaked, frenetic sound. After a while, January moved in close to Wally and held up a small pill between her fingers, pale green with a little question mark on it, offering to place it on Wally's tongue. But Wally shook her off with a smile and kept dancing.

Wally and the girls gave their bodies over to the music, venturing wherever the DJ led them. Before long Wally was working her body as hard as she did at Orson Dojo, her shirt soaked with sweat and clinging to her. She felt warm on the inside too, and thought she could stay there dancing all night. She closed her eyes and imagined it, the dance floor teeming for hours with those like herself who had surrendered to the mesmerizing sound, January and Bea close by through all of it.

Before long, though, something interrupted the feeling—something barely perceptible. Wally felt a shiver travel down her back, as if a door had opened somewhere and let a draft of cool, uninvited fresh air into the room. She opened her eyes and caught a glimpse of a single, unidentifiable face—was it a man or a woman?—staring at her through the crowd of dancers. The mass of bodies shifted, blocking her view, and when a gap opened up again the person was gone.

Or was never there at all. Wally stopped dancing, but her heart kept beating fast. Her sweat-soaked T-shirt felt tight and sticky, clinging to her and restricting her range of motion like a straight-jacket. The bodies that pressed up against her didn't feel good anymore, and she wiped her arms with the bottom of her shirt, trying to shed the sweat that strangers had rubbed off onto her.

The spell was broken. January and Bea wrapped her up in hugs again as if they could pull her back into the music. Wally felt bad that she was about to disappoint them, but then she remembered that they were completely high and by the next morning would have only a vague sense memory of it all.

Which was one of the reasons Wally hated dope.

"I'm gonna bounce," she yelled over the music.

"NO!" the girls objected. But Wally gave them each a reassuring kiss on the cheek and bolted from the dance floor. Once she was clear of the crowd, she took one last look around to see if there really had been someone watching her, but all she saw was a sea of enchanted, anesthetized faces, lost in the music.

4.

WALLY GRABBED THE SUBWAY HOME—OTHER YOUNG women might feel intimidated by a late-night subway ride into Brooklyn, but Wally carried herself with such an air of physical confidence that she rarely felt threatened in situations like that. She felt an aching sense of loneliness, though, as she sat by herself in the nearly empty train. *It's too much to carry by yourself,* Greer had said, and he was right. Of the people she loved, who was left? Claire was gone. Her best friend, Tevin, was gone. Jake and Ella were living far upstate at the Neversink Farm, earning a fresh start for themselves. Wally's adoptive father, Jason, had made repeated attempts to be part of her life again, but she wasn't ready yet to make peace with him after he had abandoned her and her mom to start a new family.

That left only Tiger—the sole, undeniable connection between her past and present—but Wally had no idea where Tiger was, or even if he was still alive.

When she got home, Wally opened her laptop and logged into the Ursula Society site. Since working at the Society, Wally had been using every possible resource to find her brother, but so far she'd come up empty. The first thing she checked was a running database labeled TIGER TRAP—a set of self-running searches she'd set up that ran twenty-four hours a day. The program continuously scanned dozens of resources, including law-enforcement systems all over the country, using a logarithm to sniff out Internet activity with a combination of keywords, including *Klesko*, *Tigr*, Wally's own name, plus references to the thirty or so ongoing criminal cases—in the United States and abroad—in which Tiger and her Russian father were named.

Some mentions came up, of course, but they were all several months old and useless by now.

Wally had become used to the disappointment. In nearly four months, the scan had come up with only one interesting lead: eight weeks earlier, there had been a series of untraceable searches using the terms *Wally Stoneman* and *Shelter Island*—even though Wally's name had never appeared in media stories about the shoot-out because she was a minor. Wally had hoped the searches were an attempt by Tiger to contact her, but the lead had gone nowhere.

Wally took a quick shower—it felt good to rinse off the sweat and body glitter that other dancers at the club had rubbed off on her, the glitter forming sparkling rainbow patterns on the white tile before swirling down the drain. She changed into the oversized pajama bottoms and tank top that she wore to bed and had begun towel drying her hair in front of the bathroom mirror when she heard a short, high-pitched *beep* from the main room.

She headed out and first checked her cell phone—assuming

that the *beep* was an app—but when she swiped the activity bar on the screen it showed that no new messages had come in. The *beep* sounded once more and Wally realized that it had come from her open laptop.

Wally sat down in front of the computer and found that the screen was on now, awakened from its sleep mode. The TIGER TRAP window had popped up and now listed one item in the "new activity" box. It described a current "visitor"—using an anonymous host—to the page Wally had set up on Facebook. This was a surprising event for several reasons, mainly because she had set up the page using her Russian birth name, Valentina Mayakova (her mother's Russian surname—Wally would never use her father's), which only a handful of people in the world were aware of.

Wally herself wasn't really into social media, but she had set up the page as a way of doing research on Society clients. For that reason, she hadn't entered any information on her profile—personal details, friends, schools, tagged pictures, hobbies—that would bring casual visitors to the page. This anonymous visitor had either landed on the site at random or had come there on purpose, running a search using the name Valentina Mayakova.

The only real content on Wally's page was a series of photos she had uploaded to the site from her cell phone. The images were of memorable places from her past—a sheltered spot under a midtown overpass, the line outside a soup kitchen near Morningside Park, a skate park just off Riverside Drive—particular spots that reminded her of the months she spent living on the street with Tevin, Jake, Ella, and, of course, Sophie. Those times had been difficult in lots of ways—and dangerous—but Wally had never felt as strong and confident as she had while roughing it on the streets of Manhattan with her crew.

Now the TRAP program was cloning the movements of the anonymous visitor, showing that he—or she—was scanning Wally's street photographs. She felt a twinge of annoyance, like her privacy was being violated, and then realized how ridiculous it was to expect any level of privacy online, especially on a site that she had left public.

Something popped up on the left sidebar, and Wally saw that the Facebook software now listed the visitor—labeled "Anonymous"—as a temporary contact. Beside the listing was a drop-down menu of options. One of them was an icon of a video camera. Without hesitating, Wally clicked the icon and watched as a small window popped up on her screen. An animated clock icon appeared, its hands spinning around as the video signals engaged.

Within seconds, the link was established and a video image appeared on her screen: a young man, handsome, with prominent features, fair skin, and long black hair. His eyes—like Wally's—were a dark gray. The sight of him took Wally's breath away.

Tiger.

He wore a look of complete surprise, as if he'd been ambushed. The two of them stared mutely at each other for what seemed like a very long time. Beyond his obvious shock, Wally picked up traces of other emotions in Tiger's expression: embarrassment, maybe even some resentment. *Why?*

Wally broke the silence.

"Tiger..."

The sound of his name snapped Tiger into action. Tiger glanced over his shoulder with a look of concern, as if to make sure that Wally's voice hadn't been heard by anyone else. When he finally turned back to the camera, his eyes met Wally's for only a moment before his hand shot forward, reaching for a mouse or touchpad.

The video image on Wally's screen suddenly went black.

"No!" Wally tried desperately to reestablish the video feed, but now all signs of her "Anonymous" contact were gone, as if they had never been there at all.

Shit.

Wally jumped onto her feet and paced around the loft, trying to settle herself down. She was mad and frustrated, and she couldn't help directing some of those feelings at Tiger himself. He'd cut off the feed on purpose, obviously, even though he had made the effort to search her out in the first place.

Four months of searching and this was what she got for it? *Bullshit.*

She continued pacing—and breathing—and after a few minutes Wally's thinking became calm enough to consider two positive things: First of all, Tiger was alive. Second, he had made an effort to reach out to her, even if it had been indirect and secretive.

And then there was the bad news: when Wally had spoken his name out loud, Tiger had immediately gone on the alert, checking over his shoulder for ... what? Or whom? She hadn't seen actual fear on his face—for Tiger to show any kind of vulnerability was unimaginable to her—but he probably had reason to watch his own back. From everything Wally knew about her brother, he had gone from one doomed, perilous situation to another all his life.

What kind of danger was Tiger in now?

5.

WORN-OUT AND DRAINED DOWN TO HER BONES, Wally finally drifted off to sleep ... until her cell phone rang, breaking the late-night silence of her loft. The caller ID read "Harmony House," the resource center for homeless youths in midtown Manhattan. During her time on the street, Wally had been a frequent visitor at the facility and had established a few relationships there.

"Hello?"

"Wally? It's Candace Chen, over at Harmony House. I'm sorry to bother you so late...."

Wally checked her phone—it read 2:40 A.M.

"That's okay, Candace. What's going on?"

"We had someone show up at our night desk. He's been beaten up pretty badly, and I think he might have been using tonight. He's very agitated. We tried to get him to agree to go to an ER or to call the police, but he was fiercely against it and we have to respect that—you know our policy. If these kids can't trust us, we might as well shut our doors."

"I understand. But why are you calling?" Wally rubbed her eyes, confused.

"So I did a little snooping. He had an address written on a piece of notepaper in his jacket pocket. It was for the Ursula Society. That's where you work, right?"

Wally sat up in bed now, the fog of sleep clearing just enough for her to realize where this was going.

"Is his name Kyle, by any chance?"

"Yep," Candace said. "His ID says Kyle Townsend, seventeen. Address on the Upper East Side. I would have waited and called you in the morning, but he's insisting on leaving now, and he's obviously in some kind of trouble. I thought that if you knew him you might be able to help figure out a plan that would keep him safe."

The smart thing for Wally to do was nothing. In the morning she could call Lewis and figure out if the Society could help Kyle, who seemed to be spiraling out of control. But that would be a cop-out.

"Keep him there if you can, Candace," Wally said. "I'll get a cab and be there in twenty."

Wally stepped out of the taxi at the corner of 41st Street and Dyer, finding the entrance to Harmony House mostly dark. The front door was locked, but through the all-glass doors she could see a security guard sitting at a desk inside the lobby—a middle-aged Hispanic man with the arms and chest of a power lifter, his muscles bulging underneath his black polo shirt. The man must have been expecting her because he buzzed Wally in before she even had a chance to ring the bell.

Before pushing through the door, Wally hesitated—she had the strange feeling that she was being watched. Quickly scanning the street, she clocked a large sedan parked across the intersection at Tenth Avenue, a streetlamp throwing just enough light down to reveal two men sitting in the front seat. The car was similar to an NYPD detective unit, but her time on the street had left Wally with pretty good instincts; the two men didn't vibe like cops. So who were they and why were they staking out Harmony House at three in the morning?

With these questions still nagging her, Wally entered the lobby to find Candace Chen waiting for her there.

"Good to see you, Wally," Candace said with her usual buoyant smile, which now seemed kind of macabre given the circumstances.

Really? Wally thought to herself. *She's perky even now?* It was the middle of the night, and Candace had been sitting up for hours with a drugged-out assault victim. What did it take to bum this woman out?

"Good to see you too, Candace. He's still here?"

Candace nodded. "He's in with our nurse."

They walked down the main hall and into the infirmary, where Kyle was stretched out on the exam table. He had an IV drip attached to the back of his left hand and an empty plastic barf tray resting on his chest. Wally leaned over him to find that his face was severely swollen and bruised, with a couple of open gashes that the nurse had closed with butterfly bandages.

"Hi, Kyle."

At the sight of her he turned his head away, looking pained.

"What the fuck are you doing here?" His voice was a little slurred. Whatever drugs were in his system hadn't yet been cleared. "Go away. . . ."

"What did you take?" she asked him.

"I didn't take anything," he practically spat the words at her. "I bought some weed from these guys near the Port Authority and we smoked it together."

Wally looked to the nurse for confirmation and she shook her head "no."

"Maybe you got more in the weed than you bargained for," Wally said. "It was the dealers who put this beating on you?"

"No! They weren't dealers; they were just guys. And then I started feeling sick and they brought me here."

"Then who hit you?"

"The cuts and bruises are at least twelve hours old, I'd say," the nurse said.

Kyle kept his face turned away, neither confirming nor denying what the nurse had said. Wally turned to Candace.

"Could I have a minute with Kyle?"

"Take your time," Candace said. She and the nurse exited the room, leaving Wally and Kyle alone.

"You went home to your father?" Wally asked. "That's how this happened?"

Again, no answer.

"Okay." She needed to try a different tack, and the memory of the two security types in the car outside Harmony House returned to her. "What you said before—when you first came to see us. That you knew things about your father. Things he'd done?"

Kyle looked Wally in the eyes now.

"Then tell me this: your father—you never told me his name...?" Kyle remained silent, still turned away from her, refusing to answer. "Whatever. If he thought he couldn't trust you, how far would he go to prevent you from blowing up his secrets?"

The fear in Kyle's eyes answered her question.

"There are a couple of guys in a car outside—"

"Who?" Kyle sat up on the table now, grimacing in pain at the effort.

"I'd guess private security."

Kyle looked unnerved, but not completely unsurprised that there were men out looking for him.

"I told you I know someone in the NYPD—"

"No! No cops! That would be worse than anything..." Kyle couldn't bring himself to finish the thought.

Shit.

Wally couldn't get past the idea that she was at least partially responsible for Kyle's condition. If she had handled him better during his visit, would he have ended up back home, getting the shit kicked out of him again by his father? Wally was determined to keep Kyle safe this time. If Lewis could hear what she was about to suggest, though, he'd go postal.

"They can't keep you here," she said, "so you should come home with me. Just for now, until we can work something out."

"I don't need your help," Kyle said.

"Clearly."

"Screw you." He shifted on the table, then reeled a little from the sudden change of position.

"After our interview yesterday," she said, "maybe you're feeling like you can't trust me, but I really just want to help."

Ignoring her, Kyle sat straight up on the exam table and took a moment to get his balance before carefully stepping down onto the floor.

"Where's my jacket?" he asked, but then he spotted it hanging by the door and grabbed it.

Now Wally was alarmed—no one could force Kyle to stay at Harmony House, and he was in no condition to head off on his own. She reached out to him and held his arm, but he shook her off with surprising strength and headed for the hallway.

"I have a safe place to take you," she said, certain her idea was a bad one as soon as she blurted out the words. "I know you don't want to go home, and I'll bet you those men are still waiting out front."

Kyle hesitated for a moment, and Wally saw her opening.

"A private place where you can come and go," she said. "Just for tonight, if that's what you want. Just for a few hours. I live in Greenpoint. There's room for you to crash with me."

Kyle took a long moment to think about this. Underneath his drug-addled defiance, Wally could see that he was scared and uncertain.

"Please, Kyle," Wally said. "We'd be doing each other a favor. This way I won't spend the rest of the night wondering where you are and what part of all this was my fault."

He didn't respond for a moment, but Wally could see him processing the idea. He finally nodded. She saw a look of relief pass across his face when the decision was made.

When they told Candace about the plan she gave Wally a dubious look but eventually agreed. Remembering the men in the car out front, Wally asked to be let out through the emergency exit at the rear of the building, which opened on an alley. At the exit, Wally peered south toward 40th Street, seeing that there was little traffic and nothing suspicious in that direction.

"Let's go," she said, leading Kyle down the alley and remaining watchful as they went. He wasn't completely steady yet, but he managed to keep up with her. They rounded the corner at 40th and headed east as Wally kept her eyes open for a cab. Tenth Avenue was nearly empty at that hour and there were no cabs in sight, so they headed south toward 39th Street, where they could see more traffic flowing.

"Are you doing okay?" Wally asked, seeing that Kyle was looking a little dazed. "We'll be out of here soon."

"I'm good," he said, sounding distant and unfocused.

They were halfway down the block when a black man in a

dark-blue suit stepped out of a recessed doorway and onto the sidewalk, blocking their path. He wasn't tall or especially big, but he carried his lean, wiry physique with a sense of confidence. Wally tensed—she didn't think this was one of the guys from the sedan outside Harmony House. How many men did Kyle's father have out here?

The man held up his hand for them to stop. The man even smiled a little, attempting to put them at ease.

"Okay," he said quietly. "There's no reason to make this hard...."

Tires squealed behind them as the large sedan that had been parked out in front of Harmony House wheeled around onto Tenth Avenue, headed straight for them.

Shit.

"Forget it," Wally said to the man. "He's not going with you."

With blinding quickness, the man's right hand shot out and grabbed Wally by the shoulder, his fingers digging deep into her muscle. His grip was powerful—like a vice clamping down on her nerves—and she felt a searing pain up and down her arm as he pulled her toward him. Wally spun to the right and brought her left arm down hard, breaking the man's grip on her.

She stepped back and saw the look of surprise and embarrassment on his face, which turned almost immediately to anger. He lunged at her again, but his rage had unbalanced him—Wally spun out of his path and crouched down, aiming a side kick straight at his knee. The heel of her foot landed hard on the man's knee joint and it buckled to the side. The man fell to the sidewalk, howling in pain and holding his dislocated knee.

"Oh my God..." Kyle said, a look of shock on his face as he stared at the writhing security man.

Wally jumped back to her feet and grabbed Kyle. The sedan kept coming and raced after them. Wally and Kyle caught a break when a delivery truck turned onto the street, blocking the sedan's way. Though they didn't turn to look, they heard the car skid to a stop and the driver's door fly open. The footsteps of the second man echoed down the street as he raced past the cursing truck driver and came after them.

Wally could hear that the man's footfalls were heavy—he was bigger than the first man—but his pace was fast and athletic, his size now slowing him down.

When they reached 39th Street and rounded the corner, Wally stopped short against the stone wall and pulled Kyle close. She listened as the second security man's footsteps grew nearer and crouched, waiting. Just as he rounded the corner, Wally twisted her body hard and struck out with a high, straight arm, striking the man in the throat.

He flopped down onto the ground, wheezing and struggling for breath, but then rose up onto his feet again, unsteady. Wally had been right about his athleticism—the guy looked like an NFL tight end, at least six foot five and well over 250 pounds with a farm-boy buzz cut and a bleached-blond goatee. His eyes burned with fury as he came at Wally, spittle dribbling out of his mouth and catching at the hairs on his chin.

He pivoted to his left side and launched a sweeping kick at her, but the size difference between them actually worked to Wally's advantage—she dropped nimbly to the ground, avoiding what would have been a devastating strike. From her prone position on the cold, filthy pavement, Wally kicked upward and launched a strike of her own, driving her boot up into the man's solar plexus. He grunted in pain and dropped, curling his massive body up in a fetal position as his body went into a kind of seizure.

"Let's go," Wally commanded, and Kyle obeyed, picking up his pace as they hustled west on 39th. A block and a half later they reached Ninth Avenue and found a taxi idling outside a Greek diner. They slid into the backseat of the cab and within seconds were headed away from the scene, the cabbie glancing suspiciously at them in his rearview mirror.

"Holy shit," Kyle said again, still trying to catch up to what had happened in front of his eyes.

"Do you have a cell phone on you?" Wally asked. She wasn't about to relax until she had taken every necessary measure.

Kyle nodded and pulled an expensive smartphone out of his jacket pocket. Wally grabbed the phone and quickly snapped its back panel open. She slid both the SIM card and the battery out and tossed all of the components out of the taxi window.

"I had all my contacts in there!"

"Your father pays the bill for that phone, right?"

Reluctantly, Kyle nodded. "Yes."

"Security pros don't need to tail people the old-fashioned way—it's too easy to just track cell signals and keep their distance. That phone was burned. When you replace it, you can never use the new SIM to call any of your usual contacts. Use only VOIP or pay phones if you don't want your father to be able to find you."

The certainty of her orders left no room for argument. For his part, Kyle seemed to be struggling to come to grips with what had just happened.

"Okay," he said, sounding exhausted. "I understand."

The cab turned south, headed for the Williamsburg Bridge and Wally's loft in Greenpoint. They traveled in silence, and within just a few minutes Kyle was asleep, his head slumped against the door of the taxi.

Passing streetlamps cast flashes of light into the back of the cab and gave Wally brief, intermittent looks at Kyle's face; she'd never seen him at peace, and the transformation was disarming. Without the anger and confusion of his waking mind he looked like the guy that he still was: handsome and unspoiled, completely vulnerable, his mouth relaxed and parted just enough for a stray lock from his shaggy hair to find that place and remain there, stirring slightly with every exhalation of his breath.

It was almost five in the morning when they finally reached Wally's apartment. She put Kyle in her bedroom, and he was asleep almost as soon as his head hit the pillow. Wally grabbed a blanket and lay down on her couch, but soon it was obvious that she wouldn't be able to sleep—the adrenaline from the fight was still surging through her system.

Wally got up and sat down at her laptop again. First, she checked the TIGER TRAP program—hoping against hope that Tiger had reached out to her—but there was no sign of that. Tiger had thoroughly broken the connection between them, and apparently he wanted to keep it that way. Wally experienced a stab of hurt and resentment. It made her glad that Kyle was there to give her something else to focus on.

Wally felt a need to do something productive, and now that she knew Kyle's last name—Townsend—she could begin investigating his case. She was still certain that he was nowhere near ready to be reunited with his lost birth mother, but there was nothing to stop Wally from trying to locate her anyway. Her first step would be to find out as much as she could about Kyle's father. Using all the Ursula Society's online resources—some of them legal, some not, including a hacked database at a major credit-rating company—Wally dove in, and within an hour had put together a good-sized dossier on the man.

His name was Richard Townsend. It turned out Townsend was the CEO of MVI—Millennia Vision Incorporated—a privately held company with headquarters in Elizabeth, New Jersey. A three-year-old article in the Financial section of the *New York Times* listed Townsend and MVI as the winners of a federal contract to produce "technology related to international border surveillance." If the man was a dangerous criminal, as Kyle had suggested, then it was impossible to tell on the surface—the law-enforcement databases revealed no "wants" or warrants or ongoing cases involving Townsend.

The search was only able to come up with one clear photo of Richard Townsend, wearing a tuxedo for a benefit at the Met, four years before. He was a large, physically fit man, barrel-chested with thick gray hair and weathered skin. His cool, somber gaze was directed at the camera, and it appeared as if the photographer had intruded on his privacy.

As for Kyle's birth mother, the situation was discouraging: seventeen years earlier, the Rutland County Clerk's office in Fair Haven, Vermont, had filed two documents: First was a birth certificate for Kyle John Townsend, listing someone named Mercy Smith as the birth mother and Richard Townsend as the father. The second document was an agreement signed by Mercy Smith relinquishing all custody of baby Kyle to Richard Townsend.

It was gratifying for Wally to find an answer for Kyle so easily, but that feeling didn't last long. Wally ran a quick check for Mercy Smith and soon found that the name appeared to be an alias, with no other mentions in the database before or since. On a hunch, Wally ran a check on the doctor who supposedly delivered Kyle. The doctor had, interestingly, died in nearby Rutland, Vermont, a year and a half before Kyle was born. Obviously, any documents with his name on them had been forged.

The result was that Richard Townsend had sole legal custody of baby Kyle, with no obvious way of identifying the birth mother. Wally figured Townsend must have paid off the mother, or somehow made sure that she would get lost and never show up again. It was a dirty mess, and it told Wally a lot about what kind of person Richard Townsend was.

Wally's eyelids began to sag just as the first sign of morning light appeared to the east—she hadn't slept in twenty-four hours, and her head felt so heavy that she couldn't hold it up anymore. She shut her laptop and curled into the cushions of her sofa. In the final, bleary moments before she nodded off, Wally wished for sleep without dreams.

6.

TIGER SAT IN THE BACKSEAT OF THE STOLEN SEDAN, watching the bank.

He felt uneasy—distracted by the clumsy, accidental way he had made contact with Wally the night before. Seven, maybe eight times he had risked everything to find scraps of information about his sister, but why? He owed her nothing, and as far as he was concerned she didn't owe him anything either—they were strangers to each other, two distant, frayed ends of a rotten, corrupt lineage, with nothing between them but a shared legacy of betrayal and pain.

Tiger promised himself that he would not reach out to Wally again.

"Go minus two," Rachel said from the front passenger seat as she checked the time on her cell phone. Though she was barely twenty years old, her voice carried the authority of someone much more experienced—someone like her father, Archer Divine, who had trained her. Rachel's short brown hair was tied back to keep it out of her way, and the wiry, muscular physique she worked so hard to build seemed pumped and almost vibrating underneath her tight black T-shirt.

When they hit the bank, Rachel would become *Sally*. Within

this crew, Tiger was always *Joe*. The driver was *Steve*, and sitting beside Tiger in the backseat was *Robbie*, both of them temporary residents of Archer Divine's "Ranch," as Tiger was. He didn't know their real names and never would.

A pretty girl emerged through the glass door of the bank—what was she, sixteen? Maybe seventeen, like Tiger? She had fresh skin and shiny, shoulder-length blond hair and was wearing a bright red-and-white cheerleader's uniform. In this outfit—Tiger knew from American movies he had seen—she and her friends would dance and shout on the sidelines during sporting events, cheering for a pack of teenage boys on the field who had no idea how lucky they were.

"Go minus one," said Rachel.

As the cheerleader strolled down the sidewalk, graceful and carefree, Tiger wondered what it would be like to know this girl in real life, to call her up casually in the evening and talk about the class they were in together, to joke about the laughable awkwardness of the math teacher. Tiger would eventually find the courage to ask the girl out on a date, and he imagined the simple thrill of hearing her say "yes."

Skaska. Paradise.

"Is that what you like, Joe?" Rachel asked. "Soft and pretty, for a rough boy?"

Tiger looked into the rearview mirror and met her stony gaze. Tiger had been at the Ranch only two weeks when Rachel had come to his room late one night, half drunk. She was strong and aggressive and hungry, but there was something missing in her. The experience had left Tiger feeling cold and empty, lonelier even than when he had the cot to himself. After than night, Tiger had refused Rachel's continued advances. The rejection had left a mark on her, and every interaction between them since then was tainted with her resentment.

Rachel's glance dropped back to her cell phone, checking the time again.

"Now," she said.

They pulled ski masks over their heads as Steve hit the accelerator and drove straight ahead, skidding to a stop in front of the bank. Rachel, Robbie, and Tiger slid out the passenger-side doors and sprinted into the bank, breezing past the startled locals of the small New England town.

The customers and employees of the bank watched in horror and confusion as the crew streamed into the bank, the barrels of their MP-5 machine guns held high.

"Everybody down on the floor!" Rachel shouted at the horrified customers and bank employees. "Anyone moves, they get a bullet in the head!"

The soft, middle-aged guard just inside the door made a fumbling attempt to reach for his gun before the butt of Robbie's MP-5 came down on the man's head and dropped him to the floor. The guard's handgun skidded along the floor and came to rest at Tiger's feet. Tiger grabbed the gun and covertly stuck it under his belt, hiding it beneath his jacket.

"I said DOWN NOW!" Rachel shouted again, rage in her voice.

The rest of customers and employees hurried onto the cold floor, lying facedown. Rachel leapt behind the counter and found the tall, lanky bank manager, hauling him through the door of the open vault to the safe-deposit boxes.

"Ninety seconds!" Robbie said loudly enough for Rachel to hear from the vault. That was how long it would take the local deputies—both of them now eating a late breakfast at a diner at the far end of town—to respond to the call.

Tiger and Robbie stood watch by the door as the sound of hammering echoed into the bank from the vault area—Rachel was targeting a specific safe-deposit box. Tiger didn't care. Not knowing the full details of any specific job was just fine with him; he could play his part like the professional he was, easy in and easy out.

"Sixty seconds!"

One minute and they would be heading away from town and back to the Ranch. Everything was under control—until suddenly, it wasn't.

The front door of the bank swung open—just six feet from Tiger—and the red-and-white cheerleader stepped into the bank. *Shit*. Why was she back, and why hadn't the door been locked? It was the simplest thing—one brief action in the routine to reach out and throw the bolt. Had it been his job? No... he was certain it was Robbie's.

The girl was sending a text on her cell phone as she entered, her eyes looking down at the display screen until she was three steps inside the door. Then she froze, her terrified gaze fixed on the barrel of Tiger's gun, his sights locked onto her.

Tiger needed to take the shot, but instead his eyes met hers. He hesitated.

"Your shot!" Robbie said.

In that instant, the cheerleader spun on her heels and bolted straight back for the door. Tiger tracked her, but before he could get her in his sights she was gone, out the door and racing up the street, hollering for help.

"What the fuck, Joe?" Robbie said, staring at Tiger in bewilderment.

Tiger had no answer.

Now the fallen guard—still bleeding heavily—lunged toward Robbie with a knife in his hand. Where had the weapon come from? He slashed at Robbie's leg, slicing deep into his thigh. Robbie howled in pain and dropped to the floor, arterial blood splashing out and mingling with the guard's own sticky red pool.

"*Mother fucker!*" Robbie roared through gritted teeth. He pointed his gun at the guard and fired a quick barrage into the man's chest, killing him instantly. A few of the customers and employees began weeping as blood continued to gush from Robbie's leg.

Femoral artery, Tiger thought. Nothing to be done. *Shit*.

"Sally! We're RED!" Tiger shouted, and Rachel quickly appeared from the rear of the bank.

"What the hell…?" she said, furious at the sight of Robbie bleeding out on the bank floor and the dead guard beside him.

"We're burned," Tiger answered.

Rachel stepped halfway out the door. She looked up the street and spotted the cheerleader, half a block away now and still screaming. The other locals on the street were all crouched down now—hiding in doorways or behind parked cars—their eyes on the bank door and on Rachel.

"Shit!" Rachel hissed.

Rachel turned her gun on Robbie and shot one clean round into his head, to a chorus of more wailing from the employees and customers, their sounds of fear reverberating off the cold, hard floor.

"We have company," Tiger said. A state trooper's cruiser had pulled up to the curb across the street. A fresh-faced young trooper climbed out of the driver's seat, his gun drawn and his eyes on the bank.

"Go," Rachel said.

Tiger raised his gun and strafed the windows at the front of the bank with a long autoblast from his MP-5, bringing down the entire front wall in an exploding shower of broken glass. His gun still blazing, Tiger sped out and onto the street with Rachel following behind him. The young deputy—petrified—scurried for cover.

As they ran across the street toward their waiting car, Tiger continued strafing the entire street with autoblasts, aiming high but sending a message to anyone within a two-hundred-yard radius that they should be smart and stay down. Rachel joined in with her gun as well, the storm of bullets ripping through cars and storefronts. Tiger spotted a parked pickup truck with an auxiliary diesel tank in its bed—a quick blast from his weapon exploded the tank, creating a deafening fireball.

Tiger and Rachel reached the stolen car at the curb, where Steve waited behind the wheel with an angry and bewildered look on his face.

"What went down?!" Steve said.

"Shut up and drive," commanded Rachel, and Steve did, peeling away from the curb and immediately steering toward a side street, the first leg of an escape route out of town that had been planned weeks earlier.

Through the rear window of the car, Tiger took one last look up the street, where the locals were already beginning to poke their heads up and converge on the scene of the heist. Far up the street—at least two hundred yards away, Tiger spotted the red-and-white cheerleader.

The girl was still running.

They dumped and burned the stolen car in a ravine a few miles to the north, then walked a mile overland to the interstate truck stop where they had parked the SUV.

It was nearly dark when they arrived at the Ranch. It was an old, seven-story brick warehouse at the edge of a vast oil-storage facility in New Jersey, just a short boat ride across Upper Bay to Manhattan. The lower windows of the warehouse were boarded up, with motion-sensitive security cameras mounted high up at every corner. Its parking lot was surrounded on all sides by a twelve-foot-high fence. Four feet of razor-sharp concertina wire ran along the top.

The motorized gate rolled open and Steve pulled the SUV inside. The parking area was large and filled with several vehicles, including a red Cadillac SUV and a gray Humvee. A basketball hoop stood at one corner.

"We'll debrief tomorrow." Rachel's tone was curt as they stepped out of the SUV, and she addressed Tiger. "My father will want to hear it all."

Tiger glanced up to the windows on the sixth floor of the warehouse and saw the figure of Archer Divine himself silhouetted in the window, the glow of a cigarette in his hand. The psychic weight of Divine's disappointment radiated downward upon them.

Tiger climbed the inside staircase to his room on the third floor. His area consisted of a vast, musty storage room, unfurnished except for a small woodstove that vented through an air shaft, a single bed, an old sofa, and a folding card table with a radio, a desk lamp, and a small collection of books resting on it. Some cardboard file boxes that held Tiger's few possessions were stacked by the bed. One wall of the room—the south side—was almost entirely comprised of windows, dirty and yellowed. The air was thick with a musty, oily smell, residue from the heavy machines that had once been bolted to the floor but had been gone for decades.

Tiger found a loose brick in the north wall and pulled the bank guard's gun out from under his jacket, sliding it into the empty space before replacing the brick. Tiger was not a prisoner on the Ranch—not exactly—but he and the other tenants were required to follow a strict set of rules: no leaving the Ranch except on sanctioned missions, no communication at all with the outside world, no computer access, and no personal weapons of any kind.

The stated penalty for breaking the rules was banishment from the Ranch with total loss of earnings—no matter how much had been accumulated. Tiger's theory, however, was that the punishment was more final. As far as he could tell, no "banished" men were ever seen or heard from again. Would Divine let a disgruntled former worker out loose into the world, with inside knowledge of the Ranch's activities to trade on the open market? Not possible.

Tiger lit a fire in the woodstove and lay back on his bed. He was restless, his mind flooded with images of the day: Robbie lying on the bank floor, blood spilling from him. The terror in the cheerleader's eyes when she looked down the barrel of his weapon. The image of the girl escaping, running hard up the street and not looking back.

The memory troubled him. He would not make the same mistake again.

Tiger eventually slept, waking in the darkness of very early morning. The clock on his radio read 3:20 A.M. He remembered the promise he'd made to himself the day before—that he would abandon any ideas of nurturing the vague, irrational connection he still felt toward his sister—but once again he felt powerless to resist the impulse. Tiger got up, dressed, and opened a window, stepping out onto the creaky, rusty, old fire escape. He quietly made his way upward, climbing the fire escape two steps at a time.

He reached the sixth floor and pried one of the casement windows open, stepping carefully into the Ranch's "operations center," a large, open, and high-ceilinged room that included a kitchen-and-dining area, a communal lounge with a big-screen TV, a tall gun vault—locked, of course—and a row of locked offices at the inside wall. Tiger crossed the floor slowly and quietly, avoiding loose floorboards on his way to Archer Divine's office. Seven seconds of work with his lock pick and Tiger was in the room, waiting for Divine's personal computer to boot up.

Tiger logged in. The password (BOZEMAN45) had been sold to him by another tenant named "Parker." Tiger didn't know how Parker had come upon the password, only that it worked. Tiger considered checking in on Wally's Facebook page, but his previous venture there had nearly resulted in disaster—without thinking, he had clicked on the "accept" button and allowed her to initiate a video call with him. When she had said his name out loud, the speakers on Divine's computer had blasted *"Tiger?"* throughout the sixth floor of the Ranch. He had been lucky that no one had come to investigate the sound.

Instead, Tiger opened the browser, navigating to the New York City traffic-information site that he had visited several times before. The time was now only 3:40 A.M., but the site carried reviewable footage of its cameras for the previous seventy-two hours. Tiger clicked on the link for a traffic cam on Lexington Avenue, uptown.

Within seconds, a live video was streaming on the monitor screen. The bottom-left corner of the image showed the west sidewalk on Lexington and a subway entrance, very quiet now with only an occasional pedestrian passing through the frame.

Tiger opened a drop-down box and selected a time frame to review—choosing 7:50 A.M. the previous morning. After a few seconds of buffering, the video of the intersection came to life, a throng of early-morning commuters streaming in and out of the subway entrance. It had been a sunny, relatively warm spring morning in the city, the commuters wearing fewer layers of clothing than they had on previous days.

Tiger watched and waited, keeping his eyes glued to the image. He began scrolling forward, scanning the images in triple time, all the while listening for signs that others in the compound were up and about. All was quiet.

When the camera clock read 7:59, another surge of

commuters emerged from the subway and onto the Lexington Avenue sidewalk. They moved in a mass, everyone in a hurry. But once they were a few yards away from the stairs the crowd began to separate. Tiger slowed the image to normal speed, and there she was.

Wally Stoneman—his sister—wore skinny jeans and a light-green sweater, a colorful scarf tied around her neck. Her familiar messenger bag was slung over her shoulder. Her bright blond hair, short and intentionally disheveled, made her stand out among the other uptown pedestrians. Wally walked south on Lexington, apparently in a hurry. Her image grew closer and closer to the traffic cam, until Tiger caught a clear look at her face. She seemed aggravated, and Tiger wondered what had put her in such a state.

Tiger froze the image and zoomed in on Wally's face. What was he looking for? Even he couldn't say. If he was hoping for some kind of insight into his own nature, it was a waste of his time—the two of them were different species, shaped by circumstances that could not have been more opposite. The inexplicable bond he felt toward her was still present, nagging him, but the need to connect with Wally seemed more and more like a sentimental miscalculation. It was a mistake as great as the one he had made the previous day when he had hesitated too long at the trigger.

Tiger heard a faint noise from somewhere out in the main room and froze, listening intently. He remained motionless and still for two minutes, maybe more, before deciding that he was in no immediate danger of being discovered.

Enough. Tiger closed the browser and ran a security sweep of the hard drive, careful to eliminate all traces of his activity. When he finally shut down the computer and made his way back out onto the fire escape, he knew with certainty that he would not make this secret, late-night pilgrimage again.

It was time for Tiger to move on and never look back.

7.

WALLY SLEPT QUIETLY AND DEEPLY, FINALLY WAKING at nearly 11:00 A.M. to the smell of fresh coffee. Looking through the sliding glass doors onto the roof, she saw Kyle sitting up straight in a patio chair, drinking coffee from one of her mugs. The morning sun looked warm and inviting, but Kyle's upright posture suggested that he was waiting, not relaxing. Wally pulled on a hoodie and poured herself a cup of coffee, then went outside to join him.

"Hey," he said. "I needed coffee. I hope it's okay."

"Sure."

"I took a shower too—there was an extra towel."

Kyle looked clean and put together, certainly better than he had the night before. He'd replaced one of the butterfly bandages on his face, and the rest of his injuries were mostly just bruises, darker now and less inflamed.

"Wally, I'm really sorry for everything yesterday," he said, sincerely. "At your office and definitely at that other place, I can't remember the name."

"It's called Harmony House."

"Right. I'm embarrassed. You have no reason to believe this, but how I was yesterday is nothing like I normally am."

"You had a bad day." A huge understatement, Wally figured, but she still felt as though her ineptness at the interview had made things worse. If they could start the day with a clean slate, why not?

"And I made your day suck too, even though you were obviously just trying to help. I would have just bugged out of here this morning, but I wanted to apologize in person. I'm sorry."

Kyle's entire demeanor was different that morning. Studying him as he spoke, Wally noticed a kind of clarity—even confidence—that he hadn't shown before.

"I appreciate that," she said. "But we're here and safe now."

"Yeah, about that—my head was obviously a little messed up last night. But if I remember things right, you seriously kicked the asses of those guys. That was, like, hard-core cage-fighting action. What's up with that?"

"I've had some training. But what you saw was mostly about surprise—they didn't expect that kind of resistance from me, and I used that to my advantage."

"That's one way of putting it," Kyle said with just the hint of a mischievous grin. "I think the second guy might be on a feeding tube right now." He paused, looking serious again, and stood up. "Anyway, I appreciate everything. And what comes next, I have to do that on my own."

Something about the finality in Kyle's voice made Wally uneasy. "Hold on," she said, "what are you planning to do?"

Kyle sighed, looking a little guilty. "I'm sorry. I used your laptop. I saw the information you put together on my father."

Wally's eyes went to the dining table—she'd left her laptop there last night, open and still logged in to her accounts. She felt a rush of anger toward him but also toward herself because she had forgotten to log off her accounts.

"That's a total invasion, Kyle!"

"I know, you have a right to be pissed off. But I didn't look at anything private—"

"It's *my* laptop, Kyle! It's *all* private!"

"I know, but you were still asleep, and I needed to know if you'd started any of your research stuff. Now I have an idea where to start looking for my mother."

"What are you talking about?" Wally was still angry, but she couldn't help being curious about what Kyle had spotted in the file.

"First of all, I know her name: Mercy Smith."

"It's an alias."

"Yeah, I read your notes. But it's a place to start. On top of that, I'd never seen my birth certificate before. I put some things together."

"Like what?"

"It says I was born in Fair Haven, Vermont. I looked on Google Maps and that's in the Adirondacks. It reminded me of something I'd forgotten: Around the time I was born, there were a few years when my father didn't live here in the city. He has a fishing lodge up in the Adirondacks. The timing fits—it's almost definite that my birth mother was with him then. I'm sure there's something up there for me to find."

"Okay, fine," Wally said. "So give me a chance to follow up on that."

"I'm going there now."

"Kyle, you have to trust me… this is a mistake. I've reviewed thousands of the Society's cases—family members separated for years and then finally coming together. More than half the time it doesn't work, and usually it's because expectations are too high. The more you *need* the reunion to work, the more certain it will be to fail you, in some way. That's the reality. There's just too much pressure on everyone."

"Okay, then tell me this: if you were me, would you wait for just the right time, or would you run down any possible lead as soon as you could?"

"I'd wait," she lied.

"Ha," he said. "I only met you two days ago and I already know that's bullshit."

Busted. She couldn't deny it.

"It's only like three hundred miles to get there," he went on. "That's one easy day of driving. Whatever I find, I don't even have to use it right away. But I have to go."

"One day of driving? You have a car?"

"I have money."

"You're going to *rent* a car? Have you ever tried? Cash doesn't do it. You're not old enough, so you'll need a fake ID, like mine, which could get you busted all by itself. Plus a credit card to secure the rental, and then you're in the system. Your father will find out immediately."

Kyle looked frustrated—he obviously hadn't thought everything through.

"I'll hitch," he said defiantly. "I'll take a bus. Whatever..."

"You don't think the fishing lodge is one of the places they'll be looking for you?"

"No way. As far as the old man knows, I hate that place."

"Why's that?"

Kyle went silent for a moment, the dark expression on his face conveying a memory of something he'd rather forget.

"It doesn't matter," he said, his voice bitter. "I'm not asking permission. I waited here to tell you my plans face-to-face because you've been good to me. I wouldn't have survived these past days without your help, and I really appreciate it. But I *am* going."

He was obviously determined, but when Wally looked at him she could see he was feeling other things also: fear, doubt, excitement. She knew how intoxicating those feelings could be. Who knew what he would find at the fishing lodge? It might be something that would change his life forever—for better or worse. At least he was showing faith in himself.

"I'll trade you," she said.

"What does that mean?"

"The place you ended up last night, Harmony House? The woman you saw there is named Candace Chen, and situations like yours are totally in her wheelhouse. She could set you up with a place to live that's safe. She could get you counseling, legal help—all kinds of things."

He shook his head. "I can take care of my own problems."

"Yeah, you can, but everyone needs a little help to start out. So here's the trade: I'll take you to Vermont, set us up with a car. We go up and find whatever there is to find, and when we get back to town you'll just sit with Candace and hear what she has to say."

"That's it."

"Yeah, hear her out. That's it. It's a win-win for you."

Kyle met her proposal with silence, apparently wrestling with the offer. Wally herself had one reservation—if Tiger reached out for her again, she would be out of contact. But it would be worth it if she could help Kyle and make up for the damage she'd done.

But he was still hesitating.

"Hey, Kyle?"

"Yeah?" He looked up at her, a pained look on his face as he struggled with the decision.

"Don't be an idiot." She cracked a little smile.

He smiled a little in return.

"Deal," he said. "For real, I'll be happy to have company. I'm actually a little nervous about what I might find up there."

Wally liked hearing this—the fact that he was feeling doubt meant he was capable of being realistic.

"That's a good way to start," she said.

Thinking about the road trip ahead, Wally felt an unexpected spike of excitement, as if an adventure was something she'd been craving all along without knowing it. She hadn't left the city even once in five months—not since Shelter Island—and suddenly the idea of escape was intoxicating.

She would have to lay a little groundwork first. Wally went inside and picked up her cell, dialing Lewis at the Society number. At some point, Wally would bring him up to speed on what was going on with Kyle, but now wasn't the time—he would disapprove of almost every step she'd taken so far, especially her decision to bring a client home with her.

"What is it, Wally? You're late."

"If it's okay, Lewis, I need a couple of personal days."

"I understand. I thought you might experience some emotional blowback after your encounter with the young man... what was his name? Kyle?"

"Yeah, Kyle. It'll only be a day or two...." she said, feeling slightly shitty for not being honest. Wally sat down on one of her desk chairs as she waited for Lewis's response, tapping her heel on the floor anxiously like a delinquent schoolgirl waiting outside a principal's office.

"Take your time away," Lewis finally said with an impatient sigh, "but you'll have to toughen up in the future. We deal with failure every day, but we just keep working."

His tone was a little patronizing, and it bugged Wally enough that she almost told him that she already was working a case, with or without his approval. *Almost*.

"I know you're right," she said instead. "Thanks for understanding. I'll see you in a few days."

Wally went back inside and threw a few things into her messenger bag as Kyle stood by waiting, then grabbed a light jacket. She was ready.

"One quick stop," she told Kyle as they locked up her apartment.

They walked down one flight together, and Kyle hung back as Wally knocked on January and Bea's door. It was January who answered, wearing pajamas with her hair up in a ponytail and a green tea deep-cleansing mask spread all over her face.

"What up, Stoneman?"

"Do me a favor and check on Tevin?" Wally asked, passing her friend a spare key to her apartment. "I'll be gone for just a couple days, but if you could give him some frozen fish once or twice, that'd be great."

"Okay, but where—" January caught sight of Kyle, hanging back by the staircase. She leaned in close to Wally to whisper in her ear excitedly. "*You slut!*"

"I'll check in if I can," Wally said, glaring at January to make her behave.

8.

"Don't bother, girlfriend. The snapper will be fine."

THEY RENTED A CAR IN BROOKLYN, USING A CREDIT card with Lewis's name on it that she was only supposed to use for Ursula Society business. Wally had no reason to think that Richard Townsend's security men had identified her yet, but they would eventually and she didn't want any transactions on her personal account that might help them find her—or Kyle.

As the two of them surveyed the menu of available cars, Wally noticed that one was a Lincoln Town Car—in white. It was a bittersweet reminder of Tevin, and how happy he had been when he had slid behind the wheel of an identical rented Town Car five months earlier. It had been a rare and exciting treat for him—a poor kid from Harlem—and his face beamed with pure happiness as he drove them out of the city and upstate, a route nearly identical to the one Wally and Kyle would be taking that afternoon.

The last trip Wally and Tevin had taken together in that car was to the Brooklyn Navy Yard, where everything went wrong. Tevin had died there, gunned down without mercy by Wally's own father, Alexei Klesko. It had been the worst moment of her life....

Until Shelter Island.

"There's a chance the road will still be rough," Kyle said, his voice snapping Wally out of her dark reverie. "Four-wheel drive might be a good idea." They chose a Ford Explorer, in blue.

Wally was careful not to include the GPS option in the rental—it was possible for their movements to be traced that way—but once they were inside the SUV, Kyle used a screwdriver from the vehicle's tool kit to pry the LED panel out of the dashboard.

"What are you doing?" she asked.

"Saying you don't want GPS doesn't really do anything," he said. "They keep it active for themselves so they can track their car."

Once he had slid the panel out, Kyle immediately located a SIM card and pulled it out, holding it up for Wally to see.

"We're officially off the radar," he said, tossing the SIM card into the glove compartment.

"Smart," she said. "How do you know how to do that?"

"Half the guys at Sexton have helicopter parents who need to know every detail of their kids' lives, and that includes being able to trace them and their cars with GPS. Sometimes a guy needs to run silent."

Wally took this as a good sign—Kyle apparently had some skills to contribute and was obviously thinking about their situation. Maybe he'd be more of a help on their fact-finding mission than she'd thought. She pulled out her own phone and shut off the GPS, just in case.

They made one quick stop at a convenience store, where they loaded up on a ridiculous amount of junk food and half a dozen cans of energy drinks—enough to keep them wired for the drive. Wally used the ATM in the store to withdraw a thousand dollars in cash. It was probably more than they would need, but she didn't want to make any Internet transactions once they were moving.

By the time they were officially on the road—Wally taking the first shift behind the wheel—it was early afternoon, with five or six hours of driving ahead. Wally plugged her phone into the stereo and streamed a playlist of Radiohead from Spotify. The music filled the Explorer with a trancelike soundtrack that fit well with the landscape rushing past them.

"It's all happening," Kyle said, a hopeful look on his face.

"Yeah, it is," Wally said.

It felt fun and exciting to break free of the city, but Wally reminded herself that she had gone way off the reservation. She was dealing with Kyle and his case in exactly the wrong way, and she had lied about it to Lewis, who trusted and cared for her. It wouldn't do any good to beat herself up about it—that would be a waste of time, now—but she vowed to be smarter and more conscientious as things moved forward.

A couple of hours into their drive, another thought came to Wally: their route to the Adirondacks would take them just fifty or sixty miles east of Neversink Farm, where Jake and Ella were now living. The thought of seeing them again was tempting, but it also made her anxious—they had loved Tevin as much as Wally had, and it had partly been her selfishness that had killed him. She wondered if they had forgiven her yet, or if they even thought of her.

"Would you be cool with a minor detour?" she asked Kyle.

"Sure. Where to?"

"My friends live on a farm north of Utica. If we just stay on the interstate it'll only add an hour or so."

"Sounds good. I'll be glad if you get something from this trip too."

Another hour of driving took them to the exit at a town called Mohawk, and from there they drove country roads north into a stretch of lush green pastureland. For miles, one farm flew by after another, with lakes and scattered woodland in between. A turn onto a long dirt road eventually led them to a two-story white farmhouse on top of a small hill, overlooking a lake. The sign at the open gate read NEVERSINK FARM.

They paused at the gate and looked the place over.

"Wow," Kyle said. "This is the real deal, right? An actual farm."

"I guess so," Wally said. "I've never been here before."

"Did your friends grow up here, or what?"

"No, it's a kind of residential thing for at-risk youths. Kids from the street and all that. They work the farm and go to school. A fresh start. Which is what my friends needed more than anything."

"That actually sounds good. I wonder if they have room for me," he joked.

They pulled into the dirt driveway and motored up to the farmhouse, where they parked and climbed out of the Explorer. Two other vehicles were parked there, both of them well-used and rusted old Ford pickup trucks. Several other buildings sprawled over the property, including a huge red barn—of course—and another building that looked like it might be a bunkhouse. The pasture held sheep and goats and about twenty head of cattle, as far as Wally could tell.

The setting was beautiful and calm—like a perfect landscape painting, Wally thought. She imagined Jake and Ella—two city kids—working this farm in overalls and flannel shirts. She couldn't help smiling at the idea. They were adaptable, for sure. They would thrive as long as they were together.

An unassuming man in his forties came out to meet them. He wore canvas work pants and a T-shirt. His clean-shaven face was weathered and creased, evidence of a life lived outdoors doing hard work. He shook their hands as he introduced himself.

"I'm Stan Hooks," he said, squinting at them.

"Hi," Wally said. "I'm Wally, and this is Kyle. Sorry to just barge in—I know you probably have set visiting times, but—"

"You're Wally Stoneman?" Stan wanted to know.

She was taken aback. "Yes."

"Jake and Ella have told a few stories," Stan explained. "You're something of a legend around here."

Hearing this, Wally felt a huge rush of emotions: relief, happiness, regret. Jake and Ella still thought of her, and they still cared for her. How had she *not* known that would be true? Why had she kept herself at a distance from them for so long, when what she needed most in the world was friends she could trust?

"If it's all right, I'd like to see them."

"I'm really sorry," Stan said. "Most everyone is down in western Pennsylvania for a few days. It's a 4H event—they're showing our hogs and taking some classes. Jake and Ella are going to be really disappointed they missed you."

Wally's heart sank a little. She couldn't imagine anything better at that moment than to have her friends' arms around her. To come so close and miss them made her heart ache.

"Me too," she said. "Let them know I stopped by?"

"I'll be sure to," Stan said. "I know it'll make them happy that you tried."

After leaving a short note for her friends, Wally and Kyle got back on the road. Wally felt a wave of sadness as they pulled away, Stan Hooks waving goodbye in the rearview mirror. Her disappointment was obvious enough for Kyle to see.

"You okay?"

She was on the verge of tears, actually, but she waited for the feeling to pass before answering.

"Yeah, just sad. The good thing is, I had some questions—some things that were weighing me down. I think I just got the answers."

"Good answers?"

"Yeah, I think so."

They made it back to the rural highway and stopped at a gas station to fill the thirsty Explorer and take bathroom breaks. From there, Kyle took the wheel. The highway led them north into the thick of the Adirondacks, a winding road through dense, green forest, broken up by occasional lakes and abundant streams that were flowing full from the runoff of winter snow.

After an hour or so—by then it was late afternoon—Kyle turned the Explorer off onto a two-lane dirt road, rutted and rough. They followed this track for five slow, bumpy miles until the road ended, becoming a private drive with NO TRESPASSING signs everywhere.

"Private road?" Wally asked. "Does that mean this is all yours from here?"

"All my father's, yeah. It's a lot of land. We have a local guy who comes in the spring to grade the road, but he obviously hasn't been through yet."

The dirt was even rougher now, and several times they were forced to stop and clear fallen branches out of the way. When the private drive finally ended, the first thing Wally saw was the enormous lodge constructed of actual logs—like something out of a Ralph Lauren ad, she thought—two stories high, with a large main section and long wings stretching out at both sides. Just a hundred feet from the porch of the lodge was a big lake. It spanned at least a mile across and there were no other homes visible on the shore.

"Wow," she said. "It's like some kind of mountain paradise."

"I know."

They climbed out of the car and stretched. The air was very quiet, but then a soft, mournful sound came to them from the water.

Wally looked across the water and could see a pair of birds floating a hundred yards out, their elegant necks silhouetted against the reflection of the deep-orange sun, hanging low in the sky. Wally followed Kyle past the house and toward the lake, where an old and weathered wooden dock reached fifty feet or so out onto the water. Crossing the gravelly shore, they reached the dock and began to walk out toward the end, the wood under their feet creaking loudly and echoing out over the water.

Wally could see that, for Kyle, returning to this place was a powerful experience. He seemed drawn to the lake by an invisible force, his eyes never leaving the water.

"How long since you've been back here?" she asked.

Kyle ignored the question, instead skipping a few yards ahead and peeling off his clothes. It all came off—boots, socks, sweatshirt, shirt, and cargo pants, until only his boxers were left. Then he sprinted as fast as he could and dove athletically off the edge of the dock, disappearing with hardly a splash under the surface of the lake.

Wally reached the end of the dock and scanned the surface of the water. The ripples from Kyle's dive radiated away, eventually quieting altogether, until everything was still and silent again. How much time had passed since he'd gone in? Fifteen seconds? Twenty? Wally started getting nervous—she stepped to the very edge of the dock and peered down into the water.

"Kyle?" Wally called out, a hint of panic in her voice.

No reply. Ten more seconds passed, but it felt more like ten minutes.

"Kyle!" Now she was genuinely scared for him. She kicked off her shoes—fully prepared to go in after him—but just then he burst to the surface in front of her, rising high out of the water and splashing back down again, hyperventilating from the cold of the water yet wearing a wide, happy smile on his face.

"Woo!" he hollered, elated and breathless. "It's so cold, but soooo awesome!"

"That was NOT funny," Wally yelled back, but something about his goofy grin was contagious and she grinned back at him despite herself.

"What? You missed me?" he teased.

"Absolutely not," she said, folding her arms squarely in front of her.

He responded by smacking the surface of the lake, splashing cold water on her.

"*Asshole,*" Wally objected as she jumped back, laughing with him.

He wiped the water from his eyes and spun slowly around, taking in the whole panorama of the lake and the lodge.

"It's weird," he said. "I don't know if you have a place like this, but I can be away for a long time and forget the feeling it gives me—then as soon as I get back in this water it's like I never left."

Wally sat down at the edge of the dock and rolled up her jeans, submerging her feet in the water until it lapped at her legs all the way up to her calf muscles. *Did* she have a place like that? The old apartment on the Upper West Side, maybe? She had some good memories from her life there, but not enough to make it a home, exactly—she had no desire to ever go back there. Wally wondered if there was a place from her earliest childhood in Russia that would make her feel that way, but if there was she had no recollection of it.

"I have that with a few friends," she answered. "I can be away from them for a while, but the moment we're together again we pick up like we were never apart."

She was thinking about Jake and Ella, of course. She wondered if it were still true, if the three of them really would meld naturally when—and if—they were all together again.

"Yeah," he said. "It's the same kind of thing. It's good, you know?"

Slowly kicking her feet in the water, Wally found herself wondering if that was the way she and Kyle would feel about each other someday—*where the hell did that idea come from?* There was definitely something different about Kyle now, as if he had begun to rediscover himself. Wally figured she could get used to this new, confident version of him.

Kyle 2.0.

"Do you have a boyfriend?" he asked, his directness catching her off guard.

"Uh..."

"It's not a complicated question," he said, a mischievous smile on his face.

"Well, no," she said. Her face felt a little hot, suddenly, and she prayed that she wasn't blushing enough for him to notice. She pulled her feet out of the water and hugged her legs close to her chest. "Not lately."

"C'mon, that *can't* be true," he said. "There's no one special you're close to?"

An image of Tevin suddenly flashed through Wally's mind, piercing her heart. "I was sort of involved with this one guy," she said. "But it didn't end well."

"Painful breakup?"

"You could say that."

"Well?" he asked after a moment, treading water in front of her. The late-afternoon sun shimmered off the drops of water on his powerful shoulders.

"Well *what?*"

"Aren't you gonna ask me? It's only polite."

Wally sighed dramatically. "Fine. Do you have a girlfriend?"

As soon as the question passed her lips, Kyle held his hands up out of the water in a gesture that said "back off."

"Easy, woman!" he protested. "I don't need you pressuring

me. My god, we've only known each other for like a day and a half!"

"Hilarious," Wally said in an irritated tone, but again she couldn't help smiling.

He chuckled with self-satisfaction. He kicked his way to the dock, grabbing the edge and gracefully lifting himself out of the water. Before she even realized where her eyes were directed, Wally noticed that Kyle's boxers were practically transparent. She looked away quickly, but if Kyle was embarrassed he didn't show it. He wiped some of the water off his body with his hands and stepped—still half wet—back into his clothes.

"Now I'm cold and hungry," he said. "Let's get inside."

Wally opened her mouth to speak but found that she was at a loss for words. She climbed to her feet and followed Kyle toward the lodge.

9.

KYLE FOUND THE HIDDEN KEY TO THE MAIN HOUSE and led Wally in through the door on the back porch. It was dark and nearly freezing inside, much colder than the outside air. The windows were covered with exterior storm shutters, and the room filled with light as Kyle went back out onto the porch and swung them open. Inside, Wally raised the windows, letting the fresh air in to chase away the thick, musty atmosphere of the old lodge.

"It gets pretty rank in here over the long winter," Kyle said. Wally actually liked the smell. It was like breathing in history.

The center portion of the house was a "great room," a big open space two stories high with solid log beams across the ceiling. White linens were draped over large, masculine leather pieces of furniture; plush sofas and high-backed chairs huddled like a gathering of ghosts before a massive stone fireplace. There were trophy fish mounted all over the walls but no other game. A big picture window faced the shore, and with the shutters now open the orange glow of the setting sun filled the room, spotlighting the myriad particles of dust in the air that had been unsettled by Wally and Kyle's arrival.

"The power is out," Kyle said. He left the room for a few minutes and then returned, carrying four brass oil lamps. "It happens every winter. I guess they haven't had a crew out here to fix the lines yet. I like the lamps better anyway—it's more like camping out, you know? The stove and the water heater are propane, though, so I have those going. In an hour or two there'll be hot water."

Kyle lit all four of the lamps and placed them at various spots around the large room, spreading a mellow yellow light. There was a large pile of split wood and kindling next to the stone fireplace, and Wally sat nearby watching as Kyle built a fire, arranging the various tiers of wood so expertly that once he lit the pile with a single match it grew fast, burning large and hot within minutes. He did all of this easily and naturally, as if he was born doing it. Kyle was taking care of her, and it felt good to be taken care of. It was a feeling Wally wasn't altogether used to.

The two of them teamed up to pull the linens off the furniture and fold them into a neat pile, until finally the great room was finished and all the dust had settled. They sat cross-legged in front of the fire, watching the flames grow larger, their shoulders occasionally touching.

"Hmm," Kyle murmured.

"What?"

"I was just thinking—did we stop for groceries on the way up?"

"Uh... do you *remember* stopping for groceries?"

"Come to think of it, no," he said. "That was bad planning. I'm starving now."

"Those five double-sized energy drinks you tossed down didn't provide lasting sustenance? Are you sure?"

He winced a little at the memory. "Don't remind me! I'll hurl."

"A big place like this must have something in the pantry."

"Yeah," he said, "there's usually something."

Kyle jumped up and headed for the kitchen, Wally right behind him. They found a large walk-in pantry to one side, fully stocked with the kind of staples—canned goods, rice, and a whole lot of freeze-dried things—that would survive long periods of time without going bad. There was nothing even remotely fresh, of course, but it was enough to feed a dozen people for weeks.

"Whoa, this is a lot," Wally said. "Is your dad some kind of survivalist nut?"

Kyle shrugged. "He's definitely got a paranoid side. What kind of things can you make?"

"I'm excellent at reheating pizza. How about you?"

"I can cook fresh trout over an open fire."

"You're officially worthless, then," Wally said, but she spotted a box that read PANCAKE MIX and pointed it out to him. "There's something. With a little teamwork we can put together some respectable flapjacks. How hard can it be?"

Harder than they thought, as it turned out. They had the mix, but the instructions on the carton required eggs and milk to complete the recipe. They went back to the pantry and found freeze-dried eggs and cans of something called "condensed milk," which they opened to find a gooey substance that looked and felt like shampoo. For half an hour they each experimented with proportions of the ingredients, coming up with their own versions of the batter. Kyle's came up way too thick and Wally's much too runny.

"Mine looks like the foamy stuff that floats on the East River," Wally said. "Totally pathetic."

"Speak for yourself," Kyle said. "I think mine is pretty close."

"Are you kidding me?" Wally said. "Look at what you've made there. Were you one of those kids in elementary school who used to eat paste?"

Kyle dipped his index finger into his "batter" and came up with a gob of the stuff... which he immediately flicked at Wally. It hit her on the cheek and stuck there, cold and disgusting on her skin. She felt a sudden fight-or-flight rush of adrenaline.

"*Ooooh*... big mistake," Wally said mock-threateningly. "Now you'll suffer my wrath!"

Wally scooped up a handful of the watery slime she'd made and hurled it at Kyle, splashing it all over the front of his shirt. He looked down at the stain in exaggerated horror.

"You will pay dearly for this," he shouted, grabbing a spatula and scooping a mega-sized gob of batter out of his mixing bowl.

Before he could get a clean shot, Wally grabbed her own bowl and ducked out of the kitchen, letting out a high-pitched squeal—*where the hell did that alien sound come from?* she wondered—as she raced across the great room and hid behind one of the couches.

"That was the girliest scream I've ever heard," Kyle said, coming after her and throwing more mix. She dodged the projectile and answered with another handful of her slime, which struck him in the face.

"How girly was that?" Wally taunted him.

Kyle kept coming after her, and they traded a barrage of shots as they chased each other around the furniture. An unexpected rush of delight ran through Wally as she bobbed and weaved to avoid getting hit, answering every attack from Kyle with one of her own. Wally had years of martial-arts training, but it turned out that none of those hand-to-hand tactics were very useful against high-velocity clumps of pancake mix. As she raced past the fireplace Kyle managed to land a massive glop of the crud on her chest.

"Wait, hold on!" she said, standing up in full view and spreading her hands wide in a universal gesture of peace. "Truce, okay?"

"Now that I've got you on the run..."

"No, I mean it," Wally pleaded, apparently sincere. "Aren't we better than this, Kyle?"

"Are we?"

Wally responded by laughing as she heaved everything that was left in her bowl at Kyle. A big splash of the slime struck him across his face as she ran away, letting out another squeal—*seriously, where the hell did that sound come from?*—and hid in a bathroom in the nearest hallway, locking the door behind her. Within seconds, she could hear Kyle arrive outside the door, breathing hard.

"The window in that bathroom is stuck and can't open more than a few inches," he said through the barricade, "so if you want out, you're going through me."

"Okay, then," Wally said, catching her breath. "Truce for real this time."

"Easy for you to say—you got the last good strike."

"Okay, fine. I come out, and you take your best shot. Then we're done."

"Cool," he said. "Let's do it."

Wally opened the bathroom door slowly and stepped out, shutting her eyes and bracing herself for the impact of the expected glob. When a few seconds went by and nothing happened, she cautiously opened her eyes and saw that Kyle had fashioned his remaining mix into a round white ball of glop, stuck harmlessly to his nose and accompanied by a blank expression on his face.

Wally laughed out loud and doubled over, accidentally wiping her crusty, batter-covered hands on the thighs of her pants.

They retreated to the kitchen and—refusing to be defeated—teamed up to mix a batter that finally looked right. Within fifteen minutes, they each had a big stack of syrupy pancakes on their plates, which they took out to the main room to eat. Calm now after their battle, they sat across from each other on opposite couches, eating quietly in front of the fire as the light outside faded from dusk into darkness.

"Can I show a girl a good time or what?" Kyle asked with a wink.

"Don't quit your day job," Wally said.

As they ate, Wally sensed that Kyle's mood was changing—he was quiet and clearly thinking about something serious. She guessed that he'd remembered the real reason they'd come to the lodge in the first place. She waited for him to speak again, and it turned out that her instincts were right.

"So... the door over there?" He nodded toward a closed door at the far side of the great room, opposite the kitchen. "That's my father's den. If there's anything here that has to do with my birth mother, it's probably in there."

"Okay." Wally could sense his hesitancy.

"But I was thinking... we don't have to do that right away, do we? I mean, tomorrow is soon enough, right?"

"Sure," Wally agreed, and he visibly relaxed. "The past few days have been pretty intense."

"Yeah. It's nice just to hang for a little. If there's more drama on the way, I'd just as soon not deal right now. What you were saying before, about me needing to be ready for this thing with my mother to work? I think I'm starting to understand what you were talking about. It's kind of scary, to tell you the truth. Almost anything could happen next."

It felt good that Kyle was willing to be so honest with her. She could feel herself drawn to him, her chest tightening a little as she watched him, the light of the fire flickering across his handsome but troubled features, his hair falling gently over his eyes the way it had while he had fallen asleep during the cab ride.

"Tomorrow is soon enough," she said.

It was fairly early when Wally found her eyelids drooping. Kyle retrieved some blankets and pillows, arranging them on the two main leather sofas in the room. They crawled under their covers and Wally closed her eyes, listening to the crackle of flames in the fireplace and the insistent chirp of crickets outside the lodge.

"Thanks for coming with me, Wally," Kyle said, his voice soft.

"Good night, Kyle," Wally said, snuggling deep into the soft cushions of the couch. She felt warm and happy as she drifted into sleep.

10.

TIGER POWERED THROUGH HIS EARLY-MORNING workout, breathing hard and dripping sweat. The roof of the warehouse was the perfect place for him—he didn't need any special equipment, and he preferred the cool, open air to the stuffy gym downstairs. Wearing only cargo shorts and a black tank top, he pushed through his fifth set of crab-walks, push-ups, lunges, crunches, planks, and dips and finished with twenty chin-ups on a pipe he had repurposed from the building's rusted old plumbing.

Muscles burning with lactic acid, Tiger paused and mopped his face with a towel. He then chugged half a liter of springwater. He would finish his workout down in the gym on the second floor, where there was a treadmill he could use to run his sprint intervals. Some of the other men—most at least eight or ten years older than he was—would probably be down there now, using the full set of free weights that the ex-military types seemed to prefer, going for pure bulk instead of the lean, quick-twitch flexibility that Tiger sought.

He paused for a moment before heading down, reluctant to leave his outdoor sanctuary on such a perfect morning. The air was so breezy and clear that the Statue of Liberty looked close enough to reach out and touch. When he finally turned toward the door to the stairway, Rachel was standing there silently. *How long had she been watching him?*

"We're ready," she said.

Tiger toweled himself off quickly and followed her down the stairs in silence. The time had come for him to explain his actions during the bank job—his failure to take out the cheerleader when he had the chance. Tiger knew that Archer Divine's verdicts could be harsh and swift. In the days since the failed heist, he had considered fleeing the Ranch, but he already had four months of hard and dangerous work invested there and very few options awaiting him in the outside world. If he stayed with Divine, he would have enough savings within a year to pay for what he needed: a new identity. A fresh start.

Tiger had chosen to risk Divine's judgment.

He and Rachel emerged onto the parking lot and, to his surprise, walked out the main gate onto the quiet street outside. Tiger had never left the Ranch on foot, and it felt liberating. They followed the road south, just past the warehouse to an empty lot, the razed remains of an ancient brick warehouse scattered about. They stopped and waited, and soon Tiger heard it: a helicopter approached from the east, flying low and fast over the bay. Within seconds it reached the lot and touched down, and Tiger and Rachel shielded their faces against the debris sent flying by its massive, deafening rotors.

The passenger door of the chopper slid open and Divine was there, waving him in. Tiger climbed inside and took a seat, noticing that Rachel did not climb in after him. As the helicopter rose into the air, Rachel held her ground in the swirling wind and watched as he went, wearing a strange little smirk on her face that made Tiger uneasy. Tiger reached to shut the side door, and at the last moment Rachel raised her hand and gave him the slightest wave goodbye, the weirdly satisfied look still on her face. Tiger cautioned himself to be on alert from that point onward.

The helicopter flew south, staying low and fast over the water. It was just the three of them—the pilot and Archer Divine seated in front, Tiger in the back. He had no idea where they were headed.

The pilot wore a dark aviator jumpsuit—and an HK45 automatic on his hip—but Divine was dressed in jeans and a spotless khaki cargo vest over a dark flannel shirt—an outfit fit for a casual stroll on the beach. The civilized veneer could not disguise the animalistic bulk of the man, however. Barrel-chested and powerful at the shoulders, Divine had large hands worn from physical labor. His fingernails had been manicured and polished to a subtle gloss. His head of thick gray hair was windblown. Both Divine and the pilot had large aviation headphones on.

Divine turned slightly in his seat and pulled off his polarized sunglasses, fixing an unwavering gaze on Tiger. The man didn't look angry, as far as Tiger could tell, but there was nothing particularly human in his eyes, either—only curiosity, as if Tiger were a puzzle he needed to solve. Divine pointed to the set of aviation headphones that hung beside Tiger—he slid them on, and they nearly silenced the deafening thrum of the helicopter rotors.

"Is there something about our arrangement that you didn't understand?" Divine asked Tiger, his voice over the headset scratchy and filtered.

"No," Tiger answered. In the outside world, Tiger was a wanted man with few options. Under Divine's protection here at the compound, he could stay hidden from law enforcement and earn enough resources to make a clean start in life. This was the bargain he and the other tenants had struck.

"Your hesitation on the bank floor was an embarrassment, and it cost us."

Tiger didn't answer. What was the point? In that blink of an eye, consciously or not, he had made a choice. He would live or die with it, *bes sozheleniya*—with no regrets.

"I expected better results from the son of Alexei Klesko."

Tiger was taken aback. Divine had never mentioned his father, and he had no reason to think he or his team at the Ranch had made the connection. Tiger had one contact in America, the phone number of a friend of a friend that he could use in case of trouble. When he had escaped from Shelter Island five months earlier, Tiger had called that number and was referred to Divine. *Of course*, Tiger realized—his contact would never have passed him off to Divine without first knowing his entire background.

"You know Klesko?" Tiger asked.

"I know *of* him. And, of course, we do deep background on everyone before they are invited to come to the Ranch. Yours was easy enough to uncover."

"I have nothing to do with my father," Tiger said, feeling a flicker of resentment rising up inside of him. He hated that even in his absence his father was still an unshakeable influence in his life.

Divine continued studying Tiger for a moment before turning back around in his seat and facing forward. As the helicopter raced south, the terrain below changed to barren marshland. Within a few minutes, Divine pointed to a location ahead and the pilot nodded, setting down on a dirt road that ran through the marsh. It was dense and overgrown with tall, vine-covered trees that ran right up to the side of the road.

Once on the ground, the pilot powered down the chopper and soon everything was silent again. Divine and Tiger climbed out of the machine. Divine pulled a small duffel bag from the footwell of his seat and took out two guns, an MP-5 machine gun and an HK45 like the pilot's. Divine took the MP-5 and handed Tiger the .45 automatic. It felt heavy—fully loaded—but to be sure, Tiger popped the mag and checked the load: one in the chamber and thirteen in the mag.

Divine began walking down the narrow dirt road and motioned for Tiger to go with him.

"I have a theory," Divine said. "Where you come from you're

royalty—prince of the streets, son of a legend. You didn't have to earn anything. You don't actually have the inner resources for this kind of work."

"Da poshel ty." Fuck you. Tiger knew it could be dangerous to stand up to Divine, but being perceived as weak carried risks as well. His experience with his father had taught him that.

Divine took no offense at Tiger's defiance—he just smiled to himself a little. After just a few minutes of walking, a clearing appeared ahead. A small, half-rotted cottage stood in the middle of it. As the two of them approached the cottage directly, there came the sound of breaking glass and then automatic gunfire—someone inside the cottage was shooting at them.

Tiger was surprised, but both he and Divine remained calm, taking cover behind a tree at the edge of the property. Tiger noted that the gunfire was scattered and undisciplined, none of the shots passing closer than four or five feet away from them. The shooter was a panicked amateur.

"The target in your failed bank job was an unauthorized copy of some account ledgers," said Divine. "Our organization is mentioned in those documents, putting us at risk. Inside this cabin is the accountant who assembled the ledgers and kept the extra copy for himself. If he isn't available to testify about the work he did, his deception will be harmless."

And now Tiger understood. It was an opportunity to make things right.

There was another barrage of automatic gunfire from the

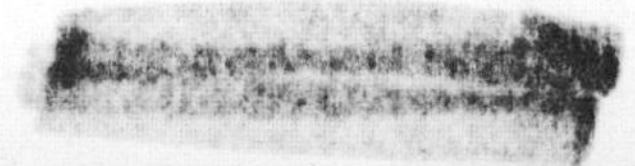

cottage—erratic, again—and then the sound of rapid footsteps. Tiger looked in time to see a lone man sprinting away from the back of the cottage, across the clearing and into the surrounding trees.

"Go," said Divine.

Tiger took off running, crossing the clearing in a matter of seconds and plowing into the trees. He ducked and dodged his way through the woods, but branches and vines still tore and pulled at him, lacerating his face and neck and his lower legs, which were bare below his cutoff fatigues. It was no matter—Tiger could handle the minor punishment, and he was sure that the woods would take an even greater toll on his desperate prey.

As he raced on, Tiger considered the ways in which this encounter might play out, knowing it was possible that Divine's intention was to leave both the accountant *and* Tiger dead in the woods to rot. If the situation evolved that way, he would be ready.

There were a few more gunfire bursts in Tiger's general direction, but none of them came close to finding their mark. When the gunfire went quiet, Tiger stopped in his tracks and remained absolutely still, listening. The woods were silent now. He waited. A single birdcall sounded from far away. A mosquito buzzed around Tiger's left ear. There came a sound of whistling wings from fifty yards away as two or three birds flit away from their perch, followed by the sound of something snapping under the weight of a footstep—a fallen branch, maybe—and then the sound of footsteps again, running somewhere through the trees ahead.

The woods were too dense for Tiger to see the man. He held his ground and closed his eyes, taking a single deep breath and releasing it halfway. He raised his gun up in his right hand and stabilized it on the open palm of his left, bending his knees slightly into a shooter's posture. With his eyes still shut, Tiger concentrated and listened, slowly turning his body to the right as he followed the sound of running footsteps with the muzzle of his HK.

Tiger fired three quick shots into the trees. A cry of pain came from up ahead, and the sound of a body crashing down onto the forest floor. Tiger began walking, soon hearing a whimpering cry just ahead, and a dragging sound. A hundred yards along Tiger found the man, clawing his way over the forest floor in agony. His face and arms were slashed and scraped from the sharp forest brush, and his left thigh was bleeding from a bullet wound.

"*Oh God…*" the man pled through gritted teeth. "Tell me… just tell me what you want…."

"Stop moving," Tiger said, and the man became still. His weeping continued, quieter now.

He was small and wiry, wearing a pair of pleated office pants and a short-sleeved dress shirt. He hadn't shaved in a while, and his eyes looked hollow and dark, as if he hadn't slept in days. A mark on either side of his nose revealed that the man wore glasses, but they were nowhere to be seen. He squinted in Tiger's direction, trying but failing to make out the face of his tormentor.

"Who are you?" the man begged.

Soon the sound of footsteps came up behind them and Divine appeared beside Tiger, looking down at the man on the ground with no more interest or concern than he would show for a rat caught in a trap. The fallen man looked up and squinted hard, finally able to recognize Divine.

"*Oh God*..." the man groaned in dread. "It was a mistake!"

Desperate and fumbling, the man pulled his wallet from his pants pocket and flashed it open, revealing photos inside of twin girls, bright-eyed with curly dark hair, no more than seven years old. "I have a family! Tell me what to do! Anything, I swear!"

Divine set his boot on the man's leg wound and pressed down. The man screamed.

"*Oh God*..."

"Few are granted such an opportunity at redemption," said Divine to Tiger.

Tiger looked down at the accountant, wounded and sniveling on the forest floor. He had no feelings for this man, who had made his own choices in life and would have to pay for them like anyone else. Tiger's only regret was that his target had no fight left in him—there was no honor in killing a defenseless man.

"So?" said Divine.

It sickened Tiger to do the man's bidding in this way, but

the accountant would die, regardless, and Divine's way would almost certainly be slower and more painful. Tiger raised his gun and fired three shots into the wounded man, two to the chest and one between his eyes, sparing him a slow torturous death.

11.

WALLY WOKE TO THE CRACKLING SOUND OF THE FIRE, stoked with new logs and warming the big room. She peeled the wool blankets off herself and sat up, feeling thick in the head the way she usually did when she overslept. Kyle was gone from his sofa, his blankets folded into a pile with his pillow on top. The sound of a whistling teapot came from the kitchen.

"Kyle?"

He appeared, looking relaxed and upbeat as he set a cup of coffee down in front of her.

"Somehow I've become your coffee bitch," he said.

"I'm feeling a little groggy. What time is it?"

"Almost ten. It's easy to sleep late here. It's so quiet, and the morning light hits the other side of the lodge."

They ate instant apple-cinnamon oatmeal for breakfast, Wally slowly waking up with the help of the strong coffee.

"I have an idea about a hike," he said. "There's a rocky point where I used to swim. It's really nice."

"A hike?"

"Not too far. It's the best time of year for it—too early for the bugs to be out. They're like kamikazes once summer comes."

He watched her with a hopeful look. His expression held a subtle sense of urgency that Wally picked up on. His anxiousness about going into his father's den and beginning the search for his birth mother had obviously carried over from last night.

"We're procrastinating, right?" she asked.

"Pretty much," he admitted.

"Okay. A hike sounds good."

They took a game trail through the woods that surrounded the lake. As she followed him along the path, it became clear to her—again—that she was witnessing Kyle in his natural element. The tortured guy she'd met in the city had given way to someone who was comfortable in his surroundings, navigating his way along the circuitous route as if he'd been born to it.

A full half hour passed before Kyle spoke.

"Is Tiger a person or an animal?" he asked.

Wally stopped in her tracks, taken aback.

"What do you mean?"

Kyle stopped and turned back to her. "In your sleep. You said something about Tiger. Like it was a name, not a thing."

"Tiger is my brother," she told him.

Another rule broken. Caseworkers at the Society were instructed not to share details about their personal lives with clients. She had violated the guidelines by allowing Kyle into her well-defended life, and now all the walls were coming down. Wally felt a little uneasy about it, but Kyle had trusted her with so many of his own secrets, and it seemed only fair to trust him back.

"What did I say?" she asked. Wally had no memory at all of dreaming. "In my sleep, I mean. What did I say?"

"Nothing that I could make sense of. But... did he run away? It was like you were calling after him."

Wally remembered again the moment on Shelter Island when Tiger had disappeared into the woods, wounded and bleeding and on the run. It was just moments after he had saved her life by gunning down their father, Alexei Klesko.

"Yes, he ran away."

The trail took them over several small rises—with occasional views of the surrounding terrain—and down into marshy streambeds, where Wally smelled lots of aromatic plants, such as wild mint and something like licorice. The air was warm but not humid, and Kyle had been right about the lack of bugs—Wally didn't feel a single bite.

Kyle pushed the pace, and before long they were both breathing hard.

"I was wondering something," she started.

"Yeah?" he asked, continuing to push down the trail.

"When you said your father wouldn't think that you would come here...I think you said, 'For all he knows I hate it there.' But that doesn't seem to be true at all."

"Yeah. When I was a kid, we used to come here as a family—me, my mom, and dad. Back when things were good, this was our happiest place."

"It's perfect here for a kid."

"It was. But then sometime when I was around eleven or twelve, they started not getting along. After a while, they were living separate lives with me in the middle. My mom didn't want to come out here anymore, but my father made me go with him. Divide and conquer, you know? That would have been all right if we spent that time together, but he always had friends up here, drinking a lot and talking bullshit nonstop. They would start card games that ended up going on for days, and it was pretty much like I wasn't even there."

"I'm sorry," Wally said, reflecting on the days when her adoptive parents were splitting up. "Adults get so wrapped up in their own problems, they forget about all the collateral damage they're doing."

"There were other women," Kyle said, sounding embarrassed. "A lot of them."

"He was cheating on your mom."

Kyle nodded. "And by having me here, he made me his partner in crime, you know? I could either hide what was going on from my mother and become as much of a liar as my father was, or tell her everything and be responsible for breaking them up. I didn't tell her. As I got older, I refused to come anymore."

Kyle's voice had become tense, and when he was done Wally

was silent for a while, giving him a chance to shake it off as they trudged on through the trees.

"I'm sorry," she finally said. "I didn't need to bring that up."

"No, it's good. Sooner or later I'm going to have to learn how to think about things without letting myself get all worked up."

"Okay," she said, "but I'm sorry anyway."

After a few miles, the trail led to the shore of the lake, where a rocky point stretched out onto the water for a hundred feet. A large, flat boulder marked the end of the point.

"I always called this Big Rock," he said, "and I always came here alone. There was never anyone around to give it another name."

She stepped to the edge and looked down into the impossibly clear water of the lake, the rocky bottom visible even though it looked to be very deep down, maybe thirty or forty feet. They sat down on the rock and took off their shoes, the fresh air feeling good on Wally's feet after the long walk.

"I don't see any other houses along the lake," Wally said.

"No, it's all ours, four hundred acres. My father likes having his own domain up here, as far as he can see."

"Private."

"Very," he said, and began pulling off his clothes.

Wally suddenly felt shy. Her attraction to Kyle had been growing since they'd arrived at the lodge, and it seemed obvious that swimming with him would take the connection between them to another level. She didn't know if she was ready for that.

Kyle perched himself at the edge of the rock and looked down into the water.

"I'm not going to lie to you," he said. "This water will be damn cold. The good thing is, there's no one around—you can scream as loud as you want."

Kyle dove in with a splash, then surfaced just a few seconds later with a yell.

"*Woooooo!* That feels good!"

He looked so happy, and all at once Wally was annoyed at herself for being such a wuss. She was hot and sticky from the hike, and she wanted to be in the water with Kyle. A lot. She quickly stripped down to her underwear and plunged deep into the clear lake. The shock was instantaneous—the water was colder than she would ever have thought possible, stinging every inch of her body all at once, and suddenly there was no air in her lungs. She kicked hard, gasping for breath as she burst up through the surface. Kyle's face was the first thing she saw, laughing out loud at her wild-eyed expression.

"*That's* what I'm talkin' about!" he yelled.

"Oh my God!" she said, having to take a quick breath of air before each word. "That's! The! Coldest! Thing! I! Ever! Felt!"

Wally was a strong swimmer, but the icy jolt of the plunge made her regress to a childhood state—she splashed around in a helter-skelter dog paddle, trying to keep her head as far out of the water as possible. Kyle swam up to her and put his hands on her waist, giving her a little boost up in the water.

"Okay?" he asked.

"Yeah..."

The two of them faced each other in a half-embrace, their breathing slowly starting to normalize. As they stayed in this position, kicking hard to tread water, Wally could feel the water between them slowly growing warmer as it borrowed the heat from their bodies. Without warning, Kyle inched forward just a little and kissed Wally quickly—gently—on the mouth. His lips were as cold as ice, but his tongue was warm, and a thrilling sensation passed through her body, making her dizzy. Kyle pulled away and grinned at her—not cocky, exactly, but teasing.

"Okay—now I've lost all feeling in my legs," Wally said, eager to take the focus off what had just happened.

He let her go, and the warmth of the oasis between them gave way to a fresh current of icy lake water that hit Wally's skin again, chilling her to the core. She scrambled out of the water, still trembling but exhilarated. She struggled to regain her breath, and appreciated the warmth and solidity of Big Rock beneath her. She lay down and stretched out on her back, pressing as much of her body as she could to its smooth stone surface.

She watched as Kyle swam a few hundred yards out into the lake with a powerful racer's crawl, then turned back to shore. She had wanted to continue kissing him, but at the same time she'd felt unmistakable relief when he'd pulled back. The reason why wasn't so complicated. The last person she'd cared about—that way—was Tevin, and the pain of losing him was still with her every day. How could she risk that kind of pain again, and so soon?

Kyle reached Big Rock and climbed out of the water, lying down beside Wally. Their arms touched, cold droplets of water tickling her skin as they rolled off his sleek body, sending shivers through her. Kyle was still breathing hard from the exercise, and each deep exhalation pressed him closer to her, her body responding with every touch. She wondered if he could possibly know the effect he had on her, the raw magnetic force of him.

She looked at Kyle and saw him smiling over at her. The two of them lying there together—it felt perfect.

12.

THAT NIGHT, WALLY AND KYLE RAIDED THE GAME cabinet in the great room. It was stocked full of playing cards, dice, and faded, dusty board games that hadn't seen the light of day since Kyle was a kid. When the sun went down and the temperature dropped with it, Kyle built another big fire. They avoided another pancake-batter tragedy by making pasta for dinner.

The two of them ate in front of the fire while playing Candyland—it was goofy but also more fun than Wally expected. The simple act of rolling the dice and moving the colorful plastic pieces around the board transported Wally to an innocent, contented time in her life, and the game seemed to have the same effect on Kyle—his mood was lighter, as if there was nothing weighing on him at all.

"You seem like you're feeling good," she observed, keeping her voice casual.

"I do feel good," he said. "I've sort of arrived at a decision, and I've been wanting to tell you, but I was worried you'd be disappointed." He rolled the dice and moved his gingerbread man ahead four spaces, avoiding Wally's eyes.

"What did you decide?"

He nodded toward his father's den. The door had been like an unwelcome guest during their short time at the lodge, its presence constantly looming.

"I think you were right all along," he said. "I'm not ready. I don't know what's in there, but whatever it is can wait."

Wally was taken aback by this reversal—*what had changed?* She felt a little frustrated, having taken two days away from her life because Kyle had absolutely insisted on visiting that room, but could she complain? Not really, since he now seemed to be following her advice.

"Okay. I mean, if that's how you're feeling—"

"I dragged you all the way up here."

"It hasn't exactly been torture." Wally was surprised to hear herself saying that, but it was true—she'd had a really nice time.

"It's because of you," he said, his eyes meeting hers. "You've taken my mind off the stuff that was driving me kind of crazy. It's so easy to get caught up in bullshit, and you helped me set it all aside."

"It's not what we expected, I guess," Wally acknowledged, "but I'm glad it turned out that way. Funny how things work out sometimes." She felt genuinely touched by what he'd said.

He nodded, his expression serious.

"I will find her," Kyle said. "Sometime. Will you still be around to help me?"

"Of course."

It was getting late. The two of them made up their couches, and Kyle put out the lamps, leaving the flickering light from the fireplace to cast a warm yellow glow in the huge room. Wally lay awake, watching Kyle for a long time. She couldn't see his eyes but was sure he was still awake too, and thinking about her. She thought about the two of them lying on Big Rock together and how that moment was a perfect version of something she had never really experienced before. She climbed out from under her blanket and took the few steps to his couch, where she knelt down so that her face was near his.

"Hi," he whispered. His eyes were obscured by shadow, but she could feel them focused on her.

Wally leaned forward slowly, her pulse accelerating, and gently kissed Kyle on the lips. She felt his muscles tensing as he brought one hand to the back of her neck, drawing her closer, while the other moved down to her waist and lingered there. The kiss was long and slow.

"I'm glad," he said when she finally pulled away. "Before, in the lake, I thought—"

"No," she interrupted. "That's what I wanted too."

"If you—"

She silenced him with another kiss, this one even more passionate than the first as she allowed her misgivings to fall away completely. Wally felt their hearts and bodies reaching out to each other, the electric rush of it surging through every inch of her body and threatening to overwhelm her.

The fire had been fading for a while, and without its heat the room had grown cold. She climbed onto his couch and slid in beside him. When she felt his hands on her bare skin—just one touch—she felt it over her entire body.

The fire had died down to a few glowing embers, but bright moonlight spilled in through the western windows of the great room. From the sound of his breathing beside her, Wally could tell Kyle was deep asleep. She slipped out from beneath their blankets and shivered, finding the air in the room much colder than she'd expected. Quietly, she pulled her clothes and boots on, then headed for the closed door in the corner of the room. On the way, she grabbed one of the oil lamps and a box of wooden matches and decided to bring her shoulder bag also, in case she found anything she wanted to take with her.

Kyle wasn't ready to learn the full circumstances of his birth, but Wally was. He'd asked her to take on his case, and now that her curiosity had been engaged there was no way she could resist the opportunity. The door in the corner was unlocked, and she stepped inside. The room was pitch black, and she realized that Kyle hadn't taken the shutters off the windows for this room—there was no moonlight—no light of any kind. She closed the door behind her and lit the oil lamp.

Nothing about the medium-sized den jumped out as unusual

or particularly interesting. The decor matched the rest of the lodge: plush leather furniture and wood-paneled walls covered with artwork, mostly watercolor landscapes or ink drawings of fish. Apparently, Richard Townsend was not a sentimental man—there were no family photos anywhere, just a few random snapshots of him holding up large salmon and trout from the lake and nearby streams.

To one side of the room was a heavy oak desk, and Wally soon discovered that the desk drawers—three on each side—were locked. There was an unlocked, shallow center drawer, and Wally fished around inside. It contained a bottle of mouthwash and a half-used tube of Preparation H—*blech*—plus some prescription heart medications that had expired the year before. She discovered several pairs of cheap reading glasses and an old switchblade knife with a bone handle. The item she'd hoped to find—a key to the locked drawers—wasn't there.

Wally opened the jackknife and started working the lock on the top-right drawer, using the strong tip of the knife as a makeshift key. No luck. She then turned the blade on its side and slid it into the space between the drawer and the desk frame. The blade dug into the lock bolt and Wally edged it up, bit by bit, until finally the bolt rolled over with a loud click and all three drawers on that side of the desk were unlocked.

The contents of those drawers seemed to be all about the lodge itself—receipts and invoices from locals who had worked there over the years, from plumbers to groundskeepers and grocers. An expanding file held the statements for a checking account at a bank in Fair Haven, Vermont, the same town referenced in Kyle's birth certificate. The checking account had been used to pay invoices for the local services, but not recently.

Wally put the file down and moved to the drawers on the left side of the desk. Using the survival knife again, it took her less than a minute to open those as well. The top drawer had only one item in it, a framed photograph of a smug-looking Townsend holding a large lake trout in his hands. The glass over the photo was cracked. Townsend—or someone—had broken the frame and had probably set it aside to be fixed at a later time.

Wally scanned the room, and her eyes settled on an empty spot on the wall behind a banquette, directly across from where she was seated. She noticed that another photo—mounted next to that empty space—was hanging slightly askew. This struck her as curious, considering that every other item in the room seemed to be perfectly in place and squared away.

She stood and carried the oil lamp across the room to the banquette, propping her knee on the bench cushion as she leaned in for a closer look at the tilted photograph. The image was of little interest—yet another shot of Townsend and a trophy fish—but Wally noticed that the weight of her body on the bench made a distinctive creaking sound, as if the boards were loose beneath her. She set the oil lamp aside and removed the cushion from that section of the bench. Wally leaned her weight onto the boards once more and heard the creak again, the wood loose and flexing beneath her. She reached under the edge of the bench and pulled up—the boards flipped open on a hinge to reveal a hidden space beneath.

The first thing she saw were the guns: two pump shotguns and two big-game hunting rifles with scopes, plus one handgun, a SIG SAUER automatic. Wally's adoptive father, Jason, had owned several guns himself, and he had insisted on educating her from an early age about the handling of weapons—a safety measure. He took Wally on regular trips to a local firing range, where she'd learned the basics of shooting and maintaining several types of guns, and her mother, Claire, had continued the practice even after the divorce.

Wally pulled the SIG SAUER out of the cache and caught the musky scent of gun oil. The weapon's firing mechanism had been cleaned sometime within the previous year. The clip was fully loaded with fourteen rounds. The rest of the weapons appeared to be in the same condition. Aside from the guns, the cache contained multiple boxes of ammunition to match each of them, plus two military-grade survival knives in nylon sheaths.

The hidden armory was not necessarily a sign of anything sinister: the lodge was probably empty for most of the year, and its remote location meant it would be vulnerable to break-ins and vandalism. Townsend could have bought a real gun safe, but something like that would immediately attract the attention of a burglar. The hidden cache made sense.

There was one other item in the secret space: a regular

cardboard shoe box with the brand name of a popular work boot on it. Wally pulled out the shoe box and sat down on the banquette, placing the box on her lap. Wally sensed that something significant would be inside. She felt the familiar rush of excitement move through her, the downy hair on the back of her neck rising in response to the visceral thrill of the chase.

Wally opened the box. Inside were at least a hundred snapshots—some regular photos and many Polaroids—of women. They weren't porn shots or anything, just regular candid shots of women on the porch of the lodge, in fishing boats, at the dining table, cooking waffles in the lodge kitchen. Some must have been taken by a third party, because Townsend himself was included in a good many, often with a sly, drunken grin on his face and his arm around the woman. By their condition, Wally figured that none were recent, and in fact were probably well over ten or fifteen years old.

The Richard Townsend in the photos was at least that much younger than the most recent newspaper photo of him that Wally had found. He looked to be in his early forties and still quite lean, lacking the barrel chest that more-recent shots revealed. In the photos, his hair was still dark or salt-and-pepper gray, rather than the full silver of his latest photos. Wally was struck by how much he looked like Kyle in the shots, a similarity that was harder to see in some of the later images.

For their part, the women seemed happy enough to be in Townsend's company. From small details—clothing, hairstyle, makeup—Wally could also tell that they came from various socioeconomic groups. A few looked like they might be local women, while others had a prissy, refined look that suggested Townsend might have brought them to the lodge from the city.

There had been a time in his life when Richard Townsend was quite a player, and the lodge had been his getaway bachelor pad. The age of the photos suggested that his wild years had coincided with the time of Kyle's birth. Almost every one of the many, many women was a potential candidate to be his biological mother. Wally checked the photos front and back, finding no labels or marking that would help identify them individually.

For Wally it was an exciting discovery, but to Kyle it would feel like a disaster—the odds of tracking down more than a handful of these women were slim, and it would be nearly impossible to identify Kyle's birth mother without more clues. Wally emptied all the photographs into her messenger bag and included whatever documents from the desk might be helpful later on. She wouldn't tell Kyle about any of them, for now. Wally regretted the necessity of the lie, but it seemed like the right thing to do.

She was about to restore the banquette seat to its original position when she heard a sound—what was it? It was soon followed by the distinctive sound of footsteps, just outside on the porch. She froze. Was Kyle out there looking for her? Wally moved to the door of the den, opening it just enough to see that Kyle was still asleep on the couch they had shared. She closed the door again and stood still, listening. She soon heard another series of footsteps outside, louder and closer this time. A second person, larger than the first.

Wally tried to imagine who they could be, other than more of Townsend's men. They could be thieves who had come to burglarize the lodge, assuming it was too early in the season for the place to be occupied. In that case, they would have seen the rented Explorer parked outside and abandoned their plan. Could they be hunters, poaching the private land? Poachers often "spotlighted" deer from vehicles late at night, but then they wouldn't be on foot, scouting out the lodge. Neither of the options seemed likely, and Wally wondered how Townsend's men had tracked her and Kyle there. She had been so careful.

13.

WALLY'S MIND SPUN, SIFTING THROUGH HER OPTIONS. First things first: she returned to the cache and pulled out the SIG. She chambered a round as quietly as she could, then retrieved a box of ammo for the weapon and placed it in her jacket pocket. She also grabbed one of the survival knives, slipping the sheathed blade inside her right boot.

Her first thought was to go back into the main room and wake Kyle up, but it seemed likely that the intruders were watching through the windows. Crossing the floor in plain sight would make her a vulnerable target. For now, they probably had no idea where she was, and that was an advantage.

Now another sound came to her: more footsteps, this time from above. At least one of the men had found his way into the lodge and up to the second floor. How? He was slowly moving from room to room as if making a systematic search.

Her heart racing now, Wally felt trapped inside the den. She needed to get outside, where she would be free to move. Wally slid the gun under the belt of her pants and swung her messenger bag over her shoulder. She chose one of the windows and unlocked it. She pushed the sliding window upward. It squeaked a little, but Wally raised it just a bit at a time, making sure the noise was kept to a minimum. It took almost a minute, but she finally opened the window enough to be able to crawl through.

The outside shutter was still closed. She pulled the survival knife from her boot and carefully slid the blade between the two shutter doors. She moved the blade upward until it hit the outside latch. As delicately as she could, Wally raised the knife blade more until the latch flipped over, making a slight rattle, but no more. The shutters were unlocked.

There were no more sounds of footsteps outside, so Wally blew out the oil lamp and edged the shutters outward, just enough to poke her head out and get a look around. The grounds outside the window—bathed in bright moonlight—were clear. As quickly as she could, Wally rolled headfirst out the window and eased herself onto the ground. She closed the shutters behind her and pulled the SIG out from behind her waistband.

With the handgun held high in front of her, Wally stalked methodically around the lodge. She encountered no one—both men were probably inside by now. She made her way back to the porch and surveyed the main room through the window. One of the oil lamps was now lit, and the blankets on the couch were thrown back. Kyle was nowhere in sight. Wally's heart sank. Was he looking for her, or had the men already grabbed him? Could he be hiding somewhere in the lodge?

Her thinking was interrupted by a chilling sight: the second security man from outside Harmony House—the farm boy tight end with the blond goatee—emerged from the kitchen and crossed the floor of the main room. He moved carefully, a cold and focused expression on his face and a gleaming steel .44 automatic raised high in front of him. His eyes scanned the room as he walked, searching. From where she crouched on the porch outside, Wally could see the dark bruising on the man's neck from the devastating clothesline maneuver she had used to strike him down. Most men would still be in an intensive-care unit after an injury like that, and to see him hunting her was unnerving. He reached the far end of the room and disappeared from view, moving in the direction of the lodge's staircase.

Something else about the sight of the man got Wally's attention: when he and his partner had confronted her and Kyle outside Harmony House, neither had shown a weapon, even after Wally had wounded them. Clearly the men's mission had been to retrieve their boss's son unharmed, and they hadn't risked bringing weapons into that situation.

Something had changed. The men had come with guns this time, and Wally considered the reasons: Kyle knew incriminating things about his father's business, and said that Townsend would do anything to keep him under his control. Maybe the old man had decided his son was beyond saving—especially now that he had involved Wally, an outsider. If getting rid of Kyle was the new mission, Wally figured the goatee guy was more than ready to make it happen... and disappear her at the same time.

"Let me go!"

Kyle's terrified cry sounded from the second floor.

Shit. Wally moved immediately toward the doorway and grabbed the handle, ready to charge in, but stopped herself short. Going straight up the staircase would be stupid... and probably what the intruders were hoping for. From her circuit around the lodge, she remembered a firewood rack on the east side that stood at least six feet high—within reaching distance of the overhanging eaves.

Wally shrugged off her messenger bag and set it down at the base of the wall. She slid her gun back inside her waistband and clambered up the heaping woodpile, pulling herself up onto the eave. The lodge had a narrow roof that ran all around the building, between the first and second floors. There were two shuttered windows on that side of the lodge, and Wally moved as quietly as she could along the shingled surface to the nearest window. She flipped open the latch and swung the shutters open. She tried to lift the window, but it didn't budge at all—locked. She sidled along the cedar shingles to the second window, opening those shutters and trying the window. It was tight, but Wally pushed upward with all her strength and the window slid open just enough for her to slip through.

She heard Kyle yell out in pain, the sound sending a chill through Wally. The cry was muffled and distant—he was somewhere at the far side of the lodge and he was suffering.

Moving carefully but with a new sense of urgency, she crawled in through the window and reached down to feel the floor underneath. It was covered with some sort of rug, but there was no furniture in her way, so she lowered herself to the floor of the completely dark room. She could light her way by the glow of her cell phone, but when she reached for her messenger bag she realized that she'd left it behind. Maybe that wasn't such a bad thing: a light would reveal what was ahead, but it would also give away her position. She decided she was better off moving covertly in darkness, even if that meant feeling her way along.

Wally had no idea what sort of obstacles were in front of her, so she decided to stay as low to the floor as she could. She began sliding slowly across whatever room she was in, feeling the way in front of her with her hands. She edged around a single bed and a storage trunk, finally reaching the far wall. Her hands found a closed door. When she reached up and pushed it open, the door creaked loudly. She froze, but if anyone heard there was no response.

She crept through the open doorway and found herself on a wood floor, its surface rough and heavily grooved from decades of use. She spotted a dim, yellowish light far ahead—it looked like light from one of the oil lamps leaking out from under a closed door, at least fifty feet away. The second floor had one long hallway that ran the length of the building, and the room with the light in it was at the far end. She could hear movement in the room, and the sound of murmured speech. She couldn't make out the words, or who was speaking.

As she crept on, Wally's senses of hearing and touch became hyperalert, helping her navigate along the nearly pitch-black hallway. It seemed like every movement and sound in the entire lodge reverberated through the wood and up into her body. She heard a very faint scratching sound and stopped to listen. The sound grew closer and closer until it was upon her, and a small creature—a mouse or rat—scurried over her right hand. Wally couldn't stop herself from recoiling at the repulsive feeling of tiny claws on her skin, and her hand clenched around the grip of her gun, nearly firing a round before she brought herself back under control.

Wally cursed silently, and took a moment for her breathing to return to normal. She continued on and began to think about her strategy once she reached the closed doorway....

"I came alone! There's no one else here!" Kyle shouted desperately from behind the closed door. His words were followed by the sound of a fist landing hard on flesh and a groan of pain.

Shit. Kyle was behind that door trying to cover for her, and was being brutally punished for it. Wally's blood raged—her first impulse was to break into the room with the SIG blazing, but she knew she had to be smarter than that.

What was the best way to go in? If she found another room on this hallway, she could climb back outside and onto the eaves, working her way around the lodge until she had a view into the room where Kyle was being held. Wally could use that position—outside in the darkness, looking in—to her advantage.

She inched along—feeling the wall for a doorway—but had only moved a few feet when her hand located an object sitting on the floor in the middle of the hallway. It was a rubbery-feeling rectangle about a quarter of an inch high. Easy: a smartphone, with the screen facing down.

One of the intruders must have dropped it. The phone could end up being a good source of information about Townsend's security team. Without thinking twice, she grabbed it. The screen lit up and instantly cast a dim blue glow all around her.

The guy with the goatee was crouched low—right in front of Wally—a large, unlit flashlight in his hand and a cruel, shit-eating smirk on his face.

"Hello, bitch," he said.

Before Wally could react, he pointed the flashlight at her eyes and switched it on. Her world went completely white—the pupils of her eyes had been dilated from so many minutes spent in total darkness, and the powerful beam blinded her.

In a flash, Wally jumped to her feet and raised her SIG, firing random rounds at the spot she had last seen goatee guy but aiming high to make sure Kyle wouldn't accidently get hit—*Blam! Blam! Blam!*—then spun herself around in every direction and kept firing blindly—*Blam! Blam! Blam! Blam!*—until a fist crashed down on her forearm, sending the gun flying.

A muscled arm reached around her chest and pulled her in, but Wally spun free and kept spinning. She performed a series of high strikes at face level with knee-high sweeps mixed in. One of the kicks landed hard on the guy's chest, and Wally heard him stumble backward. She used that momentary advantage to turn and run back down the hallway in the direction she had come, but after just a few steps she heard a tumbling sound behind her and then something rolled under her feet—*the big flashlight*—and she stumbled.

She smashed hard into the floor, and when she sprang back up it was right into the grip of two powerful arms. They wrapped around her from behind, reaching under her armpits and then up around her neck. Two massive hands clasped together behind her neck to complete an unbreakable headlock, and then the person lifted her body up until her feet were off the floor, hanging free. He had to be at least a foot taller than she was. Wally flailed and kicked, but the hold was firm and her resistance futile.

To conserve her energy, Wally commanded her body to relax. Her lungs were burning, and she struggled to regain her breath. Soon she felt *his* breath on her cheek—hot and humid, smelling of minty-sweet chewing tobacco.

"That's it," a deep, calm voice whispered into her ear. "Just relax..."

Wally felt a tickling sensation just behind her ear as the words were spoken—facial hair. His goatee.

"How's your throat?" she snarled, still struggling for air.

"It still hurts bad," the man said in a deep southern accent. He tensed his arm muscles so that Wally's arms bent awkwardly at the shoulder joint, sending a hot, searing pain through her entire body. Wally gasped, trying to breathe her way through it, feeling like she might pass out anytime from the pressure he applied to the arteries in her neck.

She was determined to keep her brain working no matter what.

"You know, Alabama," she spat, taking a guess, "you look like a white-trash moron with that goatee."

She felt him react to the sound of his new nickname and figured her guess had hit the mark. This was good. If she could unnerve him in any way, she might create an opportunity for herself.

"Yeah," he chuckled, his sickly-sweet tobacco breath swirling around her ear, making her gag. "Alabama is right. Good guess."

"You seem like someone who has some legitimate skills," Wally kept at him, "maybe even elite. Military, right? A job like that has real meaning, especially during wartime. But look where you are now—you've traded on that service to become an errand boy for some rich asshole. That must leave you with an empty feeling."

"It's gonna get bad for you, little girl," he said, his voice sounding more stressed now.

Wally struggled again, trying to break free from the hold even though she knew it was pointless. Her eyesight had begun to return, and slowly the doorway at the end of the hallway came into focus. A man stood there, an oil lamp in one hand. Wally couldn't make out anything in the room behind him.

This second man was Asian with a short, stocky build and long black hair swept back. He walked down the hallway toward them, stopping a few feet in front of Wally and looking her body up and down.

"This is the one?" the Asian guy said flatly. "This little thing took you down?"

Alabama hesitated before answering. "Yes."

"That's an embarrassment. You have a hundred and fifty pounds on her."

"He's hurting me," Wally croaked to the second guy. Speaking was difficult from the tight headlock, but she made the effort to sound even worse. "I feel sick."

"Like I give a shit," the Asian guy said, expressionless.

But now Wally could see his mind working on the question of her well-being. She had an opening. Wally suddenly began struggling again, twisting and writhing in Alabama's arms, and he tightened his grip. She made a choking sound for a moment, then went completely limp, her eyes shut and legs dangling loose. She held her breath. The men were silent at first, but she stayed with it. Ten seconds, twenty. Forty. Wally's chest began to ache badly, and she wondered how long she could keep it up. She must have started to turn blue or something, because the Asian guy finally spoke up.

"Jesus," he said to Alabama. "Is she really out? If you break her, you bought her—you can answer to the man yourself."

Wally's lungs were about to burst, but she held tight. She

heard some movement—it sounded like the Asian guy was crouching down, and then a slight metallic tone: the oil lamp being set on the floor. The man stood upright again and Wally could feel him moving close. He laid his hand on her rib cage, feeling for movement.

"She's not breathing...." he said, sounding anxious. She opened one eye very slightly, enough to see that he had moved in close.

"Back off!" Alabama warned.

Too late. Wally flexed her muscles and brought her right knee up as hard and high as she could. It struck the Asian guy in the mouth, and Wally could feel the man's teeth shattering on impact. Blood spurted in every direction as he reeled back, howling in pain and rage. He quickly regained his balance and lunged at Wally.

"No!" Alabama yelled, reflexively turning aside to sidestep the oncoming charge. At that moment, the attacker struck outward with his elbow—aimed at Wally's face—but she managed to move her head to the side just an inch. The point of his elbow glanced off the side of her head and struck Alabama squarely in the throat, connecting with the wound that Wally had given him two days earlier.

Alabama yowled in pain—he tried to keep hold of Wally but she wrestled free of his arms and dropped to the ground, scrambling toward her SIG, still lying on the floor ten feet away. She dove for the weapon, grabbing it and rolling onto her back in one motion, facing upward now with the gun in front of her. In those few seconds, the Asian goon had reversed course and was coming straight at her. Wally blasted three shots, two hitting him in the chest and the third in the face, just below one eye. The man fell lifeless to the floor, but behind him Alabama had regained his balance and came at Wally, his face a mask of burning rage.

She aimed at him and squeezed the trigger, but the SIG jammed. *Shit!*

Alabama dove for her, but she rolled to the side and he missed, his massive physique a disadvantage as his momentum carried him past her. Wally scrambled to her feet again but could hear him behind her, rising up again and coming back at her. She took three steps down the hallway and reached for the oil lamp on the floor, its wick still burning brightly.

She swung around and hurled the lamp at Alabama. He ducked, but the lamp struck the wall behind him and shattered, the oil bursting into flames and splashing onto the upper right side of his body, his arm, neck, and face now on fire.

Alabama screamed in pain and fury, flailing wildly. He dropped to the ground and rolled, trying to snuff out the flames. Wally leapt over him and sprinted toward the room at the far end of the hall. There she found Kyle struggling to pull duct tape off his wrists. He looked disoriented but otherwise unharmed.

"Wally…"

"We can't go back that way." She motioned toward the

hallway where they could see Alabama blocking the way, still rolling around frantically on the floorboards—the flames on his clothes and skin were almost snuffed out.

Wally grabbed a wooden chair and repeatedly swung it against one of the windows in the room. The glass shattered, and she jabbed at the space again and again until all the shards of broken glass were cleared from the opening. One more shove with the chair was all it took for the shutters to crash open.

Wally and Kyle heaved themselves through the broken window, rolling onto the shingled roof outside. The moonlight was bright on this side of the lodge, and they could see a clear space below them. Without taking time to debate the choice, they both jumped, hitting the earth ten feet below and rolling. The touchdown was painful.

"Are you okay?" Wally asked, scrambling to her feet and hauling Kyle up with her.

"I'm good," he grunted. And they ran.

They raced back around the lodge and over the back porch, toward the waiting Explorer. Wally peeled off to retrieve her messenger bag from beside the firewood rack. She dug into the bag as she ran to the car, locating the keys to the Explorer just as she reached it. She pressed the "unlock" button on the fob and the locks clicked open.

She climbed in behind the wheel and Kyle slid in beside her. She backed the car up quickly and then threw it into drive. As they peeled away at high speed, some motion from the direction of the lodge caught Wally's attention: Alabama burst through the porch door and charged after them, the right side of his body and clothes charred black and still smoking. In his left hand was the big steel gun she'd seen him carrying before.

Wally and Kyle ducked low in their seats as they raced away, and a rapid series of gunshots rang out behind them—a full clip. At least four or five metallic *thwunk* sounds signaled that the Explorer had been hit, but none of the car glass shattered, and both Wally and Kyle escaped harm. The shooting stopped when they were about a hundred yards away. Kyle turned his head to get a last look at the lodge.

"It's burning," he said flatly, void of emotion.

Wally saw a flickering orange light up the second floor of the lodge, where the flame from the lamp she had shattered was growing. A house made of logs stood no chance, especially without a fire company within twenty miles.

"I'm glad," Kyle added.

14.

WITHIN A HALF MILE, THEY APPROACHED A NEW JEEP Grand Cherokee, black with fake wood paneling. It was parked along the side of the road, right where Townsend's men would have left it to be sure they were not heard. Wally pulled to a stop and climbed out, leaving her door open and the engine running. She peered in at Kyle, who still looked shell-shocked.

"Stay inside and keep watch down the road, okay?" she told him.

He didn't argue. Wally pulled the survival knife out of her boot and sliced the air nozzles off the Cherokee's tires, the air rushing out as she did each one. The doors to the car were locked, but she used the heavy steel butt of the knife to break the driver's-side window and let herself inside. There wasn't much to find: trash, a map, a container of antacid pills. One cell phone had been left there in the driver's door compartment—a cheap burner—and Wally took it. She popped the trunk and found two sleeve-style gun cases there, one with a shotgun inside and one with an assault rifle. She didn't want either, so she left them. There was nothing else.

She climbed back in the Explorer and they sped onward, retracing the route that they had taken to the lodge two days before. Wally snuck a look in Kyle's direction, and in the glow of the dashboard lights his expression appeared vacant and numb. She could relate to his stressed-out condition—her hands were clammy, and they gripped the wheel as if it were a lifeline. Her jaw felt permanently clenched.

The images of the battle in the upstairs hallway of the lodge—the battle for her life—flooded back. She had killed a man. Shot him dead at point-blank range. A human life. She'd set another man on fire. *Oh my God. Oh my God.*

Wally hit the brakes and the speeding Ford took a hundred feet to skid finally to a stop on the dirt road. She flung her door open and tumbled out, dropping to her knees. With a massive heave, she began puking, one violent purge after another, until there was nothing left and her throat was burning from the acid. After a minute she caught her breath and stood to find Kyle near her. Something about her distress had jolted him out of his stupor. He looked halfway alert now, and he was worried about Wally.

"Are you okay?" he asked.

"No." She absolutely was not okay.

She reached inside the car and pulled out a bottle of water. She gargled with it and spat it out three times until the taste of puke in her mouth was nearly gone. When she'd steadied herself, they drove on in silence. Kyle fished around and found a pack of gum, passing two slices of peppermint to Wally and taking two for himself.

It was forty minutes before they reached the highway, where Wally came to a full stop on the shoulder of the road. All she wanted was to think clearly, to be smart. Anything else was too much to ask.

"I'm sorry," he said. "For everything. For getting you involved."

Part of Wally wanted to comfort and reassure him, but in the back of her mind she'd been trying to figure something out, and she had to confront him about it.

"Kyle, I need to ask you something," Wally said. "We talked about the rules: no cell phone calls, no—"

"At that gas station," he blurted out.

"What did you do?"

"You were paying for everything, and... I just felt weird about it. I wanted my own money—"

"What did you use? An ATM card?" Wally felt an eruption of anger growing inside her.

"It's a secret account. My mother set it up for me, like a special thing between the two of us so my father couldn't always use money to control me. He didn't know anything about it—"

"*Kyle*. Your father knows whatever he wants to know! Get that through your head! You came to me for help, but you ignore all my advice. I take time out of my own life to come up here—against my better judgment—and in the end it's all a waste of time because you don't have the guts to follow through. On top of that, you do a stupid thing like using the ATM card and because of that I *killed* a man?! Are you fucking *kidding* me?!"

Wally felt herself about to lose control and stopped, pulling herself back from the edge. She took a few deep breaths and turned back to Kyle. He looked scared and ashamed, the way he was when Wally had first seen him in the hallway outside the Ursula Society, only worse.

"I'm really sorry," Kyle said weakly. "I don't know what else to say."

"Okay," Wally said, trying to keep the anger out of her voice. "You didn't mean any of it, I know. I'm just…" She couldn't finish the thought, because if she continued it would undoubtedly turn into another tirade, which would be pointless now.

"Let's just keep going," she finally said. "I think we should take a different route home, just in case."

He nodded in agreement. Wally turned north, planning eventually to loop back east and take another highway back to the city.

As they drove on, something in the passenger-side footwell caught Kyle's attention: Wally's messenger bag had fallen open, and the photographs she had taken from Townsend's secret stash had spilled out. Wally watched from the corner of her eye as Kyle picked up the photos and slowly sifted through them, a look of both fascination and dread on his face. For a moment she thought about stopping him, but that would be pointless now.

He switched on the overhead cab light so he could get a better look, studying the images closely as he leafed through them, transfixed.

"Where did you find these?"

"Your father's den. While you were asleep. I probably shouldn't have done it without asking you."

"There are at least a couple dozen of them," he said, sounding grieved. "And there are some I remember who aren't here, so there are probably others." Wally could see him working through the implications of it. "I'll never find my birth mother, will I? I won't even be able to figure out which of the women she was."

"Honestly, I don't know," Wally agreed. "It will be difficult."

After that, Kyle remained quiet for a while, deep in thought. Wally drove on, following the curving two-lane highway west—nothing but dark, impenetrable forest on either side of the road for miles—until they reached an intersection with a larger highway that could carry them south. There was a busy truck stop there, and Wally pulled over.

"I can barely keep my eyes open," she said, feeling herself start to crash as her adrenaline rush finally bled out for good. "I need to get something."

It was just past four in the morning by then, still entirely dark. Diesel fumes filled the air as Wally and Kyle walked together into the truck-stop store, splitting up at the restroom doorways.

The ladies' room was empty. Wally peed, then leaned over the sink and gave her face and armpits a thorough rinse. When she was done, she went out into the store and found a large can of energy drink—a nasty, carbonated green one that she knew would jolt her awake—and a bag of trail mix that included chocolate, nuts, raisins, and enough other things to fill up her recently evacuated stomach.

Kyle wasn't in the store, so she paid for her stuff and went to the car, which was also empty. Leaning against the hood of the car, Wally munched on a few handfuls of the trail mix and popped open the energy drink. She waited and snacked for several minutes before she started to wonder what the hell he was still doing in the men's room.

Wally set her food down in the car and went back inside the store. No Kyle. She went to the men's room and knocked on the door.

"Kyle. What's up? You okay in there?"

No answer. Wally was starting to feel uneasy. *Screw it*. She pushed through the men's room door and went inside. It was pretty disgusting in there—much filthier than the women's—but Wally found no one there, even after checking every stall. She went back out into the store and checked every aisle again. No Kyle.

Wally returned to the car, worried. There she saw something—a scrap of paper—pinned to the windshield under one of the wipers. Had it been there before, and she just hadn't seen it? It was a blank lotto card from inside the store, and Wally opened it to find just a few words scribbled there in pencil:

Forget it all, Wally. I'm done.

Shit! Wally walked to the edge of the highway and looked in both directions, thinking she might see Kyle trying to hitchhike up or down the road. She didn't. She realized that vehicles were regularly arriving and departing from the stop—at least one or two every minute—and Kyle had plenty of time to talk his way into a ride.

He was really gone.

What the hell? To come all this way, to go through everything that they had—together—and then this? She wondered if he'd left because of her tirade or because of the hopeless situation with his birth mother. Both, no doubt. It broke her heart a little, but mostly she just felt angry, plus overwhelmed and exhausted in every possible way. All she wanted now was to get in the car and drive, as fast as she could, back to the city, where she would sleep for three days straight.

Wally gassed up the Explorer and climbed in, turning south as she pulled out onto the dark, nearly empty highway toward home. Her burner phone still had the music-streaming program, and she created her own channel of loud, throbbing house mixes that would help keep her awake and hopefully drown out some of the emotional noise in her head.

She drove fast, stopping only once for another tall energy drink and a couple of granola bars to fill the aching void in her stomach. She reached the city in four-and-a-half hours, inching her way across the Triborough Bridge and down the Brooklyn-Queens Expressway with the early commuters. Her first stop was the rental-car agency, where a polite young Hispanic guy named Hervé walked around the Explorer with an iPad in his hands, checking for damage.

Hervé paused at the rear of the car and gave Wally a significant look. She checked out the area that had caught his attention and saw the large bullet holes that were now ventilating the rear hatch of the SUV, courtesy of Mr. Alabama and his big, shiny .44.

"That's why I always get the extra insurance," she told Hervé.

"I think maybe I'm supposed to report this to the cops," he said.

"Not necessarily," Wally said, handing him five twenty-dollar bills from her wallet.

Hervé took the money.

Wally walked the last few blocks home, climbing the stairs to her rooftop apartment two at a time, desperate to collapse onto her mattress. Everything else—Tiger, Kyle, Lewis—they would all have to wait. She reached her landing and pulled out her keys, ready to unlock the door—then stopped short. There were noises inside the apartment. Footsteps, moving lightly inside. She remained still, head cocked and nerves alert, concluding that there were two separate sets of feet moving in there.

Shit. Had Townsend found out who she was and where she lived already? Her last sanctuary in the world had been invaded. Her heart sank at the thought. The SIG was still in her bag, the clip full of ammo again, but the idea of going strong against yet another team of armed goons was inconceivable to her. The only smart option was retreat. She would back down the stairway and call Greer—it was time for his buddies from the 94th Precinct house to earn their salaries.

Wally took one step away from the door—ready to run—but then she heard music. Her boom box was suddenly playing an old-school favorite, "Rock the Casbah" by the Clash, followed by an outburst of laughter—high-pitched and as familiar to Wally as the sound of her own voice. Wally fumbled with her key, finally fitting it into the lock after what seemed like ages. She pushed through the door and entered, just in time to hear Ella bitching at Jake.

"Don't open it! What if she's saving them for something special?"

"Special *olives*?" Jake answered in exasperation.

Wally hurried into the room to find Jake and Ella in the kitchen, Jake holding a jar of gourmet stuffed cocktail olives that had been sitting in her fridge for months. Huge grins broke out on their faces when they saw her, followed by expressions of concern—Wally knew she looked ragged and drained after the events of the past few days. Ella flew across the room and threw her arms around Wally in a bear hug, nearly tackling her to the floor with the impact.

"Oh my God," Ella said, her voice tearful.

"I love you, Ella," Wally said, and felt tears of relief and grief and happiness all mixed together tumbling down her cheeks. It was a release of the feelings she had been keeping inside for months.

Thank you, thought Wally. She had no idea who or what she

was thanking, but somehow that didn't matter. *Thank you.*

While the girls held each other tight, Wally snuck a peek at Jake, who watched them with a smile on his face and the jar of olives still in his hand.

"So… can I open these?" he wanted to know.

15.

WALLY SLEPT FOR NEARLY TWELVE HOURS. WHEN SHE finally woke, she ambled into the main room to find Jake and Ella wrapped up together on her couch, watching a British sitcom on TV. Wally dropped down easily beside them on the couch.

"You look so much better, Wally," Ella said.

"I don't know if I've ever been that tired before," Wally sighed, leaning her head against Ella's shoulder.

"Sorry for busting in," Jake said. "We didn't have anywhere else to crash."

"Are you kidding? I've had so many surprises over the past few days, and this is the only good one. I'm so glad you guys are here."

"Stan told us that you'd stopped in at the farm. He could tell you were pretty disappointed that we were gone, and we were worried that something was going on with you. He signed off on a couple free days for us."

"You can stay?" Wally asked, embarrassed by how happy she was to hear it.

"For a while, anyway," Jake said. "So, what's been going on?"

"No, you guys go first," she told him, eager to avoid thinking about her experiences of the past few days—she could feel the memories of it pressing on her, ready to overwhelm her if she let them. "That farm is such a beautiful place, and Stan seemed like a good guy. He said you were off to a 4H thing?"

"It was really awesome, actually," Ella said, her eyes lit with pure enthusiasm. "They taught us all about hydroponic farming. I know it probably sounds boring, but—"

"You can grow food year-round," Jake said. "Even upstate, in winter. You can put together a farm that's totally self-sufficient. It's like your own little country."

"I love it," Wally said. "That's awesome you're so into it. It sounds really cool."

"Jake has become Stan's right-hand guy," Ella said proudly. "He's totally crushing it."

To see her old friends doing so well was such a great surprise. The three of them had come together just over a year and a half earlier, a group of runaways on the streets of New York City who—along with their other friends, Tevin and Sophie—had formed a tight family unit. Relying on each other, the crew had survived—no, they had *thrived*—for nearly a year, until everything had come apart violently. For Ella and Jake to be sitting there with Wally in her little Greenpoint apartment—alive and healthy—felt like a miracle.

Jake was a former football and wrestling jock from Ohio. He'd always had a dark, skeptical nature and was constantly frustrated with the world and with himself. Seeing him now—so confident and positive—made it obvious he'd found a sense of purpose. As for Ella, she had always been flighty and ethereal—*magical Ella*—and that lovely, unaffected part of her nature was still there. Her time away, though, had added an aura of substance to her. In the past she had relied on Jake for everything, almost as if she might float away without him to tether her to earth. The Ella sitting before Wally now had become her own anchor. She had grown up.

"I've been wanting to see you guys for so long," Wally said, feeling herself beginning to choke up.

"That's what we wanted too," Ella told her. "But we didn't hear from you and we figured... I don't know what we thought. Why didn't you call?"

Wally hesitated. She had avoided this moment for a long time, but there could be no more hiding.

"I was so ashamed," she finally said, surprised by the pent-up tears that spilled out. "I was responsible for what happened to Sophie and Tevin—I know that. I was afraid that if I reached out to you guys, I'd find out that you couldn't forgive me. I wouldn't have been able to handle losing the two of you."

"You cared about Sophie and Tevin as much as we did," Jake said. "Things got out of control, but you didn't ask for that to happen. You would have done anything to keep them safe—we know that."

"Except let go of my obsession with finding my mother. I let it block out everything else. Our friends died because of it. It should have been me."

"None of that matters now," Ella said.

"How can that be true?" Wally asked. "After everything that happened, how can you say that?"

"It just can," Ella said. "You didn't mean for any of it to happen. We were devastated when Tevin died, but so were you. It doesn't mean we should lose each other too. Yeah, maybe we needed some time to get past everything, but we have. That's love."

"*That's love*," Wally repeated, letting it sink in. She laughed through her tears. "I've read about it, sure."

"Yeah," Jake said. "You can be a pain in the ass, Wally, but we actually love you anyway. And we're here now."

Wally nodded. "We're all still here."

"Hey," Wally said as she began to recover from the intensity of their reunion, "how did you find my place, anyway?"

"We called your friend the cop," Jake said. "We had no choice."

"You called Greer?"

"Yeah," Ella said. "He's kind of a weird dude, but he gave us the address. Said it warmed his heart that we were looking for you—he actually used that phrase. What's his deal?"

"He's even more of a pain in the ass than he used to be," Wally said. "He means well."

"And you need to get a new dead bolt on your front door," Jake said. "Took me less that twelve seconds to trip it."

"Seriously? I paid good money for that thing...."

"We also met your new downstairs friends," Ella said, making an obvious effort to disguise her jealousy and disapproval. That wasn't much of a surprise—Wally couldn't really imagine Jake and Ella getting along with January and Bea, at least not at first.

"January and Bea, you mean."

"Wally, they're like brain-dead sorority party girls," Ella said.

"Trust me—they'll grow on you if you give them a chance."

"Hmm." Ella didn't sound convinced.

They were all starving, so they had pizza delivered just after midnight: pepperoni and pineapple on a thin, crispy crust with grilled vegetables on the side. As they ate, Wally laid out every detail of the past five months of her life—her ongoing search for Tiger, her work at the Ursula Society, and, of course, Kyle. She described her whole ordeal with him, from his first appearance at the Society to the explosion of violence at the lodge. Kyle's sudden disappearance in the middle of nowhere was the final, frustrating act of the story.

"Holy shit," Jake said when she was finished.

"I killed that man at the lodge," Wally said, astounded by her own admission. She'd experienced terrible violence before—and had committed some brutal acts of violence herself—but she had never taken a life.

"You had to make a choice," Ella said. "I'm glad you were strong enough to do it. Not that I'd ever doubt that. You did what you had to do, or you might not have survived."

"I know you're right, but I don't really know how to explain it. It's a sick feeling, no matter what. I feel like I left something behind up there. Now it's gone up in smoke with the lodge and everything else."

"So what do you do next?" Jake asked.

"I just want to sleep some more," she said. Already she was exhausted again. "You guys take my room, okay?"

They were about to object, but she insisted. Wally guessed that she had a fitful night to look forward to—it was usually that way when her thoughts were spinning like this—and she wanted to be able to move around the apartment without worrying about disturbing them.

Once Jake and Ella were tucked away behind the closed door of her bedroom, Wally took a long, hot shower and changed into more comfortable clothes. She turned out the lights and curled up on the couch, pulling a warm blanket over herself.

In the dark silence of the room, her thoughts turned to Kyle. However angry and disappointed she was with him, Wally couldn't help wondering where he was right then and if he was safe. At the same time, worrying about Kyle made her angry with herself.

After all, Kyle had been the cause of the trouble at the lodge, and he'd left her behind.

Like Tiger. Why couldn't she just let go? What was the point of living in the past? It was a landscape of pain and anger and regret, a scorched earth.

The sound of a ringing telephone interrupted her thoughts, but the ringtone was unfamiliar. She looked to the dining table, where her cell phone was charging. It wasn't ringing. Wally concluded that the offending phone must be Jake's or Ella's, but then realized its source: her messenger bag, slung over the back of a chair at her dining table.

Only then did Wally remember the burner phone that she'd taken from the Jeep Cherokee that Alabama and the other gunman had parked near the lodge. Wally climbed off the couch and opened her messenger bag, still full of the photos of all the women that she had found in Richard Townsend's secret cache. Sitting under the photos was Alabama's phone, and it was ringing. There was no caller-ID information on the screen.

Wally hit the answer button, saying nothing. After a moment of silence, a man's voice spoke out, sounding tired and impatient. Wally guessed that he was middle-aged—probably a smoker and drinker, judging by the roughness of his voice.

"Do you have her?" the man said.

Do you have her? The caller thought he had Alabama on the line, or Alabama's partner, who would never answer a phone again.

Do you have her? Have *whom*? Was he asking about Wally? But that didn't make any sense. Townsend had sent those men to retrieve his son, Kyle ... hadn't he?

"Speak, goddamn it," the man said. "Do you have the girl or not?"

A chill shot through Wally. The man on the other end of the line was asking about *her*—it had to be. Which meant that every assumption she had made in the past few days had been completely wrong.

Wally's mind reeled. She was still half asleep, but certain memories began to slip into place. The man waiting behind Harmony House had reached for *her* first, not Kyle. When Alabama had her in a choke hold and it looked like Wally might be hurt, the Asian guy had freaked out.

Those men hadn't come for Kyle—they had come for her. But why? None of it made sense.

"What the hell is wrong with you? Do you have the girl or not?"

"Not quite, asshole," Wally answered.

The other end of the line was quiet—the silence broken only by the sound of breathing—and then the man hung up.

Wally, numb, let the phone drop to the floor. What was she supposed to do now? The phone call had scratched the surface of something, but what? She was obviously in some sort of danger. Whatever it was that this man wanted from her, it was vitally important to him. She couldn't expect him to stop.

More men would come.

She suddenly realized that the burner phone was giving away her position. She was about to remove the battery, but first she checked the phone for other content. There were no contact numbers listed and the call history had been erased. It was a cheap model, so there was no GPS that she could use to track the movements of Alabama and his partner. The last folder in the storage card was for photographs, and there were two photos stored there. Wally opened up the first one—the image was small but sharp.

It was a picture of Wally, taken from a distance with a telephoto lens. It took her a moment to figure out where it had come from, but to one side of the frame she could just make out an incredibly large, muscular arm, the short sleeve of a black T-shirt stretched tightly around it—the bouncer at Cielo. The photograph had been taken just two nights earlier, outside the dance club as Wally and the other girls had passed through the entrance.

The image made Wally remember the strange feeling she'd had inside the club: the sense that there had been eyes on her. It turned out she was probably right, that Alabama or one of the other men had followed her there, maybe even planning to grab her that night if they had the chance. Wally remembered that a cab had just pulled up to the curb when she'd stepped out of Cielo. Maybe that bit of lucky timing had saved her—for the moment. Life was a game of inches.

There was still another photograph stored in the cell phone, and she opened it next. What Wally saw there, on that tiny screen, took her breath away. The picture was a straight-on shot from the waist up of a young man in a white T-shirt standing against a bare cement wall. His face was completely expressionless, as if he was posing for a passport photo. His hair was shoulder length and black, and his eyes—like her own—were dark gray. She had stared into those eyes just two nights ago for a fleeting moment before she had spoken his name aloud and he had ended the encounter.

Tiger.

16.

WALLY WAS WAITING WITH COFFEE AND DOUGHNUTS when Jake and Ella emerged from bed the next morning. The sight of her sitting at the dining table—impatience written all over her features—put them on alert.

"What?" Jake asked. "What happened?"

She told them everything: from the late-night phone call to the photograph of Tiger on the burner phone and the game-changing conclusions she'd arrived at. Just a day earlier, Wally had debriefed Jake and Ella about everything that had been going on with her. Now, less than twelve hours later, she had a very different version to tell.

"So, the men who came at you outside Harmony House—" Ella began, processing it all.

"—and up at the lodge," Wally added.

"AND up at the lodge... they were after you, not Kyle?"

"And the pictures in the phone tell me that they aren't just after me," Wally said, "but Tiger too, wherever the hell *he* is."

And then Wally told the two of them what she had left out before: the surprise face-to-face, late-night meeting she'd had with Tiger on Facebook. Wally was nervous about how Jake and

Ella would react when they heard how *all-in* she was in her search for Tiger. It had been Wally's obsessive need to find her Russian birth mother that had brought so much chaos to their lives just five months ago. But their reaction took her by surprise.

"It's not like a shock or anything," Ella said. "He's your brother—of course you want to find him. And you are, after all, *you*."

"Truth," Jake chimed in.

"There are days I wish I wasn't," Wally said. "Believe me."

"As long as you protect yourself..."

"I will," Wally said, thankful for her friends' acceptance.

"First thing," Jake said, "we have to find out what we can about these assholes who keep coming after you."

We have to find out, Jake had said. *We*.

"Yeah," she agreed gratefully. "We don't have much to go on, but—"

Wally held up the burner phone that contained the photos, letting them speak for themselves.

"This is what we've got," Wally said. "What do we do with it?"

It took a moment, but soon Ella's face lit up with excitement.

"Paige!" Ella said. "I haven't seen her in so long...."

Paige Jefferson. The Cell Phone Whisperer. Of course. Why hadn't Wally already thought of her?

"Her shop opens at ten," Wally told them, and checked the time. "Which gives us an hour."

"Let's hit it," Jake said.

"There's something else I have to do, though," Wally went on. "After figuring everything out, I realized how messed up all of this was for Kyle. There's a crew of gunmen out there, and all along we figured they were after him. No matter how much of a psycho his father is, it turns out that hanging with me was probably the most dangerous thing he could have done. Plus, I totally went off on him when we were driving away from the lodge. He's got to be tied up in knots by now."

"There really was something there, huh?" Ella asked, reading Wally. "You and Kyle?"

"I think so," Wally said, although nothing was clear anymore. "I don't know. I guess I'd like it to be something. There were moments..."

"What are you going to do?" Jake asked.

"I have to get him some real help," Wally said, her mind made up. "I've only made things worse for him. It's the right thing to do."

While Jake and Ella got ready to go, Wally grabbed her cell phone. She had weighed the situation and was clear on what needed to be done. It was true that being with Wally had put Kyle in harm's way, but that didn't change the fact that his conflict with his father was still explosive.

First, Wally punched the code into her phone that would prevent the person on the other end of the line from seeing her phone number come up on caller ID. Then she dialed 911.

"This is 911," a woman's clipped, stern voice sounded on the other end of the line. "Please state your emergency."

"Hi, uh..." Wally made her voice sound as young and scared as she could. "My good friend hasn't been to school in like a week, and no one has heard from him. I'm really scared about it. I tried to call his cell and his home number, but there's no answer at either one."

"I understand," the woman on the other end of the line said. "But this is an emergency line. I can give you the number for Social Services—"

"I told our dean at school, but he said it was none of my business. The thing is, Kyle's father is physically abusive. He beats him all the time, and it seems like no one cares. Almost anything could have happened to him."

There was silence on the other end of the line, and Wally couldn't be sure her report was being taken seriously. Her only goal was to be absolutely, positively certain that New York City authorities paid a visit to Kyle's home, and soon. She'd heard lots of stories about terrible domestic situations falling through the cracks at Social Services, and she was prepared to say anything to make sure that didn't happen. Also, the call was untraceable, so there was no way in hell there would be any blowback against her for making a false report.

"I was visiting his apartment last week," she went on, "and his father had, like, a lot of drugs in the house. I mean, a lot, packed like bricks? In tall stacks. Plus lots of guns lying around. Big ones. It didn't seem very safe."

"Okay," the operator began, sounding very alert now, "let's start by getting your information—"

"I always see those signs on the subway, right?" Wally continued. "They say, 'If you see something, say something.' So I guess this is me, like, saying something."

Before the 911 operator could respond further, Wally recited the Townsends' Upper East Side address and hung up the phone. She couldn't be sure if her call to the authorities would immediately make Kyle's situation at home better or worse, but at least his case would be in the hands of people whose actual job it was to help.

17.

WALLY, JAKE, AND ELLA CAUGHT THE L TRAIN INTO Manhattan and then transferred to the downtown 6, joining hordes of commuters jammed together on the morning trains.

"It feels good to be crowded and squished again," Ella said with total sincerity. "There are more people in this train than in the entire town near the farm."

They got off at the Bleecker Street station and walked one block north, where there was a small, independent cell phone shop called Soul Cell. As they walked, Wally checked the street and sidewalks behind them to be sure they weren't being followed—the menacing phone call in the middle of the night had put her on high alert. Whatever it was that Alabama and the other goons were after, she had no reason to believe they would stop coming for her.

Do you have her? the man had asked. Replaying those words in her mind still sent a chill through Wally. What the hell was going on, anyway? The only thing she knew was that she finally had a major lead in her search for Tiger—the photo of him on the burner phone—and her chances of finding him probably hinged on the legendary abilities of Paige Jefferson.

It was a few minutes after ten when the three reached Soul Cell, just in time to find fifteen-year-old Paige Jefferson opening up the shop by herself. Paige smiled broadly at the sight of them.

"Jake? Ella?" Paige beamed at her old friends.

Wally managed to stop in at Soul Cell from time to time, but Paige hadn't seen Jake or Ella since they had moved upstate. The three of them crashed into each other on the sidewalk, wrapping each other up in a group hug.

"You're opening up shop without your folks?" Wally asked when the love fest finally broke up.

"Dad's working a freelance IT gig today," Paige said, "and Mom had some tax stuff to take care of downtown."

Paige's mother was a Jamaican immigrant who had worked for years as a nanny and housekeeper, eventually saving enough money to open her own business, Soul Cell. The small shop catered mostly to the cellular needs of the students at NYU, just a block away. Mrs. Jefferson was a large woman—three hundred pounds or so—and usually wore some sort of African wrap as a dress with her hair in a massive dreadlock ponytail. She and her husband had home-schooled Paige since the age of ten, but their daughter was a typical enough New York teen in most ways... except for the thick dreadlock ponytail hanging halfway down her back, like her mother's.

The three of them stood by while Paige opened the shop and set up for business, lighting the floor-to-ceiling display cases full of hundreds of phones and accessories. When she was done, she invited them all into the backroom repair area. Paige had a well-earned reputation as a sort of cell phone savant—Wally and her friends had always called her the Cell Phone Whisperer. She could fix damaged phones and retrieve lost data where others failed, including some miraculous feats in which she had revived phones that had been swamped in water, trampled in mud, and lost in some unmentionable places that Paige didn't usually like to talk about.

"What's up?" she finally asked when her worktable was clear and ready to go.

Wally pulled out the cell phone that had Tiger's photograph in its memory and handed Paige the phone and the battery that she'd removed.

"It's Korean," Paige said, examining the phone closely. "A burner, obviously, but not bad quality. No great features or anything, but reliable. We don't carry it here, but it's probably sold in forty or fifty tristate locations. Why did you pull the battery out?"

"Well," Wally said, "I'd say there's about a fifty-fifty chance that if you fire up that phone, thirty minutes later some armed creeps will show up at the door of your shop looking to hurt me."

"Huh," Paige said, apparently unimpressed. "You know what we call that around here?"

"What?" Jake asked.

"Tuesday," Paige said with a sly smile. "Just kidding. Hold on a sec—I can make sure we're not traced."

She reached up toward the wall, where a small, homemade-looking black box was mounted, with only an on-off switch on its front and a small indicator light. Paige switched on the device and the light glowed red.

"Signal jammer," Paige said. "Look outside."

The four of them looked out through the shop to the busy sidewalk out front. Streams of commuters and students were moving in both directions, many of them either speaking or texting into their cell phones. Within seconds of Paige's activating the jammer, the pedestrians began stopping in their tracks, glaring at the suddenly useless devices in their hands with looks of betrayal.

"I so love that!" Ella said. "Look how lost they are—it's like you ripped out their souls or something."

"I know," Paige said, giggling. "Pathetic. It's oddly satisfying to be a Tower God."

With the jammer in full effect, Paige placed the battery back in the burner phone and turned it on. Within twenty seconds the device had fully booted up. Paige's fingers ran over the controls with lightning speed as she explored the workings and storage of the device.

"We have a call history that is set to erase automatically," she said, "so it appears blank. We have no GPS feature, but there may be some location-related metadata stored in the RAM, depending. We have two downloaded files, which are photographs. One of you Wally, dressed for clubbing and the other picture...whoa. This guy is hot!"

"Easy there," Wally said. "That's my brother."

"Really?"

"Yeah, I know. He's pretty good-looking. And screw you for being so surprised that we're related."

"Okay," Paige said finally, setting the phone down on her worktable and giving Wally an attentive look. "Tell me the story."

Wally paused. She had known Paige for nearly two years, but their relationship was really just based on business. During her time on the streets, Wally and her crew—including Jake and Ella—had earned money trading in black-market calling cards, and Paige and her mother had occasionally dealt with them. Wally and Paige shared a mutual trust, but it had never gone deeper than that.

"I've been looking for my brother for a long time," Wally said. "His name is Tiger, and this photograph is the best lead I've found. Although, to be accurate, it sort of found me."

"What do mean?"

"I had a run-in with some men—"

"The gunmen that are supposedly after you…you weren't kidding about that?"

"Not kidding at all. This phone came off one of those guys. I have no idea what they want from me—all I know is that they have something to do with Tiger. Whatever you can dig out of the phone might be my only way of finding him."

"But no pressure," Jake added.

"Yeah, sorry about that," said Wally.

Paige thought about it. "Well, like I said—there may be some metadata stored in here, off the directory. Depends on the carrier. It'll take me a while to dig it out of the memory, so I'll have to get back to you on that. For now, let me find the CID and see if I can get you the point of sale—I have connections with most of the distributors."

"That would be great."

"I'll make you a deal," Paige said with a sly smile. "I'll help you however I can, and once you find Tiger you can introduce me."

"Paige, I'm shocked," Ella said, faking a gasp. "I didn't know you were such a diabolical slut."

"Everyone needs a hobby."

"Done, then," Wally said. "I think you'd be good for him."

Paige held up her finger in a gimme-a-second gesture, and headed into the back office of the shop. Within just a few minutes, she returned with a discouraged look on her face.

"I don't think this will help you much," she said, holding up a napkin with a few scrawled notes on it. "That unit was part of a delivery of two hundred cell phones that were jacked two weeks ago from a truck up in Harlem—on Frederick Douglass Boulevard. I talked to the distributor and he said their delivery guys get hassled by local gangs up there all the time. The shipment was never recovered, so there's no way I can tell you who that phone was sold to."

The news didn't have the negative effect that Paige had

anticipated. During their time as a crew, the three of them had done a fair amount of "business" in that area of the city, and their street knowledge was still intact—the three of them looked at each other, calculating the possibilities.

"GMB runs those streets," Jake said.

"What does that stand for?" Paige asked. "Or do I not want to know?"

"GMB—the Get Money Boys," Ella said. "Hard-core bangers."

"Whatever they ripped off, they always fenced it with Panama's smoke shop," Jake said. "Back in the day, anyway."

"Panama's long gone," said Wally, "but if someone else is running his shop now, maybe we can still track the phone."

"I guess we're going to Harlem," said Ella.

18.

"JUST LIKE OLD TIMES," JAKE SAID WHEN THEY boarded the uptown B train, which would take them all the way into Harlem.

"Yeah, it's strange going back to Panama's," Wally said, the idea of returning to the smoke shop already putting her on edge. "It feels like time travel."

Back then—before everything came apart—Wally and the crew went to Panama when they wanted phone cards to sell on the street. When they had something to sell, Panama fenced it for them, and when they needed fake IDs or wisdom about what was happening on the street, Panama was their guy. What they didn't know back then was that the 131st Street Smoke Shop was *"up,"* meaning it was under surveillance by law enforcement who were trying to sting gun dealers off the street. The man they knew as Panama—a huge, menacing man of nonspecific race—was actually an undercover ATF agent named Cornell Brown.

Wally had watched two people die that November morning on Shelter Island—Panama and her mother, Claire.

They got off the train at 125th, and five minutes of walking took them to the intersection of Frederick Douglass Boulevard and 131st, on the southwest side of Harlem. The neighborhood had cleaned up some, but Wally and her friends knew that the criminal undercurrents of those streets had never gone away, and probably never would.

The 131st Street Smoke Shop was shut up and dark. A hand-lettered sign hung on string behind the door—CLOSED. Loose trash and smoked-down cigarette butts had piled up against the doorway, likely swept there by the wind. The debris gave the impression that no one had entered the shop in a week, at least. Wally peered in through the window and could see that the shop looked the same inside as always, fully stocked and ready for business. She banged hard on the door, hard enough to clang the bells hanging inside to announce a customer. But there were no signs of life inside.

"Well, that pisses me off," Wally said.

"Closed in the middle of the day," Jake said. "Good way to go out of business."

"Unless your business is something else," said Wally. "Let's check out back."

They stepped over the low chain running across the entrance to the small, empty parking lot beside the smoke shop. When Panama had been running the place, most of the real business had been run out of the back entrance, which bordered on St. Nicholas Avenue and the park beyond. They walked to that entrance, not surprised to find it locked with a strong dead bolt.

"Do you have something?" Jake asked Wally, and she fished

around her messenger bag, coming up with a Leatherman multi-tool. She handed it to him, and he used a combination of the main blade and his plastic ID to work on the dead bolt while Wally and Ella stood watch.

"Are we sure this is a good idea?" Ella asked, sounding practical, not scared. "Even if they did sell the phones, they do everything in cash. I don't see them keeping a list of their customers."

"Yeah," Wally agreed, "but we came all the way up here, right? Unless Paige can dig out more for us to work with, tracing the sale is all we have."

They heard a loud *thunk!* as the dead bolt turned over. Jake turned the doorknob and, just like that, the three of them were inside, closing the door behind them.

A few dirty skylights in the ceiling of the large, crowded storeroom cast a dim yellow glow through the space—enough for the three of them to make their way without turning on the lights. As their eyes adjusted, they discovered that the large room was filled with a massive stash of electronics and home appliances—flat-screen TVs, laptops, music players, Bluetooth headsets, and microwave ovens—hundreds of boxes of contraband stacked all the way to the ceiling with only narrow aisles in between.

"Holy shit," whispered Jake. "I could shop here."

They made their way to the center of the room, where a partially open space had been left to make room for a long folding table. Several crates of brand-new iPads and iPhones were on the table, still in their original boxes with the Apple insignia on the outside. Wally noticed that the crates were only halfway unloaded, as if the work had been interrupted.

"I guess that's why they aren't bothering with the storefront anymore," Wally said. "Here's where all the magic happens. Do you guys see any crates for burner phones?"

"Over here," Ella said. She pointed to a wall of boxes labeled with every cell phone brand name, plus several with labels in mostly Asian characters. "They're definitely in the burner business."

"Weird, though," Jake said. "It's hard to imagine the Get Money Boys in here, running inventory."

"They'd have someone else working this side of the operation," Wally said. The moment the words were out of her mouth, sounds of movement came from the deep, dark aisles on the other side of the storeroom.

Wally heard the distinctive *click!* of a bullet being chambered in an automatic handgun.

Shit.

The Get Money Bitches—girl associates of the Get Money Boys—came rushing out of the far, dark aisles of the storeroom. They were a quick, overwhelming force of nine or ten fearsome-looking young women with half a dozen drawn guns between them. They were various builds, most of them black, and ranging in age from fourteen to their early twenties. Some had shaved heads and baggy gangsta clothes that almost made them look like men, while others wore elaborate makeup and had their hair done in feminine weaves and rows. All moved quickly and looked angry.

Wally, Jake, and Ella instinctively turned to run, but they only made it a few steps before the girls were on them, attacking furiously. Wally felt hands grabbing her by the shoulders in an attempt to drag her down to the floor, but she spun around and landed a series of high kicks—driving back one girl and knocking a 9mm Beretta from the hand of another. But when she looked back around for her friends she couldn't see them anymore.… Had they split in another direction? She could hear the sounds of fighting somewhere nearby—Jake was grunting and growling as he struggled with the GMBs.

"Jake!" she called out, feeling a blast of rage at the possibility of her friends being hurt.

Wally tried to head in the direction of Jake's struggle, but two more of the GMBs came hard at her from the far end of the aisle—that made a total of four ready fighters who would be almost unbeatable in such a cramped space.

"You're done, girl!" one of the GMBs said.

There was only one direction for Wally to go—*up!*—and she started climbing the wall of crates on either side of her, jamming her hands and feet into the narrow spaces between the cardboard boxes. She made it six or seven feet up the wall when several strong hands grabbed her ankles and calves, tugging her down. Wally managed to kick their hands away a few times and held strong for three or four seconds, but soon her muscles were burning from the effort and her strength gave way.

The hands pulled her down and dragged her by the feet back to the space in the center of the storeroom. Jake and Ella had already been corralled, lying faceup on the floor, with the GMBs standing around them in a circle. Wally counted seven drawn guns, now pointed at the three of them.

"Wait—" Wally was silenced by a hard kick to her ribs.

Facing Wally, Jake, and Ella from above—her Glock handgun drawn and chambered—was a young black woman over six feet tall. Her hair was cropped short and she wore a tight white wife-beater, her powerful arms covered with tattoo sleeves, inked and scarred. She wore loose black jeans cinched at the waist with a black leather belt.

"You *crazy*?!" the woman yelled at them. "You know where you are?! You came to rip off the GMBs?!"

Wally realized that she knew the woman standing above them—knew *of her* anyway. Her name was Afrika Neems, and her boyfriend was the alpha male of the Get Money Boys.... Wally couldn't remember his name. Plenty of the city's gangs had female associates, but the Get Money Bitches were considered to be almost as powerful within the GMB pecking order as the men.

"We didn't—" Wally began, only to be subjected to another hard kick.

Jake tried to get up to defend her, but as soon as he moved he took five or six brutal kicks that knocked him back down.

Wally forced herself to keep speaking, even if it meant taking more hits.

"We didn't come here to rip you off," she said.

"Bullshit!"

Two more kicks. Wally struggled for breath.

"You're Afrika, right? I've heard about you..."

Another kick to her ribs.

"Everybody heard about Afrika," one of the other women said.

"But you didn't hear enough," said another, "or you'd have stayed yo' white ass far away from here."

"I heard about you from Panama. We used to trade with him."

No kicks that time. Afrika gave Wally a longer look.

"Trade what?"

"Nothing. Phone cards. Just for walkin' around money. Small-time."

"Well, that's too damn bad then, 'cause today you done small-timed yo' ass into hella pain. We got the Boys comin' in today, and I *know* what they gonna do wit you."

A few of the other girls acknowledged her words with nods, some of them obviously looking forward to witnessing whatever punishment the Get Money Boys would deliver.

"We just came to ask a question...."

"Well you betta ask now, and I hope it's a good one," Afrika said, "'cause you done *died* for it today, white girl. Busting in on the GMB? You outta yo' fuckin' *mind*...."

Wally thought now, for the first time, how to ask if the Get Money Boys had stolen the shipment of burner phones, and if they remembered who they'd sold them to. She immediately realized how ridiculous and meaningless that question would sound now. Their actual lives—hers, Jake's, Ella's—were on the line.

"Best speak up, girl," Afrika said. "Ain't no Panama here, and 'til he come back we make the rules here."

Did Wally hear that right? *Until Panama comes back?* What was she talking about? Panama—Special Agent Cornell Brown—was dead, beyond question. Like the three of them would be soon, if Wally couldn't talk their way out.

"Can we just talk to Panama?" she asked, probing for information that she might be able to use. "He'll tell you we're okay. Where is he?"

"Panama got warrants," Afrika said. "He gone. He got people in Louisiana, so maybe he there. Don't know, don't much care. The smoke shop is *ours* now. Like *you* is ours."

Wally's mind spun as she processed the implications: the gang didn't know Panama was dead, or that he had been undercover for the ATF, obviously. Which meant that they didn't know the smoke shop had been under surveillance. Law enforcement had managed to keep all of it under wraps, which could not have been easy, and they'd managed to plant some story about

Panama being on the lam somewhere in Bayou country. But why?

She could only think of one answer.

"You need to get out of here now," Wally said. "We all need to go."

"Say what? Bitch, you get crazier and crazier."

"Okay," Wally said, "then just let me stand up for a minute. I need to show you something. I'm not going to do anything stupid."

Afrika thought about it.

"Please," Wally added.

"I s'pose you can't do nothin' stupider than breakin' in here in the first place."

Wally stood up slowly, her body aching from the many kicks and her fall from the wall of crates.

"I need a radio," she said.

"What the *what*?" Afrika said.

"Please," Wally said.

Afrika thought about it, her eyes studying Wally skeptically, but then gave another nod. Wally looked to a shelf nearby, where an old boom box sat. It was an old-school beast of a thing with a manual tuning dial and cassette player. It must have been there for years.

Wally hauled the boom box off the shelf and silently prayed that there were working batteries inside. She hit the power switch, and the radio came to life, blasting classic soul—the Isley Brothers.

It's your thing, do whatcha wanna do…

I can't tell you…who to sock it to.

Wally turned the tuning dial, passing over news channels and rap and several stations with mariachi music until she finally landed on an unused frequency. The radio was nearly silent then, except for a slight hint of static. Wally raised the boom box up high over her head and paced around the storeroom.

Afrika and the other GMBs looked at her like she had lost her mind.

"Crazy white girl…"

Wally kept her focus, and continued moving through the large space. She held the radio up to the wall, the shelf supports, and the old landline phone on the wall—but nothing happened. She paused, reconsidering her strategy. Her eyes pored over the large space, searching.

The GMBs were focused totally on Wally now, leaving Jake and Ella free to pull themselves up off the floor. They stood and watched their friend with baffled expressions on their faces—the two of them obviously had no idea what she was up to either.

Wally looked straight up—a simple aluminum work lamp hung above the central worktable, its thick orange power cord running all the way up to a beam in the ceiling. She set the boom box down for a moment, cleared a small amount of space on the worktable—carefully pushing aside several thousand dollars worth of iPads—and climbed up onto the table herself, the boom box in hand. She raised it up toward the light fixture, and when the radio was within a foot of the lamp its speakers began to emit a loud, high-pitched screech, similar to feedback from a concert sound system.

Wally pulled the boom box away from the lamp, and the noise stopped. She pushed the box back toward the lamp and the screeching began again.

Now Wally looked straight at Afrika Neems, who took a moment to process what was happening. When she finally did, her eyes widened as the revelation sunk in.

"There's mikes?!" she shouted, incredulous. "This place is *hot*?"

"This place is hot," said Wally. "Panama was a cop."

It was the only explanation she could think of—why law enforcement would go to so much trouble to hide the fact that Panama was involved in the Shelter Island shootout, and that he was with the ATF. The police wanted to keep up surveillance on the smoke shop. It had taken Wally all of two minutes to find one of their radio mikes, but it was likely there were half a dozen more buried in the walls and fixtures of the shop.

"Holy hell," Afrika said, a look of dread on her face. "We're outta here. . . ."

It was a jailbreak, then—without looking back, all the Get Money Bitches made for the exit, not bothering to pocket an iPhone on their way out. The shop was hot, so *everything* was hot. What they needed to do was put as much distance as they could between themselves and all the stolen merchandise.

Wally, Jake, and Ella were right behind them, and by the time they reached the parking lot, the GMBs had split up, rushing off in ten different directions. Wally looked east and saw that Afrika Neems was about to cross St. Nicholas Avenue, headed as fast as she could in the direction of the park.

"Afrika!" Wally called out, and the girl stopped to turn around and face Wally. "Two weeks ago, a crate of two hundred burner phones were jacked on Frederick Douglass. . . ."

Wally waited for Afrika to acknowledge the statement, one way or the other, but she remained silent.

"I just need to know where they ended up," Wally said.

"What's your name, white princess?"

"Wally Stoneman."

"He was a tall white man, Wally Stoneman," Afrika said after taking a moment to make up her mind. "Tall and strong, like a football player. He bought the whole case of burners, all two hundred. Whoever he works for must have lots o' things goin' on. . . ."

"Anything else?"

The young woman took a moment to think.

"He a *cracker*," she finally said. "Up from down deep, there. Georgia, Mississippi . . ."

"Or Alabama maybe?"

Afrika nodded. "Or Alabama, maybe. And that's all I got."

Wally thanked her with a wave but wasn't feeling exactly triumphant. What she'd heard only confirmed what she already knew—for everything she'd put herself and Jake and Ella through, they had no new handle on how to find out exactly what Alabama wanted from her and Tiger.

Wally turned away and rejoined Jake and Ella. They headed south on Douglass, making their way back toward the 125th Street subway station.

"That was cool, Wally," Ella said. "Where'd you learn that, with the radio?"

"From Nick," Wally said, referring to her old boyfriend—her first boyfriend, really—a hard-core junkie. "When he got paranoid, he thought the cops were listening in on us wherever we went. He carried a little handheld radio with him, just to do sweeps. Never found a bug."

"Hey." A voice from behind them made Wally wait and turn, her defenses up.

Afrika Neems was hurrying to catch up with them.

"Are you gonna see that man again?" she asked, a little breathless. "The cracker?"

"I'm gonna try," Wally said.

"Then watch your ass," Afrika warned, looking a little spooked. "He asked me if we could get any punch...."

"*Punch*?"

"Some on the street call it that. Or just *plastic*. A kind of explosive. You can maybe find the real thing, but it can be traced so some fools make it on they own. It's some serious shit. Five pounds o' that would take out a whole damn city block. I didn't have none, but your cracker had money so *someone* is gonna get it for him."

"Okay," Wally didn't know what this information would mean for her, but it couldn't be good. "Thanks again."

Afrika just nodded, then turned on her heels and made her way back north toward St. Nicholas Avenue. Wally, Jake, and Ella continued south on Douglass. Just when they'd reached the corner of 128th and Douglass, two unmarked cop cars sped toward them and squealed to a stop right in front of them. Four very unhappy-looking plainclothes cops stepped out of the cars.

"I think they're offering us a ride," Wally said wryly, reacting to the men's glares.

Jake and Ella laughed without humor. *What now?*

19.

"A THREE-YEAR OPERATION!" DETECTIVE ATLEY GREER howled. "NYPD, ATF, FBI . . . a joint task force focused on at least four organized-crime groups doing business at the smoke shop. They were just two or three months from making their cases, and you brought it all down in five minutes!"

Wally had never seen Greer like this—all vexed up. She figured the grief must be raining down in buckets from his higher-ups in the precinct. Outwardly, he was his usual self, a reasonably fit guy in his forties who could almost be called handsome, except he always looked like he'd lost his shaving kit and slept in his suit. His eyes, however, were lit up like Christmas right now. Greer was genuinely pissed off. It was almost intimidating.

"The GMBs were going to kill us," Wally snapped back. "As in *kill*. Where were your fat-ass surveillance guys while that was going on? Sitting in a dark room with their thumbs up their asses, no doubt. We had to take care of ourselves, and we did."

Greer opened his mouth to dispute Wally but found no retort. He knew she was right. It took him a moment to compose himself.

"And what the hell were you doing at the smoke shop in the first place?" he said. "That place is a cesspool."

"I'm not answerable to you for my whereabouts. I have rights."

"You broke in!"

"Did I? Is someone pressing charges?"

"Okay, fine. If you didn't break in, then the GMBs are guilty of assault and possibly kidnapping, plus possession of illegal firearms. You want to make good? Then *you* press charges against the gang chicks..."

"I wish I could help you, but my memory of it all has gotten a little hazy. Probably low blood sugar. I'd make a terrible witness."

Wally wouldn't be inclined to snitch on Afrika Neems anyway, but the fact that she'd offered information about Alabama clinched it—Wally would rather be a friend of the GMBs than an enemy, any day.

Greer went quiet for a moment, looking like he was trying to chill himself out.

"You understand, Wallis," he began again, marginally calmer this time, "that the perception here at the precinct is that I have some amount of influence over your conduct. So when you go off and—"

"I didn't ask for that," Wally cut him short. "I didn't ask for your *influence*, or your probie foot patrols knocking on my door, or our little heart-to-heart fatherly advice sessions."

The words had come out sounding more harsh than she had meant, and Wally felt the smallest pang of guilt. However annoying he was at times, he'd proved he was someone she could rely on. Fortunately, Greer seemed to take her rant in stride—twenty years on the NYPD had obviously hardened him to verbal abuse. He leaned back in his chair and waited, allowing Wally a moment to collect herself.

She had considered the possibility of spilling everything to him about Alabama and the other gunman—she obviously needed all the help she could get—but now that she knew they were somehow linked with Tiger, there was no way she could involve any kind of law enforcement. Through one of the Society's sources, Wally had managed to get a look at Tiger's criminal file. Included in his sheet was information from Interpol—the international crime fighting organization—about serious charges that would be waiting for him if he ever returned to Russia. But his situation in the United States was even worse.

Tiger had come to America with their father, Alexei Klesko, and the two men had left a swath of destruction and violence across New York—much of which Wally had witnessed firsthand. On Shelter Island, Tiger had redeemed himself in Wally's eyes, but that meant nothing to the New York State Police, much less the ATF or the FBI. All of them had warrants out for Tiger, which meant that Wally would never be able to involve the authorities in her search without putting her brother in jeopardy. She wondered what Greer would do if he ever came into contact with Tiger, but wouldn't risk finding out.

"I'll tell you what else is disappointing…" Greer said.

"Oh yes, please."

"You seemed like you were off on a new and good track," he said, "and now you're palling around again with your old street crew." He motioned toward one of the interview rooms on the west side of the precinct floor, where Jake and Ella were sitting and waiting their turn to be questioned. They both looked pretty wiped out, probably still feeling the effects of the intense scene with the GMBs.

"You have no idea, Greer," Wally said with a half laugh. "If you're so concerned about the state of my mortal soul, you should be glad I'm with them. Jake and Ella are the straightest arrows I know. The dirtiest thing they're into now is pig shit, and I mean that literally."

Greer looked dubious but also weary. He sighed deeply.

"Go home, Wallis," Greer said. "And take your morally pure friends with you."

"Okay, I'll do that," Wally said, not moving from her seat. "But I was wondering—"

"Whoa, I know that tone of voice," Greer said, astounded. "You're going to ask me for some kind of favor, now? Unbelievable."

"Not at all. I was just wondering if you knew anything about an old friend of mine from school. I knew he was having problems at home—like, bad domestic stuff—but I heard that something big went off at his place today. I'm just wondering if he's okay."

Greer gave her a long, hard look. He clearly didn't believe anything out of her mouth anymore. Justifiably so.

"What's your friend's name?"

"Kyle Townsend," Wally told him.

Greer typed in the name and Kyle's address, clicking on a few options before proceeding to read through several documents. After a minute, he turned back to Wally with narrowed eyes.

"It says here that 911 received a call from an anonymous female who reported a case of domestic abuse and possession of drugs and weapons—enough to start an Upper East Side cartel."

"A concerned citizen, obviously," Wally said. "What did the police find?"

"Nothing. No Kyle Townsend, no father Townsend. No evidence of domestic abuse. Not one gram of dope, not one weapon or bullet. According to the building staff, father and son had bugged out two days earlier and haven't been seen since."

Kyle and his father were gone. Wally hated to hear this—had her 911 call actually made things worse?

Shit.

"Is there something you want to tell me, Wallis?" Greer asked, seeing the look of concern on her face. "If you're holding something back—"

"Kyle is a friend," Wally answered, "and I'm definitely worried about him. Are the cops going to do anything else? I really believe Kyle's in trouble, and his father is the cause of it."

"We'll keep the inquiry open, but that's all we can do at this point. There's no evidence at all of a crime, unless you can give us something more."

Wally thought about it. She'd heard Kyle's story, but she had nothing to back up what he'd told her. Now the two of them were gone, and Wally had no idea where. End of story.

"Shit," Wally said. "I don't know anything else, Greer. I wish I did."

The three of them had just enough energy left to make it back to Wally's apartment, stopping only to pick up a pizza on the way. They all changed for bed and turned on an episode of *The Wire* while they ate the pizza. It was a great show, but nothing they saw on the screen was more intense than what they had lived through at the 131st Street Smoke Shop.

"I'd forgotten," Jake said. "I mean, about how out of control things used to be for us back in the day."

"I know," Wally said. "I'm sorry."

"Don't be sorry," Ella said. "Not for back then, and not for today. We made it through, like we always used to. And we were there for each other, like always. That's all that matters."

January and Bea poked their heads in around ten thirty, tricked out in their club clothes as always. One look at the situation on the couch told them everything they needed to know.

"Whoa," said January. "You guys are dug in already, huh?"

"Pretty much," Wally said. "But have fun."

"When do we not?" Bea said. She and January blew Wally goodbye kisses and took off for their night on the town. Moments later, they could hear the girls down on the street, shouting for a cab and letting out a "*Woot woot*" when one stopped for them.

Ella looked at Wally and rolled her eyes.

"They're nice!" Wally defended herself. "I need friends here while the two of you are upstate milking goats or growing hydroponic broccoli or whatever."

"How would those two have done today at the smoke shop?" Ella asked, a sneaky smirk on her face.

Wally laughed out loud, unable to hold it back.

They went on watching *The Wire* but only made it through one episode, and it was obvious that Jake and Ella could barely keep their eyes open.

"Take my room again," Wally said.

"Thanks," Ella said. "G'night."

Ella and Jake headed to the bedroom, closing the door behind them. Alone in the living room, Wally stretched out on the couch and wrapped herself up in a heavy, old, cotton-knit blanket, one of the few items she had brought with her from her mother's old Upper West Side apartment. The blanket was worn and soft and comforting—a transcendent reminder of the times when she had felt loved and in harmony with Claire.

In the deep quiet of the night, Wally began to hear the sound of movement from her bedroom—it was Ella and Jake hooking up. She wondered if it was something they were able to do at Neversink Farm or if this time away gave them an opportunity they didn't usually have.

Wally wrapped herself in Claire's blanket and went outside to the roof, giving the couple some privacy. She'd always been happy for her best friends for finding each other and being such loyal partners, but Wally couldn't help feeling a little envious too. Jake and Ella made being a couple seem so easy and natural—something Wally had never experienced.

Wally's relationships with men always seemed to be complicated and elusive, just like they had been with Kyle. She thought about the closeness they had shared up at the lodge before Alabama had shown up and everything had gone to hell. Was there anything about their connection that was worth saving, or had she done the right thing by distancing herself?

Maybe both. She wondered where Kyle was now and whether he was safe.

20.

TIGER AND RACHEL WALKED SIDE BY SIDE THROUGH the neighborhood, drawing little interest from the housewives running errands or the gardeners mowing lawns. The two of them wore tracksuits and tennis shoes, and both had nylon tennis-racket cases slung over their shoulders. They carried water bottles in their hands, hydrating at regular intervals the way any young, upwardly mobile power couple would on their way home from a tough match of mixed doubles. The two of them didn't share a single word.

The western end of the housing tract was bordered by a tall, dense row of trees, the kind that are planted specifically to block an unattractive view. From the sidewalk, Tiger and Rachel ducked off through the trees, soon coming up against a tall perimeter fence. Tiger flipped the tennis-racket case off his shoulder and opened it, producing a heavy set of wire cutters. Within just a few moments, they breached the fence and entered the property.

For the next ten minutes they walked across open ground. It had once been cultivated fields but was now hard and sterile. They reached a wooded hill and ascended—it took only a minute to reach the top. They stopped there, shrugging off their bags and finding an observation spot behind a clutch of maple trees. Rachel pulled out a *snaiperskuyu vintofku*—a sniper rifle with a long-range scope—mounting it on a bipod at ground level.

Tiger was surprised to see the weapon.

"I thought we were just here to scout."

"We are," she answered. "But if we're spotted, things could get difficult."

Tiger pulled out a nonreflecting tactical spotting scope and used it handheld, crouching just a few feet from Rachel. In silence, they scanned the territory on the far side of the hill. It was a shallow valley—probably less than half a mile across—bordered on the other side by a hill almost identical to the one they were set up on. A single access road entered the property from the south. Paved with asphalt, it was sprung all over with cracks that had weeds spearing up through them. The road hadn't been maintained in many years.

At the center of the valley sat a large abandoned factory of some kind, surrounded by a high perimeter fence. The fence itself looked no more than a few years old and appeared completely intact. The factory contained by the fence, however, had obviously gone unused for years; graffiti covered every inch of the place, even the highest parts of the walls, which rose up to four stories in one section. The sheet-metal walls along the ground had been almost completely stripped away by scrappers, and what was left was completely rusted.

"It was a munitions factory," Rachel said. "It's been shut down for decades."

"Are we going in?"

"No. We're waiting."

They perched there for nearly three hours, silent and unmoving. The sun eased down behind the hills to the west, and Tiger was surprised at how cold it became once the sun had fallen out of sight. If Rachel felt any discomfort, she did not let on.

"Do you have a dossier?" he asked.

"Excuse me?"

"Have you been arrested before?"

She hesitated before answering, suspicion in her voice. "No."

"Did you go to school?"

"Yes."

"Secondary only, or college?"

"Hofstra."

"I don't know what that means."

"College."

"And what did you study?"

"Business."

They were quiet for a while before she broke the silence.

"Why?" she asked.

"It makes me curious. It seems to me there are many choices for you, many possibilities. But you choose this."

In the dimming light, Tiger could feel Rachel watching him closely.

"This is business," she finally said. "Our family business. And yours."

Tiger considered this. Of course she was right—his path through life had been determined by the circumstances of his birth. He had assumed that the pull of such things wasn't as strong in America, but maybe he'd been wrong.

Minutes later, they spotted two large, black SUVs—Ford Expeditions—entering the valley and approaching along the access road, from the south. The vehicles reached the perimeter fence and continued on to the entrance gate, just two hundred yards from where Tiger and Rachel were waiting.

A man emerged from the passenger side of the first car. He was burly looking and wore a dark suit, his hair shaved in a close buzz cut. He unlocked the gate and rolled it to the side, allowing both vehicles to enter the yard that surrounded the factory. Once the cars had stopped, things got busier: eight other people stepped out of the vehicles, two adult Hispanic-looking men and six younger people who Tiger guessed were in their mid-teens—at least two or three years younger than himself. Four were boys and two girls, and all of them equipped with weapons—assault rifles and automatic handguns.

Tiger watched them closely through his scope. The teens were of various ethnicities. One of the boys and one of the girls were black, very dark skinned. Two other boys were Hispanic, and one of each gender was Caucasian, with an Eastern European look to them. They moved with purpose, constantly scanning the area with their eyes. Despite their youth, they carried their high-powered weapons as if they were natural extensions of their limbs.

Tiger had an uneasy feeling of recognition. There was a man who was known as Sweet, a black-market transportation *pasrednik*—a "fixer"—who operated throughout Eastern Europe, Africa, and South America. His chosen name was Swede, but during his operations in the eastern Congo—delivering shipments of weapons to tribal guerrilla troops—the locals had pronounced his name as Sweet, and it stuck.

As far back as the mid-nineties, Sweet had surrounded himself with a multiethnic cadre of very young bodyguards, rootless and war-ravaged teens he assembled from areas where he did dirty business. Sweet trained the youths himself and always kept them close, valuing them for their boldness and unfailing loyalty. They were not drugged or brutalized like other child soldiers but instead were highly incentivized with cash and perks. Most of all, they were a very effective security measure. There was something inherently terrifying about a teenager with a submachine gun, a sense that bestial, bloody havoc could be set off by even the slightest miscue.

Tiger had once met Sweet face-to-face, during a weapons exchange in Gjilani, Kosovo. Only fifteen himself at the time, Tiger was part of a security team backing up one of the bosses from *Piter*... St. Petersburg. Though he was a low-level member of the team, his boss had made a point of introducing him as the son of Alexei Klesko—apparently, his father and Sweet had done profitable business over the years, and Tiger's presence as a member of his crew lent his boss a certain credibility.

Sweet was a short, pudgy man with wispy blond hair and a fair complexion that seemed permanently scarred red after so much time spent in sunny equatorial destinations. Tiger remembered the man as having an oddly warm manner, smiling more than you would expect from someone involved in the arms trade. Sweet had shaken his hand, a gesture Tiger found especially reassuring at the time, since they were surrounded by no fewer than twenty of Sweet's heavily armed teenagers.

Now, sitting undercover atop the hill in eastern New Jersey almost three years later, Tiger was nearly certain that the group of young fighters he was observing were an arm of Sweet's security force. Tiger wondered if Rachel and her father could possibly be aware of his distant connection to Sweet. He also wondered exactly how far across the planet he would have to travel to escape the influence of his father—he had a nasty suspicion that no distance would be great enough.

"What are we looking at?" Tiger asked Rachel.

"You tell me."

Tiger looked through the scope, focusing on the group below as they entered the abandoned factory together, most of them carrying flashlights now as they systematically made their way through the complex. The layout of the factory started to become clear to Tiger: the left side of the factory was low and long, thirty feet high, but obviously one large room. This had to be the manufacturing side of the plant, probably a long assembly-line system. To the right was the management side, a tall building with five separate floor levels.

Tiger watched the flashlight beams move through the complex, first along the manufacturing side—quickly—and then moving on to the taller section as the team scanned every floor. The team was moving much too quickly for this to be a search.

"A security sweep," he said. "They have something planned for this space, and this is their early recon. We're scouting them as they scout the site."

Rachel nodded, confirming his assessment.

"What are they protecting?" Tiger asked, sure he already knew the answer but interested to hear what Rachel's answer would be.

"Does it matter? Tell me what they've decided."

"The left side is a large open space, not a good place to defend anything or anyone at risk. The tower on the right is more secure—especially the upper floors—so whoever or whatever they are guarding will be found there."

The two of them watched as the team below filed out of the factory and back into their vehicles, the same big white guy locking the gate behind them and climbing into the lead vehicle before they drove away, their headlights necessary now in the dim twilight as they sped back along the access road and disappeared from the valley.

After waiting just a few minutes, Rachel stood up and shouldered her racket case.

"What are you doing?" he asked.

She reached into her bag and pulled out a medium-sized handgun—a 9mm Beretta—and held it up for him to see.

"Finding a place for this," she said, and started walking downhill, into the valley. "Wait here."

Tiger watched her progress as Rachel reached the bottom of the hill, then jogged across open ground to the locked gate of the complex. Less than a minute later—did she have a key, or did she pick the lock?—Rachel was through the gate and prowling inside the old factory building itself.

He saw the glow of Rachel's flashlight moving through the building, in much the same way the recon team's had, except Rachel moved directly to the tower side of the structure, climbing the steps to the top floor as her first order of business. At that point, the flashlight glow settled in one place and did not move.

Tiger watched and waited. He felt uneasy—he wasn't sure why—and a thought came into his head: he didn't have to stay there. He could easily turn and go, disappearing into the night and putting Rachel, Archer Divine, and the Ranch behind him for good. This possibility—that he could reclaim a sense of control and independence that he hadn't felt in months—gave him a warm feeling.

Just as easily, though, he imagined himself out in America alone. He'd be capable of surviving, but to what end? He had dreams of a new life—naive dreams, maybe—but the pact he'd made with Divine offered the only tangible route toward achieving what he wanted most. There was a price for holding on to his dream, and Tiger had been paying it.

He would not stop now. If fate threw obstacles in his path he would face them like a man, just as he had done every day of his youth, in the streets of *Piter*. Tiger held his ground and waited. Soon Rachel would return from the compound below. Before long, Tiger would certainly learn what destiny had in store for him.

He would be ready.

21.

WALLY WOKE FEELING A POWERFUL NEED TO BE productive—at *anything*. For all the danger and hassle they'd been through the previous day—finding themselves at the mercy of Afrika Neems and the rest of the GMBs, and then getting blasted by Greer for blowing up the surveillance at the smoke shop—Wally had precious little to show for it. She was as far from finding Tiger as she had ever been, and just as far from understanding what was behind Alabama's attacks.

She decided to surprise Lewis Jordan by actually showing up for work.

Jake and Ella were still asleep, so she left some cash out on the kitchen counter with a note. She hoped they'd go out and spend the money having fun. Wally left a chunk of frozen fish on Tevin's island, but this time he sulked and remained fully immersed.

"There's such a thing as being *too* low maintenance," Wally said to the snapper. "If I wanted warm and cuddly I'd have gotten a cat, but you could show me a little something."

She headed out of the apartment and made her way toward the subway. Watching her back along the way to make sure that she was not being followed, Wally scanned the cars parked outside her apartment building. She half expected to see Alabama or some similar creep waiting for her. Whatever it was the men wanted from her—or whatever connection they had with Tiger—Wally had the powerful sense that they would keep coming for her until they got it. She didn't see anything or anyone that worried her, but made a mental note to be alert and aware of her surroundings throughout the day.

It felt good to get on the G train again, just for the sense of routine and continuity, and she began to look forward to a long day of work on the Society's database. When she arrived at the office, she was relieved to find that there were no new handsome young clients waiting there, ready to turn her life upside down.

Wally made tea and got right to work, setting a huge stack of case files on her desk and plowing through them at blinding speed with little or no comprehension. When Lewis finally arrived late in the morning, Wally emerged from her trance-like work mode and found that of the twenty case files she had begun with, only one or two remained.

"Well, hello there," Lewis said, surprised to see her. "You're back with us again? How was your time away?"

"Hey Lewis. It was okay."

"You sound discouraged."

"I'm fine. I've had some personal things going on."

"Anything you want to talk about?" Lewis asked as he hung up his coat and hat.

Wally hadn't decided yet what she wanted to tell him—where would she start, anyway? With the total fiasco of her trying to help Kyle, or the part where gunmen were chasing her all over the state for reasons unknowable?

And she had killed a man—there was that. A memory that she was able to put out of her mind for hours at a time, only to have the images of that terrible moment explode back into her consciousness. One day soon she would share the details about all of it with Lewis, but now was not the time. She kept her eyes focused on the screen in front of her, worried he might read her face and realize her situation was more dire than she was letting on.

"Can I hit you back on that, Lewis?" she said. "I'm not sure I have it in me right now, and to be honest, I'm enjoying the grind of my Herculean database project."

"That's fine," Lewis agreed as he turned on his computer, readying for work.

His implicit trust made Wally feel guilty for holding out on him.

"I can tell you, though," Wally said, "that over the past couple of days I've actually had a chance to appreciate some of your smart advice."

"What particular wisdom are you referring to?" Lewis peered dryly at her over the rim of his reading glasses. "I've offered you so much."

Wally smiled. It felt good to be back in the office—Lewis was really good at pulling her out of a dark funk.

"The part about how it's not really in our power to rescue

people," she said, leaning back in her chair and meeting Lewis's eyes. "We can play a part, but ultimately they have to fix themselves. I sort of stuck my neck out for someone who wasn't ready to be helped, and it did no good at all."

Wally had absorbed that lesson from her relationship with Kyle. It had hit home when she had called 911, potentially making things worse.

"You're welcome for the wisdom," Lewis said, studying her. "But don't be too hard on yourself. The impulse to help is an essential thing. It just needs to be exercised with caution."

"You're not gonna say 'I told you so'?"

"Not hardly," Lewis said, climbing out of his chair in order to fill both their cups from the teapot. "One day, Wally, I'll bring you up to speed on my own litany of mistakes and regrets, covering the full span of my long life. I promise you—my countless shortcomings will make yours seem like small beer."

He ambled back into his office, leaving Wally to guess what "small beer" meant.

"Thank you," she said, and she meant it.

They both got back down to work in silence. Wally quickly returned to her hyperproductive mode, an almost hypnotic state in which she processed another dozen case files. When she finally came up for air, it was almost six o'clock in the evening and Lewis had gone for the day—she only vaguely remembered him mumbling a "goodbye" on his way out.

He'd attached a note to her messenger bag: "Nice to have

you back where you belong. Keep up the good work."

Wally felt pretty good on the train ride home—reenergized, maybe—and allowed herself to consider her next move. Every question remained open: Where was Tiger? Where was Kyle? How long would it be before Alabama and the others made another run at her? The burner phone she had grabbed upstate was still the only lead she had, and finding its point of sale hadn't brought her any closer to the answers she needed.

Paige had said she would try to dig more information from the phone, but she hadn't been in touch. Wally texted her, assuming it would go through once she emerged from the subway.

Anything? Wally typed. It wasn't until she emerged from the subway station that Paige's reply finally came: *Wrkng on it stay tuned.*

Wally walked the half mile home from the station, stopping in her apartment just long enough to slip into workout clothes. Jake and Ella weren't back yet. She jogged down Nassau Avenue to Orson Dojo, where she went through the usual warm-up torture and then prepared for some sparring exercises.

"Not so fast," Orson said, leading her to the far corner of the floor where he had brought in a fighting target—basically a punching bag that had padded arms sticking out at several angles. "I can't have you breaking any more of my clients."

"You're putting me in the corner?"

"Just to demonstrate consequences," Orson said. "Most people come to my dojo only for exercise, Wallis, not to prepare for war. If too many of them leave here with broken noses, I will lose all my business."

"Fine," said Wally, annoyed. "Okay if I break the target?"

"Do what you will."

Wally began her striking sequences and quickly discovered the training value of the target dummy: it never got tired, never retreated. You could beat the crap out of it and it was always ready for more. After just ten minutes of work she was so exhausted she could barely raise her arms to wipe the sweat from her forehead, and her hands and feet felt bruised from the nonstop barrage of contact. It felt oddly satisfying.

Orson stepped in then and returned Wally to the sparring rotation with the others in the class. She fit in much better from that point on, too tired and sore to do any real damage and a little more on par with the rest of the class.

By the time she made it home, Jake and Ella had crashed on the couch with the TV on. Wally spotted a couple of takeout bags on the kitchen counter, and the tantalizing aroma of food made her stomach rumble.

"How was it?" Wally asked them. "Did you get to the city?"

"Yeah," Ella said, sounding unenthusiastic as she munched a handful of pretzels. "It was okay."

Wally looked to Jake for details.

"It was weird to see some of the old crowd from the streets," he said. "The ones who were still around, anyway."

"They haven't changed, Wally," Ella said. "And I guess we were feeling like we had, a lot. We didn't fit in the same way."

"I know what you're saying," Wally said, sitting down on the arm of the couch. "Sometimes when I'm out in the city I see some of them—Leila and DJ and that group. I always want to hang with them, but when I have it's never been good. So I usually just keep walking."

Then a thought struck her. "Do you guys want to go back to the farm?" she asked. "I mean, it's okay if that's what you want—"

"No," Ella said. "I mean, eventually yes, of course. But there's nowhere else we want to be now. Just here with you."

"You're sure?" Wally braced herself for the answer. It seemed obvious now that they'd want to go back home. Because the farm *was* their home, now.

"Yeah, of course," Jake said, straight-faced. "Especially since we found this good Mexican place on the way back, in Brooklyn. We have a bag of burritos over there, just waiting 'til you got back. So we'll definitely stick around long enough to have dinner."

"You're an ass," Ella said to Jake, laughing, then turned to Wally. "Take a shower and we'll heat up dinner."

Wally did as directed, relieved that her friends weren't leaving yet. But as they ate together—huddled on the couch with

Gossip Girl reruns on the TV—she couldn't shake the weird feeling of alienation she was experiencing. Her reunion with her closest friends couldn't have happened at a better time—but there was no question that Jake and Ella were firmly on their own path, one that could easily lead them farther and farther away from her.

And where would that leave her? The new life she had begun seemed fragile, as if it could come apart at any time. Where was she really headed in her life? Would she always be the bad girl alone in the corner, like she had been at Orson Dojo that afternoon, segregated and angry?

When Ella and Jake eventually left for the farm—which they would—Wally would be left alone in her secluded, rooftop apartment with an antisocial snapping turtle. What the hell kind of master plan was that? She suddenly felt annoyed and disappointed with herself. Things had been different when Tevin was around. She'd had her person—someone to always turn to—and she missed that more than anything.

Wally's cell phone vibrated loudly on the kitchen counter, and she set aside her food to go check the incoming text.

"Is it from Paige?" Ella wanted to know.

"Yeah," Wally replied, reading the new message. "She was able to dig the phone log from the memory of the burner. It's only ten numbers, but she said she'll keep working."

Wally hit the speakerphone button and clicked a few buttons—the texting program automatically read phone numbers in texts and turned them into hypertext. All she had to do was click on the numbers one at a time, and the phone would automatically dial them. From the speakerphone came the rapid, high-pitched key tones of a phone number being dialed. After just one ring, an automated female voice sounded from the phone's speaker.

"I'm sorry. The number you have dialed is no longer in service."

Of course. Even in her distracted state of mind, Wally systematically thought the problem through. Alabama and the other gunmen wouldn't have made calls to any traceable phone numbers—Alabama had bought all two hundred stolen burners, according to Afrika Neems, and this was why. Any phone he had dialed had been destroyed and dumped by now.

"It's a dead end," she said, setting the phone down and dropping back onto the couch. She picked up her burrito and took a huge bite, even though she'd lost her appetite.

"What are you talking about?" Ella asked. "It's still your best and only lead."

When Wally didn't respond, Ella shook her head in exasperation and stood up from the couch, picking up Wally's cell phone herself before Wally could stop her. She clicked on the next number from the list.

"I'm sorry," came the reply over the speakerphone. *"The number you have dialed is no longer in service."*

"See?" Wally said. "It's all gone cold."

Ignoring her, Ella persisted and went through the list—all

with the same result. Even Ella looked like she might be ready to give up when she dialed one more time and got a new response. It was the outgoing voicemail message of an actual, active phone line, delivered in a loud, laughing, festive voice, the sounds of music and partying in the background.

"Hey! It's January! I'm too busy crushing Manhattan to answer the phone right now, so leave me a message, bitches!"

22.

WALLY, JAKE, AND ELLA LOOKED AT EACH OTHER in stunned silence.

Ella handed Wally the phone, and Wally checked out the text message from Paige Jackson again. There it was: the cell number of *her* January—party girl and volleyball jock. And it had been dialed six times over the previous two weeks by the very person who had been hunting Wally.

Wally felt lightheaded. She realized she'd been holding her breath since the message had played. She exhaled and gave herself a moment to calm down from the adrenaline rush she was experiencing. She clicked on the number again. And again came the rapid key tones of a phone number being dialed. Again, the connection was made.

"Hey! It's January! I'm too busy crushing Manhattan to answer the phone right now, so leave me a message, bitches!"

"I *knew* there was something wrong with her," Ella growled, revealing an attack-dog side that her friends had only been exposed to on rare occasions. Ella rushed to the apartment door, her eyes on fire.

Wally and Jake jumped up after her.

"Ella, stop!" Wally yelled, but Ella was already rushing down the main staircase.

Confronting January directly wouldn't necessarily be the best option—it might even be the worst—but by the time they caught up with Ella, she was already at the end of the hallway one floor below, banging on January and Bea's apartment door.

"Open up, January!" Ella hollered.

There was no answer. "We have to get in," Ella said, determined. Wally shrugged—there was no stopping Ella, and part of her needed to know more just as badly as Ella did.

Jake hurried upstairs and returned with a knife from Wally's kitchen, and from there it took him less than thirty seconds to throw the cheap door lock open. The three of them entered the apartment quietly, closing the door behind them.

"Wow," Jake commented, stunned. "They're pigs." Coming from Jake, this said something.

January and Bea's cramped living space was half full of cheap furniture—off-the-curb cheap—and everywhere were piles of dirty laundry and half-eaten fast-food containers. The place reeked of spoiled food and dirty gym clothes. An overflowing cardboard box full of empty wine and beer and vodka bottles graced one corner.

Wally realized that she had never seen more of the apartment than a quick peek through the door on their way out at night, and now she wondered if they had been too embarrassed to invite her in.

"They have no money," Wally said. Both had been trying hard to save money for college, and the wages they earned at the coffee shop were meager.

"But they're out every night, Wally," said Ella.

"New York can be a friendly city for pretty young girls in heels," Wally answered, remembering when she'd thought the same thing at Cielo only a few nights ago.

It was a one-bedroom apartment, and January and Bea's possessions were so intermingled that it was impossible to tell who slept in the bedroom and who took the sofa bed. The sofa was still open, covered by wrinkled sheets and a pile of laundry (clean or dirty?) that included many pairs of lacy, expensive underwear—who had paid for those? One wall was tacked full of family photographs—one family fair-skinned Irish and the other Hispanic—plus newspaper clippings from January's championship high-school volleyball career. One clipping included a color photo of January spiking a ball over the net, her red ponytail flopping forward from the force of her swing and a look of fierce determination on her face.

"I don't get it," Jake said. "Yeah, it's a sty, but so are half the pads of people around our age. Nothing here says they're anything more than two girls working hard and living cheap and partying their guts out. This is New York."

"That's because you—like all men—see a pretty face and assume the girl behind it is an angel," said Ella.

There was a beat-up Ikea desk in the corner with an open

laptop resting on it, but when Wally flicked the touch pad a password prompt came up. She could take the laptop and have it hacked, and as she pondered the risk of it she noticed a cardboard file box under the desk. She opened it up and found exactly what she'd expected: piles of utility bills, pay stubs from the coffee shop down at the corner, plus assorted other boring paperwork.

There was a collection of monthly bank statements amid the bundle, unopened and addressed to January. Wally opened the most recent one—it had been mailed just a few days ago—and tore it open. In the transaction list for January's debit account, Wally found a series of deposits going back one month, all wired from the same account. The deposit amounts ranged from two hundred dollars to five hundred dollars, all in even dollar amounts.

The sight of this evidence—if that's what it was—finally stirred Wally to feel rage welling up inside of her. Up to that point, she hadn't wanted to believe that her new friends had turned on her—or that maybe they'd been enemies all along. Wally felt like a fool for even considering an innocent explanation for January getting phone calls from one of the gunmen.

"These deposits for the last month add up to nearly two thousand dollars," Wally said as she flashed the document for Ella and Jake to see. "She sure as hell doesn't make that at the coffee shop."

"What do we do?" Ella asked, her voice serious.

Wally thought it through. "We'll take the bank statement

but leave everything else. For now, the girls are the only link to Alabama and the others. If they know we're on to them, they could take off—and then I'm screwed."

Jake and Ella didn't disagree. The three of them left the apartment as they'd found it—trashed—with the laptop untouched, and took only the recent bank statement with them when they closed the door behind them.

As soon as the three of them returned to Wally's apartment, she logged on to the Ursula Society's database, Jake and Ella peering over her shoulder. The Society subscribed to the same in-depth credit-analysis services that most banks and loan companies used, so they could track basic financial records pretty easily.

Using the account numbers from the payments that had been made to January's account over the previous two weeks, they traced the payments to a simple checking account in Tampa, held in the name of someone called Norton Freud Queely.

"Wow," said Jake. "Some name. If he'd gone to my high school, my friends and I would have made his life hell. Just sayin'."

"Well," Wally said, "I don't think this Norton was ever bullied."

"How can you tell?"

"Because he doesn't exist." Wally had started running

down the particulars associated with the account, and immediately found that the home mailing address given to set up the account—in Tarpon Springs, Florida—did not exist at all. The Social Security number given actually did belong to someone named Norton Freud Queely, but he had passed away in Philadelphia two years earlier.

"It's a bogus account," Ella said.

"The money in it was real enough," said Wally, "but completely untraceable. It looks like the account was set up just to deal with January, because the only action on it is the payments to her."

"Shit," said Ella. "There's gotta be something else...."

"Hold on," Jake said—he sat down next to Wally and switched to a different browser. He typed the name *Norton Freud Queely* into the search box.

"But it's not him," Ella objected. "The actual guy is two years dead."

"He isn't the one who opened the checking account," Jake said, still running through his Google search as he spoke, "but you can't tell me that the name is random. Who thinks up Norton Freud Queely?"

On the laptop screen, results for the keywords *Norton Freud Queely*, in that order, were nonexistent. The drop-down window in the Google toolbar, however, asked, "Did you mean N. F. Queely?"

"Maybe I did," Jake answered.

He clicked on the name and a whole bunch of hits showed

up, almost all of them listed in the category "News." N. F. Queely had been an investigative reporter for a weekly independent newspaper called the *Philadelphia Metro*. The most recent story that included Queely's name hadn't been written by him, but *about* him: two years ago, Queely had been abducted in front of witnesses outside a gay bar in the downtown area called "the Gayborhood." He had been missing for several days when his decomposing body was found in a local park, having been beaten savagely.

Local gay activists had raised hell as time went on, and the murder went unsolved, citing it as on obvious case of "gay bashing," a hate crime given lowest priority by law enforcement.

Jake didn't stop his search there, but kept scrolling backward through the timeline and found that several months before his death, Queely had posted the highest-profile feature story of his career, which the *Metro* submitted for a Pulitzer. It was a story detailing a rise in illegal arms shipments headed overseas from the eastern United States. For the first time in years, according to Queely's "inside" sources, American black-market arms dealers were going head-to-head with the more recent leaders in that market, including Eastern European and Russian crime organizations.

The mention of Russian organized crime caught Wally's attention. Both Tiger and Klesko had deep roots in that world, but she felt obligated to call "bullshit" on Jake.

"So just like that, we go from my volleyballing party-girl

neighbor to a bogus bank account in Tampa to international arms dealers," Wally said. "Paranoid, much?"

"It's not such a leap," Jake insisted. "Break it down: some very heavy guys—well-financed and vicious—have been coming after you. We don't know what they want yet, but we know it has something to do with your brother Tiger, because his picture was stored in one of their phones. The hitter used that same phone to call January, who we find out has been on someone's payroll—for what? Watching you, probably. That still doesn't tell us what they're up to, but it confirms that they are well-financed and determined. So the stakes are very high for them. Follow me so far?"

Neither Wally nor Ella could dispute his reasoning.

"Good. So we're still in the dark about what exactly this is all about, except for one thing: the alias used for the payments to January is the same as the name of a reporter who did a deep-background exposé on competition among American and foreign arms dealers, and the reporter was killed soon after that story ran. Arms dealing is a high-stakes business. I'm not a big conspiracy guy, but these goons coming after you, Wally—they've gotta have something to do with black-market arms dealing. I'd bet on it."

"But even if it's true, what does all of this have to do with Tiger?" Ella asked.

"He grew up inside the *Vory*," Wally said. "The Russian mob. Arms sales are a huge part of what they do, especially over the last few years. He's on the run and probably doesn't have a lot of options, so he might somehow have gotten himself into that world again."

Wally felt a terrible sinking feeling as she considered this. The only conclusion she could arrive at was that Tiger was in very deep trouble, and she was probably powerless to help him.

23.

WALLY, JAKE, AND ELLA STAYED UP FOR HOURS—they were waiting for January and Bea to come crawling back home, but they hadn't completely decided what they would do when that moment came. It didn't matter—when two o'clock in the morning rolled around and the two girls were still missing in action, Wally realized that it was pointless to wait. With the schedule the girls kept, they might not come home at all.

"What are you going to do?" Ella asked.

"Don't know, but it can wait until morning. You guys go to bed."

Both Jake and Ella eyed Wally skeptically. "You're going to sleep too, right?" Ella wanted to know.

"I swear," Wally said.

Jake raised one eyebrow—but didn't argue. They were right, of course—Wally's head was full of puzzles that needed unraveling, and in the quiet and dark of her living room they haunted her more than ever. She brainstormed ways that she might manipulate January and Bea into contacting whoever it was that was paying them—a way that Wally might follow them to a meeting—but she never settled on a plan that would work without alerting the girls that their secret connection had been discovered.

The more she thought the situation through, the more Wally felt a sense of foreboding. The list of actions that had been taken against her—and *Tiger?*—was growing by the hour: from the attack on her outside Harmony House to the attack at the lodge and now the conspiracy involving the only two friends she had made since starting over in Greenpoint.

It seemed obvious that January and Bea had been employed for two basic reasons: to monitor Wally's activity and lure her into a vulnerable situation, where Alabama and the others would finally be successful in grabbing her. Wally thought back to the night at Cielo, when January had offered her the tab of Ecstasy—or *whatever* that pill was—and now it seemed like an incredibly transparent attempt to drug her. She had finally left the club when she sensed she was being watched, and now she figured that it was her refusal of the drug and her sudden exit that had ruined their plan.

Wally heard distant thunder at around four o'clock in the morning, and soon a spring storm arrived overhead, with rain pouring down and lightning illuminating the sky. It was a full-on storm: loud and violent to match the dark thoughts consuming her heart and mind, and she didn't know what she would do to survive it all. Even with her best friends sleeping just a few feet away, she felt deeply alone.

She tossed restlessly on the couch, too hot and stuffy under her blanket and never quite finding a comfortable place among the cushions. Her mind was as restless as her body—her thoughts went from Kyle to January and Bea to the Get Money Bitches and, of course, to Tiger. She remembered that her face-to-face online encounter with Tiger had taken place late at night and decided it might be worth trying to connect with him again. She sat up and grabbed her laptop, but was immediately distracted by a blinking green light on the kitchen counter—it was the notification light on her smartphone.

Wally's notifications were set on *vibrate only*—if she was distracted with something else, she often missed the notification entirely. She turned on her screen and saw that there were seven new text messages waiting for her, with a phone number she didn't recognize listed as the source.

R U there? the first message read, and had been repeated two more times, a half hour apart. The time code showed that the first message had come in about four hours earlier—probably right about the time she and Jake and Ella had been downstairs, riffling through Bea and January's apartment. Wally had no idea who had sent the messages—the only thing she could tell was that they had been sent from a cheap phone—another burner, no doubt—since its messaging program didn't autocomplete the words like Wally's smartphone did.

Messages four, five, and six had come in a cluster, just seconds apart:

Dont blame U

Srry for everything

Gbye

And the final text, sent a few minutes after the others:

I lkd swimming w u... Never again I guess

It was Kyle. Wally felt a sudden rush of—*something*. Excitement? Anxiety? Since she'd made the call to 911, Wally had basically written Kyle off as a lost cause. The possibility that the connection between them might return left her confused but exhilarated. What was the right thing to do? For a brief moment she considered not replying to his messages at all but dismissed that idea. According to Greer, the police had found out that Kyle and his father had left their city apartment days earlier and never returned. Since she'd heard that, Wally had been wondering and worrying about what had happened to him. She hoped he was still reachable.

I'm here, she typed.

Nearly a minute passed, during which she kept her eyes glued to the screen, waiting. Finally, the phone vibrated in her hand and a new message popped up.

Sorry I left u, the message said. **So sorry.**

Wally smiled, relieved.

No matter, she typed. **You okay?**

Almost another minute passed before the next message arrived.

Afraid, the message said.

I know, she typed, and without hesitation added, **I can help. Where are you? Can you meet me?**

She immediately wondered if her offer to help had been a

mistake—considering her history with Kyle, it probably was. But Wally also knew herself, and realized that until she had a clear idea about what had happened to Kyle—and whether or not he was safe—she would never be able to keep him out of her thoughts.

There was a long pause then—at least three or four minutes. She was just beginning to believe that something had gone wrong when the phone finally vibrated again.

Come to eagle rock res, the message read. **I can get there**.

The name sounded familiar to Wally but she didn't immediately know why. She opened her laptop and checked Google Maps. Eagle Rock Reservation was near Montclair, New Jersey: it was a fairly large block of green with only a few roads along its perimeter. Not a long trip from Greenpoint as the crow flew, and traffic in the middle of the night would be almost zero.

Wally paused before sending her reply. Was this even a good idea? She debated the issue in her head for a moment, but it was no use trying to be overly rational. Kyle was asking for her help and she would go to him. That was it.

Will take me some time, she replied.

Fllw gates ave to end, the reply came back.

I'll be there, Wally typed.

24.

WALLY SLUNG HER MESSENGER BAG OVER HER shoulder, struggling with a brief internal debate: to go armed or not? The SIG SAUER she had taken away from the lodge upstate was hidden behind the bureau in her room with two loaded clips. She would be happy if she never had to hold that weapon again, but if things got to a place where she needed to defend herself or Kyle, wouldn't she rather have it? The violent clashes she'd experienced over the past several days turned out to be unrelated to Richard Townsend, but the man still loomed in Wally's imagination as someone who was *capable* of violence.

Wally had seen the results of the beating he had given his own son.

Wally found the SIG and the clips in her room and slipped them into a snug inner pocket of her messenger bag. It would give her fast access to the weapon if necessary. She snuck into her bedroom very quietly—careful not to wake Jake and Ella. The couple was blissfully asleep in a spooning embrace with Jake on the outside, his powerful arms delicately cradling Ella. From her closet, Wally grabbed a fresh set of clothes and a black raincoat. She was out the front door less than two minutes later.

Outside, Wally managed to flag down a cab. The sleepy Palestinian driver was happy to grab such a hefty fare in the waning hours of a quiet, rainy night. It was a forty-minute ride at least, and Wally was glad she'd gotten a driver who wasn't feeling chatty. She mentally rehearsed the steps she would take to make Kyle safe that night—provided he was finally willing to follow her direction. She was determined not to argue with him.

The possibility of helping Kyle—*really* helping him, this time—teased Wally. It promised to deliver a feeling of success that had eluded her for the past few days. This time, help would only be offered under her own terms. If Kyle was ready to accept some sort of rescue, then fine. If not, she would turn straight around and head home.

It had to be tough love this time.

Once they'd exited the interstate into the quiet, suburban enclave of Montclair, New Jersey, Wally used the map on her cell phone to give the cabbie an indirect route. They stopped two blocks away from the end of Gates Avenue, the location Kyle named as their meeting place. Arriving on foot—and from an unexpected direction—would allow Wally to approach the spot with some stealth, just in case there were any surprises waiting.

Rain was still coming down hard as Wally climbed out of the cab. Heavy clouds loomed overhead, and the cold predawn air gave Wally a chill. She pulled the hood of her jacket over her head and started walking at a quick pace. Because of the clouds there was no sign of light to the east, but it was now approaching six o'clock and some early-morning commuter activity had begun: expensive cars pulling out of driveways and heading toward the train station or the interstate.

As Wally approached Eagle Rock Reservation, she immediately remembered why the name had sounded familiar, even though she had never actually been there. The most obvious feature of the park was a densely wooded ridge that rose several hundred feet above the surrounding area. At some point up along the ridge—Wally couldn't see it from where she was—a lookout spot gave visitors a clear and dramatic view of lower Manhattan. During the terrorist attacks on September 11, 2001, many people had come to the park to watch the horrific events unfold. Photographs from that day still appeared in stories about the tragedy. The meeting site Kyle had chosen would be at the foot of that hill, with the reservation's forest rising up beyond.

A vehicle rounded a corner a block or so behind her, in enough of a hurry that its tires squealed on the turn. Acting purely on instinct, Wally quickstepped off the sidewalk and ducked behind the cover of a hedge that divided two of the large front yards that stretched out toward the street. She could hear the roar of a powerful engine making its way up the street in her direction.

She peered through the hedge in time to see a silver Humvee approaching along the route she had just walked. The massive vehicle moved slowly along the street as if on a search, but its windows were tinted too dark for Wally to see who was inside.

Had she been followed there? Or could the occupants of the Humvee be there in search of Kyle?

The Hummer drove on to the base of the hill—Undercliff Road—and turned right, headed for the place where Gates Avenue came to an end. It was moving directly toward her planned meeting place with Kyle. Wally's instincts told her that the spot was no longer safe. Wally pulled out her phone and texted to the number of the burner phone Kyle had used to contact her.

Get away from Gates Ave., she typed as fast as she could.

She waited, but there was no response. Was her warning already too late? Wally hurried to the corner of Undercliff Road and looked to the right. She could barely make out the silver Humvee through the rain: it was parked one block up, the exhaust from its idling engine steaming in the cold air. The rain began to fall more heavily now, and Wally hoped that Kyle had sought out a place where he was sheltered from the weather—that action might have taken him far enough from the street that he wouldn't be spotted by whoever was in the Hummer.

Wally crouched low and dashed across Undercliff and into the woods of Eagle Rock Reservation. Once under the cover of the trees, she climbed the hill for thirty or forty yards and then moved north, toward a place where she would hopefully be able to peer down onto the intersection of Gates and Undercliff.

Soon she was above the site and sheltered from view by the trees. The silver Humvee was still parked at the intersection, but Kyle was nowhere in sight. If Kyle had not been snatched up already, he was probably safe for now. Finally his answer came.

I C, Kyle texted. **Slvr hummer**.

WRU?

Up the hill, he answered.

Wally figured he must be higher up the slope than she was—he had probably been hiding out of sight already, waiting for her to appear before he showed himself.

50 yrds up slope.

Come 2 me, he typed.

The woods were dark under the cloud cover—Wally wasn't sure how she would find Kyle in the woods without calling out to him, which would be dangerous. She began climbing the hill, scanning the trees along the way for any sign of him. She climbed for over a minute, but instead of spotting him she came across a paved road that wound up the hill in easy switchbacks.

Wally rushed across the road, nearly reaching the woods on the other side when a set of powerful headlights flashed on and shined down on her from just up the way, the beams catching her before she could get into the trees. She hurried into the shelter of the woods, but the car sped down the road to the spot where she had crossed. The vehicle was a shiny black SUV, a Cadillac Escalade. Wally stopped briefly to rest as the vehicle skidded to a stop. Every door except the driver's opened up—three men climbed out and began to advance in her direction.

Wally caught a glimpse of the man in the driver's seat, his face illuminated clearly by the interior lights of the vehicle when the doors swung open. It was Richard Townsend, Kyle's father. Wally recognized him from the single photograph she had found in her initial background search of his son Kyle. He was a broadly built man in his early fifties, his mostly gray hair combed neatly back.

Wally raced on up the hill, her lungs and thighs burning from the effort as she dodged around the trees and undergrowth of the slope. She started to feel desperate, not believing for a moment that she would be able to outrun all of the men. She could hear them crashing through the dense, wet brush behind her, getting closer with every step.

Wally could see the lights of traffic further up the slope—it appeared to be the same paved road on another switchback. She headed straight for it, hoping she could reach that open space and flag down some traffic, but she smelled something familiar wafting through the air: the unmistakable aroma of weed. According to the direction of the wind moving across the slope, the source of the weed had to be to her right. Wally turned in that direction and headed straight for the smell. Her legs immediately felt stronger now that she was no longer running uphill.

She could hear some quiet voices ahead, followed by a high-pitched, giddy peal of laughter. Within forty or fifty yards, Wally burst through a patch of dense growth and startled a group of young, homeless-looking men hanging out around a small fire. All their heads turned in surprise toward Wally. She had stumbled upon some sort of encampment, a tarp strung up for cover over a fire pit with all kinds of garbage—beer cans, Doritos wrappers, and empty whippet dispensers—strewn about.

The young men looked scrawny and twitchy and burned-out, career dopers. None of them seemed to take any notice of the rain that was now coming down. One guy—probably no more than twenty but with the ghostlike aura of a meth addict—gave Wally a once-over with his creepy, sunken eyes.

"What the fuck do you want?" he said.

Wally saw an opportunity to confuse her pursuers. "Cops!" she shouted, and the dopers began to scatter in every direction, the meth-head included. A couple of them headed up the hill, but the rest scattered downhill, to the east, charging loudly through the woods in panic. Wally did the opposite—the crude fire pit was constructed with stones from a broken-down field-stone wall, and Wally vaulted over what was left of the wall, slinking down on its opposite side and pulling several branches up against her to complete the hiding spot. She waited there, motionless and barely breathing.

Within seconds, she heard the sound of Townsend's men approaching, crashing through the trees and following the sounds of the partiers, whose scattered footsteps could still be heard in the trees.

"I can't tell which is her!" one of the pursuers hollered. "You two . . . head down the slope!"

Wally heard them split up and race off after the partiers. They'd run in so many directions that there was no way her pursuers would be able to tell which to follow. After less than a minute, she quietly poked her head up from behind the stone wall. The party spot was empty. Before her pursuers could double back, Wally turned uphill again, jogging away from any direction taken by Townsend's men. As she moved, Wally texted Kyle again.

Your father is here. Stay away from the road.

A few seconds passed before Kyle responded: **Can u c radio tower?**

Wally looked up the slope. In the fading light of dusk, she could see a blinking red light up above the ridge, probably a hundred and fifty feet high. Beneath the red light she could just make out the structural lines of a tall radio tower with cell-phone-antenna panels attached at over a dozen points.

Yes.

Meet thr, came his response.

K, she typed, and started uphill in the direction of the tower. She couldn't hear anyone behind her, and figured the dope-smoking teens had thrown them off her scent. Eventually she came upon a narrow service road that led to the radio-tower facility. Rain continued to fall as Wally hustled up the road and found Kyle standing outside the cyclone perimeter fence that contained the radio tower and its maintenance building. He had a green military surplus poncho over him to fend off the rain, the hood pulled forward.

"We don't have much time," Wally started, breathless from her rush up the hill. "We have to go."

But even as she said it, something felt wrong. The shoulders beneath the poncho were much too narrow to be Kyle's—the wet nylon draped loosely, almost to the ground. When the figure turned to face Wally she saw that it wasn't Kyle at all, but a young woman with short-cropped hair and a chilling smile.

"What—" Wally began to speak but never had the chance to finish.

To her left, a man stepped from the shadow of the trees and raised his right hand toward her. Wally heard a distinct *click!* and felt an intense pain surge through her, every muscle in her body going rigid. She'd been hit by a Taser. Her motor controls abandoned her and Wally fell to the ground, aware of what was happening despite the pain and physical disorientation. She felt herself shouting but heard no actual sound. As she lay on her back facing upward, she could make out individual drops of rain as they fell out of the sky toward her, illuminated by the perimeter light of the radio tower.

Wally was completely immobilized. She begged her body to rise up and run, but there was no response. She heard the sound of vehicles approaching, then a set of tires screeched to a halt. Soon Richard Townsend was standing above her. The silver Humvee pulled up next, and Alabama—the man she had burned at the lodge—stepped out to join him.

Alabama? But he was after her, not Kyle… right? Wally couldn't think straight. What was happening? Alabama and Richard Townsend were standing side by side, looking down at her.

Townsend wore an expression as cold as she had ever seen, as if she were an object unworthy of empathy. Another man stepped forward with a syringe in his hand and stuck Wally in the neck.

As she faded from consciousness, Wally's head slumped to the side. It was only then that she finally saw Kyle standing ten feet away. If he was feeling any regret or shame, Wally didn't see it. If anything, he looked satisfied.

"Kyle," she felt herself struggling to say his name.

Within a few seconds, Wally felt everything slipping away.

25.

TIGER FINISHED HIS WORKOUT WITH TWENTY minutes of wind sprints on the treadmill. His lungs felt near to bursting as he fought through the final stretch: a four-minute sprint at ten miles per hour. By the time he climbed off the machine, he was dripping sweat even though the air in the second-floor gym was cold. He went to the watercooler and refilled his workout bottle, chugging half of it in two or three swallows.

Rachel was working out on the weight bench near the far wall, finishing off a set of presses at a hundred and seventy pounds—impressive for someone her size. As soon as she finished she sat up, breathless and flushed, and her eyes went immediately to Tiger. Rachel was monitoring his movements, and she'd been doing it all morning, hanging near him upstairs in the lounge and now down in the gym, trying to act casual as if the intersection of their daily schedules was just coincidence. Tiger couldn't figure out what was going on, but something was in the works and it made him uneasy.

He wondered what would happen if he actively tried to ditch her. As he finished his water and started doing some stretches, Rachel's cell phone rang. She took the call, turning away from him in order to have a private conversation. Tiger seized the opportunity and turned toward the door of the gym, walking calmly out onto the stairwell. His first intention was to head up to his room, but he decided at the last moment to go downstairs instead—there was a steady rain coming down outside, and he liked the idea of cooling down in the open air of the parking lot, the storm pouring down on him.

He was just about to step outside when two of the Ranch's vehicles—a black Cadillac Escalade and a silver Humvee—pulled through the front gate and came to a stop in the center of the lot. Tiger stopped in the shadow of the doorway and watched as Archer Divine and five of his men poured out of the vehicles, into the rain. One of the men was the guy everyone called Pete, an experienced mercenary who spoke with an accent from one of the states in the American south. Pete had been away from the Ranch for several weeks, only returning a few days ago with some significant burns on his face and upper torso. As expected, he offered no explanation for his injuries.

Tiger heard Rachel in the stairwell behind him, calling his name from the second-floor landing. "Joe?" There was urgency in her voice. Soon Tiger could hear her descending toward him, but his attention was focused on the activity in the lot. She arrived beside him and took firm hold of his arm.

"We're going back inside," she told him, but her insistent pull on his arm made Tiger even more determined to stay where he was, and Rachel wasn't strong enough to move him on her own.

Then Archer Divine noticed Tiger for the first time. A strange, playful look came over him, as if some sort of depraved entertainment was about to begin. Tiger now registered that one of the men exiting the black Escalade was Divine's own son, Kyle, who had also been absent from the compound for several weeks.

Divine nodded toward his son. Kyle leaned into the backseat of the black SUV and, with a small grunt of effort, emerged with a limp body in his arms—that of a young woman. There was no way to tell if she was dead or alive. As Kyle turned in Tiger's direction, the overhead light in the lot revealed the girl in more detail: she was petite, wearing a hooded black jacket over dark clothes. The hood shifted slightly to reveal short blond hair, and her head lolled back, revealing her face.

Wally.

"Easy, Joe..." Rachel said, gripping his arm with two firm hands now, but Tiger shrugged her off and rushed toward his sister, his protective instincts in full control of his actions. There was shouting—commands for him to stop—but Tiger barely even processed the words. He made it to within a few steps of Wally before several of Divine's men reached him, one of them raising a rifle up high and swinging the weapon down toward Tiger's head. He felt his legs crumple beneath him.

26.

WALLY STIRRED AWAKE, HER HEAD HEAVY AND HER vision blurred from whatever kind of narcotic she had been dosed with. When she sat up, the rush of blood almost made her pass out, so she closed her eyes and shifted her body until her head started to feel normal again. She felt no new injuries to her body—her only physical damage was the sore place on her neck where she had been tased.

Wally took in her surroundings. She had been lying on an old, dank sofa in a very large room—it looked like a storage area of an ancient warehouse, dusty and creaky and probably unused since forever. Near the sofa, a fire burned in an old iron woodstove, warming the air within a circle of perhaps ten feet. There were a few cardboard boxes placed near the sofa. One wall of the room was covered almost entirely with windows, dirty and smudged with decades of grime. Though it was dark outside, Wally could make out the structure of fire escapes on the exterior of the building. On the inside wall of the huge room was an enormous sliding cargo door. It looked like it was made of steel, and contained a more human-sized door within it, also shut.

Wally struggled to remember how she had ended up in this

place, but it was all very vague. She had been running through the Eagle Rock Reservation, chased by Kyle's father and his men. Her last memory was of Kyle's betrayal—she had done everything she could to help him, but in the end he had lured her into some kind of trap. She felt a fresh surge of anger toward Kyle, remembering the almost triumphant look he wore as he had watched her lose consciousness. She felt an intense need to meet him again, face-to-face, and make him regret his treachery, but she was also angry with herself. When she was with Kyle, Wally had given in to her emotions so carelessly. If she had been more guarded—more *herself*—maybe none of this would have happened.

First she would have to figure out where she was and how to escape.

Wally suddenly became aware of a low, barely perceptible wheezing. She scanned the area for its source and discovered that just ten feet away from the sofa in a shadowed area beneath the wall of windows stood a single bed with army-surplus blankets piled and twisted on top. The blankets covered the mattress in such a way that it took Wally a few seconds to realize that there was a person lying under them.

As quietly as she could, Wally stood up off the sofa to get a better look. From what she could tell it was a boy, but deeply asleep. She moved closer, until she was just five or six feet away from the stranger. Her heart stilled when she first saw the boy's face in profile, his features handsome and young, framed in flowing, shoulder-length black hair.

"Tiger?" Wally could barely believe it, her heart thumping hard in her chest as she hurried to her brother's side. Tiger wasn't conscious, but he was alive and breathing. His face was covered in bruises and cuts—like an ultimate fighter after losing a cage match—but nothing that seemed life-threatening. Wally pulled back the quilt; Tiger was fully dressed in cargo pants and a flannel shirt, and the shirt was very bloody around the area of his left shoulder. Other than that, she could see no signs of major trauma.

Wally shook him gently. "Tiger?" No response. She shook him again—harder—and this time he responded by bolting straight up, his eyes lit up in alarm. Wally jumped back as he launched himself off the bed and onto his feet, stumbling and dizzy at first but finding his balance quickly. Still disoriented, Tiger crouched in an attack position—and ready to fight—but then his eyes met Wally's, and he froze. Comprehension slowly dawned on him, his mind struggling to catch up. She could see the change overcome him as the reality of her presence sank in. His hands—raised and ready for battle—dropped to his sides, but the wariness in his eyes did not diminish.

"You," he said.

Wally felt an urge to reach out and wrap him in her arms, but she stopped herself. She could see him holding back, unsure how to act in her presence.

"Hello, brother," she said.

Wally watched as Tiger paced uneasily from window to window, peering out into the darkness like an animal through the bars of a cage. For him, their reunion was less important than the danger of their situation.

She knew what Tiger was seeing, because she had checked it out herself: there were two armed men on watch outside, one on the fire escape a floor above them and one patrolling the parking lot on the ground two floors below. When she had looked out the window, both men had immediately clocked her presence there. Their alert poses told her that they would be quick to react if she tried to exit onto the fire escape. It seemed likely that others were standing watch, out of sight.

Tiger had already checked the entrance door on the opposite wall—he had tried to open it but it was locked from the outside, and the act of trying to force it open had brought the sound of footsteps outside the door, someone moving closer and probably standing ready in case Tiger made an effort to break through the lock.

Wally and Tiger were prisoners with few options.

"Sit down," Wally said. "Please. It'll just take a minute."

Tiger reluctantly sat beside her on the ratty couch. Someone had left a small first-aid kit on the floor beside the sofa, and now Wally went to work tending the minor injuries to Tiger's face.

Though her face was right in front of his, Tiger averted his eyes.

She wondered what it was, exactly, that kept him at a distance. Resentment for all that she'd been given, while his life had taken a completely different course? Embarrassment that she had surprised him online, seeking her out? Or maybe distrust was his default mode—he had been raised by criminals, after all. Had anyone ever taught him how to love someone?

Wally cleaned his wounds with antiseptic, then used a butterfly bandage on the gash that crossed his strong jawline. She cut off his shirt next. Tiger never winced, even as she pulled the material off his shoulder wound, dried blood ripping away from his skin.

At least twenty tattoos covered Tiger's torso, front and back, all crudely executed in dark black ink. Some were figures—stars at his shoulders, a large cross on his chest, a Russian minaret—while others were phrases written in Cyrillic that she could not decipher.

The cut on Tiger's shoulder began to bleed again, heavily enough to worry Wally.

"This will need stitches," she told him.

She received no reply, and he kept his eyes directed away from her.

Wally poured alcohol on the wound—again Tiger showed no sign of pain other than a faint twitch of his eyelid. The first-aid kit contained a sterilized needle and thread, and Wally went to work with them. She had never done it before, but she figured it couldn't be much different from fixing a torn hem.

When she was done—twelve stitches in all and not a sound from Tiger—she bandaged him up, then found a clean shirt in one of the cardboard boxes by the window and helped him pull it on.

"You're welcome, *Tigr.*" The Russian pronunciation of his name. Wally said it with a teasing smile, hoping he would rise to the occasion and thank her. He didn't.

"Tiger," he said, with barely a hint of a Russian accent. He had been assimilating, apparently.

The two of them were quiet for a moment, awkward in each other's presence. Wally understood that she would have to be patient with him—there was a whole lifetime of distance between them, and it would take time to reach across it.

"What is this place?" she asked.

"When I came to America with our father," he began, looking uncomfortable with even basic conversation, "I brought a telephone number with me."

The mention of their father—Alexei Klesko—brought an involuntary twinge of anger and loathing to Wally.

"Someone to call, if things went bad, you mean," she said. "Which they sure did, I think we can agree."

She was referring to Shelter Island, of course. Tiger gave a curt nod of agreement.

"What happens here?" she asked, urging him to continue.

"Most men here are wanted by the law," he said. "For this man Divine, we work jobs. We are safe here. He protects us."

"This is the Hole in the Wall," she said.

Tiger gave her a puzzled look.

"It's a thing from old westerns. The Hole in the Wall was a secret hiding place. Outlaws would rob trains and then go there to lie low. I don't know if it was a real place from history or just the movies."

He gave another of his curt nods, acknowledging the comparison.

"But what's at the end of it?" she asked. "What's the goal?"

"Money, of course. And opportunity."

"For what?"

He thought for a moment. "For change."

Wally considered this. "Ah. You're a wanted man. You work for this guy Divine, and he'll hook you up with what you need for a fresh start?"

Filling in the blanks made Wally feel like a ventriloquist, forced to carry both sides of a conversation with a wooden character.

The fire in the stove had burned down by then, and the air around them was losing its heat. As Tiger got up to feed a few dry logs into the embers, the reality of her situation—the reality of the past week, really—overwhelmed her with all its force.

"This man Divine—what's his first name?"

"Archer," he responded.

"Archer Divine. Honestly, that sounds made up. Can you describe him to me?"

Wally watched as Tiger summoned a visual image of this guy Divine.

"Strong physique, more than six foot," Tiger said as he sat back down with her. "Perhaps fifty-five years old. Silver hair."

"Does he have children that you know of?" Wally had begun to feel certain she knew who "Divine" was.

Tiger gave her a curious look but nodded.

"Is there a son? Maybe named Kyle?" Her voice had taken on a sarcastic, angry tone that she couldn't control.

"Yes, Kyle. When we work, his name is "Seth," but he rarely works with us, unlike his sister. He's privileged."

Shit. As she'd begun to suspect, Richard Townsend and Archer Divine were the same person. Kyle had really done a job on her, spinning his complicated lies while all the time luring her to this place. Wally felt sick to her stomach.

"My God," Wally whispered, her mind reeling at the implications. "I am such a fucking idiot."

She stood up and paced the floor anxiously as she explained to Tiger about Kyle, how she had fallen for the tragic account of his abusive father and tried to help him find his biological mother—all of it bullshit, apparently. She kept her head turned away from him most of the time, afraid to see his response to the pathetic tale. She'd been foolish and naive.

"His father's identity—Richard Townsend or Archer Divine. Maybe one is made up, maybe both. It doesn't matter. The plan all along was to lure me out."

Wally thought about the trip to the Adirondack lodge, and the intense connection that she and Kyle had supposedly shared there. In fact, his only goal was to get her in a vulnerable place where she could be taken. The men there—Alabama, and the one she had shot and killed—had been working with Kyle the entire time. She thought about his "screams" when he had supposedly been interrogated by the men. All faked.

Wally felt her stomach turn all over again.

"Why do this?" Wally asked. "What's their game?"

Tiger didn't answer, but Wally could see he had been considering different possibilities in his mind, and all of them were dark—dark for Wally, and almost certainly dark for Tiger. Wally silently cursed herself and continued pacing. Lewis had told her to be careful, to be sure that she was making choices for the right reasons, and she hadn't listened.

"What's Divine's business?" she asked Tiger.

"We do different jobs for him," Tiger said. "But his main trade is weapons."

Like Klesko, Wally thought to herself. And Tiger too. She had read the international warrants that awaited Tiger in the real world, and many of the crimes named involved black-market weapons. Wally thought about the reporter, N. F. Queely, and the story he'd written about the intense competition among Americans trading black-market arms overseas. Maybe Jake's guess had been right—maybe Queely really had died for that story.

Maybe Divine had ordered his murder.

27.

"WOULD YOU LIKE TO KNOW ANYTHING ABOUT OUR mother?" Wally asked.

Wally and Tiger had both been there when Claire Stoneman had died, holding her in their arms as she lay bleeding in the fresh November snow on Shelter Island. Wally had lived most of her life with Claire, but for Tiger, that one tragic moment of connection was all he had to cling to. Wally felt the enormity of the responsibility she carried: Tiger's knowledge of his mother would be created now, through her words.

"*Ne perezhvai*," he said again, averting his gaze. "You needn't bother."

"Well," Wally said, "now you're just pissing me off."

He looked toward Wally, surprised by her tone.

"What's done is done," Tiger said, simply.

Wally glared at him, feeling both angry and hurt by his refusal.

"You can pretend you don't care," she said, anger decorating every word, "but that's bullshit. You've looked for information about me online—I traced your searches. We wouldn't have met face-to-face that night if you hadn't been seeking me out the same way I've been looking for you."

Wally could see him stiffen, embarrassed to be exposed in that way. She thought of a movie she had seen once about a man living alone in the wilderness who tried to forge a friendship with a wild wolf. It had taken months of the man laying out one morsel of food at a time, each day just a little bit closer until he finally could reach out and touch the animal.

"Claire held so much back," Wally began, setting out a "morsel" for him. Who knew if she would have another chance to share her memories? "She lied to protect me, so I'm always questioning how well I really knew her. I can tell you she was a good person, and she was capable of love."

Wally wanted to say that Claire had loved her, but then what conclusion would Tiger be forced to draw? That Claire had not loved him? That she had abandoned him as a child because she loved her daughter more than her son? Wally knew it wasn't true.

"She was sad a lot of the time," Wally went on, "and I never really understood why until I learned about you. I sometimes wonder at how she lived with it—leaving you, I mean. It was obvious that she carried around a ton for the rest of her life. It must have been horrible."

Tiger said nothing, but he was clearly deep in thought, the flickering light of the fire playing on the features of his face, which were delicate and hard all at once.

"You look like her," Wally told him, only just realizing it herself. And now she had his attention. "Your profile," she continued. "The shape of your nose and brow, so intense. It makes me remember her to look at you. It hurts."

She had reached him. "I'm afraid to ask you about your life," she blurted out, surprising herself. "Because I was given so much. And you were left practically on your own."

"I didn't need anyone. I made my way and asked for nothing."

"It's not supposed to be that way, you know," Wally said.

He merely shrugged. She realized that breaking through Tiger's defenses would be a long-term challenge, and she wouldn't be able do it without his help.

Noticing the similarities between Tiger and Claire had made Wally wonder something.

"Am I like him?" she asked.

Almost against his will, Tiger looked at Wally, contemplating her features. She watched as his eyes finally settled on hers.

"Yes," she said. "I know. *Ochee chornya*." Dark eyes. Deep gray, almost black. The one feature Wally undeniably shared with their father. "I think about it," she said. "About my nature, and where that comes from. I'm selfish and reckless. I've brought harm to the people I cared about most. My mother wasn't like that, so where does that come from if not from him?"

"You can believe me," Tiger said bitterly, "you are nothing like him."

By the tone in his voice, Wally couldn't tell if his words were a compliment or an insult.

She suddenly felt exhausted. Carrying on ninety percent of a conversation was brutally difficult work.

"I'm hungry," she said, scanning the room. "And I have to pee." She got up and found a filthy, crudely constructed bathroom in the far corner of the room. Once inside, she sat on the cold seat, facing the yellowed ceramic sink. A small hairbrush, a toothbrush, and a half-used tube of toothpaste rested on its surface. The dismal tableau made Wally even angrier than she was already.

"Where do they feed you?" Wally asked Tiger when she reemerged.

"The sixth floor," he said. "There are things to make sandwiches and leftover food in the refrigerator."

Wally made her way to the locked door and pounded on the dense metal surface.

"We're hungry," she shouted. "Open up!"

Tiger stood and approached her, looking cautious, but Wally signaled for him to keep back.

"It'll be fine," she told him.

There was no response to her pounding, so she began kicking the door with her boots again and again. Each hit sounded like thunder as the metal creaked and echoed through the warehouse. After half a minute, the lock turned and the door opened to reveal two people standing outside. One was a young woman with brown hair tied back in a bun and a tremendously buff physique—juiced, probably. She held a 9mm Glock at her side, one finger resting on the trigger.

The second person was Alabama, whom she'd last seen

chasing her down through the Eagle Rock Reservation. He had gauze on the side of his face and neck where she had burned him, and small dark spots had formed on the bandage where the oozing fluids from his wounds had begun to seep through.

"Alabama," Wally nodded at him. He returned her greeting with a stare so cold and murderous that it sent a shiver down her spine—but Wally was determined not to let him know that he was intimidating her in any way.

"What do you want?" the girl asked.

"We need food."

The girl mulled it over. "I'll give you one minute in the kitchen. Come with me."

She continued into the hallway, catching the silent exchange between Alabama and the girl. He relocked the door and held his post while the girl followed Wally up the stairs. As they climbed upward, Wally could see a dozen or more closed doors in the hallways of the upper floors—the only other person they encountered was another guard, tall and wiry, who raised a shotgun as Wally passed by.

"What's your name?" Wally asked the girl as they climbed the stairs.

"Shut the fuck up," the girl growled.

"Catchy."

The sixth floor was one large, open room with a kitchen-and-dining area and a lounge space with a big-screen TV. There was a row of locked offices at the inside wall, and Wally could see a large computer monitor on one of the desks—the same computer, she guessed, that Tiger had used to watch her.

Wally went straight to the kitchen area and easily discovered leftovers in a large industrial refrigerator. There was pepperoni pizza, along with some green apples. She couldn't be sure how long they would be held in the room downstairs, so she grabbed pretty much everything that looked edible, including some sweet things. There was beer in the refrigerator, and Wally grabbed a few bottles. She found an empty grocery bag and stuffed the goods inside.

Back inside Tiger's room, Wally heated the cold pizza on the top surface of the woodstove until the air was full of the salty, greasy, delicious smell of pepperoni and cheese. Wally was gratified that Tiger ate with her, at least.

They each ate two apples and drank the bottles of beer, but they were both still hungry. Wally dug through the remainder of what she had grabbed from the kitchen, including most everything from the cabinet that held the sweet things. There were some gingerbread cookies, graham crackers, marshmallows, two large jars of applesauce, and some chocolate bars.

"Oh my God," Wally said, pulling the graham crackers, marshmallows, and chocolate from the bag. "S'mores."

Tiger looked confused.

"It's kind of a dessert," she explained.

Wally found some wire hangers that Tiger had used to hang up a couple of shirts. She unbent the hangers and produced two long, thin metal skewers. Tiger watched curiously as Wally speared two marshmallows on each skewer and handed him one.

"You hold them over the flame," she said. "It'll only take a minute."

Wally held her marshmallows over the hot embers of the woodstove, and Tiger followed her lead. They watched as the heat began to caramelize the surface of the marshmallows, turning them dark brown.

"Mom made these for me," Wally said, thinking back. "The first time, we had rented a beach house for a week on Martha's Vineyard—I think I was seven or eight years old. One night we made a little fire pit in the sand down by the water's edge. As the sun went down these swarms of mosquitoes descended on us, so we huddled close to the fire and the smoke kept them away. It was so…just, really nice. Mom brought the ingredients out and told me they were called s'mores. As in, if you eat one you'll always want some more."

She could feel Tiger watching her as she relayed the memory, and couldn't help but wonder—did he have even one memory in his troubled life to equal hers? Could he even relate to the sensations and feelings that she was describing? That expression on his face, was it resentment—anger, even—as he was forced to listen to the details of happy moments between mother and child that he had been forced to live without?

When the surface of the marshmallows started to char,

Wally pulled hers from the stove and motioned for Tiger to do the same.

"Here," Wally said. "Let me."

She broke a graham cracker in two, placing a large piece of chocolate on one half. She then took Tiger's skewer and placed his toasted marshmallows onto the chocolate. Setting the second half of the graham cracker on top of the marshmallows, she pressed down on the cracker and pulled the skewer away, creating a sandwich with chocolate and toasted marshmallows on the inside and graham crackers on the outside. She passed it to Tiger.

"It's important to squeeze down now," Wally said. Tiger obeyed, pressing on the sandwich until the hot, gooey insides of the marshmallows broke through the charred outer skin and spread out onto the chocolate, melting it.

"That's it," Wally said. "You have to eat it right now."

Wally watched as Tiger bit into his s'more, a vivid expression of pleasure crossing his face as the sweet flavors mixed together. His mouth stopped moving, and his eyes glazed over as he focused all his attention on the sensation of taste, as if the flavor was some kind of revelation. Wally could feel her heart breaking—for Tiger, for herself, and for their mother, Claire. For all the moments the three of them should have shared, but had missed and lost forever.

They came for Tiger at dusk: Divine and Rachel and four of their men, all except Divine armed and training their weapons on Wally and Tiger.

"Tiger," Divine said simply. "Let's go."

Wally turned to Tiger and looked into his eyes. Had she reached him, in any way? She felt a surge of panic, all of a sudden worried that the few hours spent together were all they would ever have, and that she had failed. There was nothing in his expression to confirm her fears or reassure her, either. She stepped forward and wrapped him up in her arms, holding him as tightly as she could.

He didn't return her embrace, but he took advantage of the moment to whisper in her ear.

"The south wall," he said. "Search the loose bricks."

"But—"

"Believe nothing they say," he added. "Just run."

28.

THE HELICOPTER STAYED HIGH OFF THE GROUND, in order to attract as little attention as possible on its trip west. Tiger was fairly sure he knew their eventual destination, and if he was right it would only be a few minutes before they arrived.

"You know where we're going?" Divine said, practically shouting over the noise inside the cabin. His words were more a statement of fact than a question.

"Sweet," Tiger replied.

Divine nodded. "Sweet and I have some conflicting business interests," he explained. "And our relationship has become strained recently. Something is going to happen regardless, so I might as well control what that something is."

"I would have done the job," Tiger said. "There was no need to involve my sister."

"I'm not sure you would have—not the way I need it done."

"How?"

"I need you to show your face."

Tiger thought about this, realization sinking in. Sweet had long-time partnerships with crime families around the world, associates who would lose money if Divine managed to get rid of his rival. There would be consequences—blowback, as the Americans called it—fatal ones. If it was known that he—Tiger Klesko, son of Alexei—was Sweet's killer, blame for the incident would be placed somewhere else, somewhere thousands of miles to the east: *Piter*. The *Vory* would deny their involvement, of course, but who would believe them?

With Sweet's security team always surrounding him, a close-up killing was a suicide mission for Tiger.

"For five years I've been looking for a way to get rid of Sweet," Divine continued, a hint of triumph already on his face. "Then, five months ago you showed up at the Ranch. Goes to show you the virtue of patience."

So, Tiger thought, he had been doomed from day one at the Ranch. All the work he had done for Divine had been a waste. Tiger's hopes of a new life for himself had been foolish, and he silently cursed himself for not realizing it sooner.

He scanned the cabin of the helicopter. There were five of them besides the pilot—Tiger, Divine, Rachel, and two other gunmen he had seen before but never worked with. No chance for an alliance there. To the rear of the cab was an impressive array of weapons, both small arms and assault weapons, plus two grenade launchers—a backup plan, no doubt. If Tiger moved quickly enough he might be able to reach the pilot—there were several ways he could imagine bringing them all down, to end the mission before it even got started.

"I like your spirit," Divine said, as if reading Tiger's thoughts.

"But my instructions to the Ranch were clear—any interruption of our plan, and your sister will die."

"You're going to kill her anyway."

Instead of denying this immediately, Divine reached into a side compartment and pulled out a small stack of photographs, which he passed to Tiger. They were surveillance photos—taken from a distance with a long lens—of his sister Wally, in the company of two other teenagers, a petite Asian girl and a fit, clean-cut guy. They looked familiar to Tiger, and it only took a moment for him to realize that this same couple had been part of Wally's street crew several months earlier.

"Wallis cares very much for these two," Divine said. "Possibly even more than she cares for you. She certainly knows them better. Once you have done this service for us she'll be released, with the assurance that if she talks, her two friends will be killed. With pain. You see? There's no reason for us to hurt your sister. You have my oath on this."

Tiger didn't answer. His mind continued to turn, searching for a way out.

"I know," Divine said. "You're still not on board. You're thinking there are other options, maybe even that Wallis is capable of fighting her way off the Ranch... especially with the help of the Glock that you stashed in the brick wall? Or the combat knife in the loose grout beneath the windowsill? You thought we wouldn't shake down the room before we put you both in there?"

Der'mo. Shit.

"We're almost there," said Divine, impatient now. "If you want to protect your sister, there are no options. There's even a chance you could survive it—a slim chance, I admit, but if you're half the man your father is, you might make it."

"I'm curious," Tiger said.

"About what?"

"What makes you so sure I will trade my life for hers?"

His question was sincere. Tiger barely knew Wallis Stoneman. Though they were brother and sister, she had been given every advantage in life, while he had been set adrift. It wasn't he that owed her loyalty, or a debt. It was the other way around. Thrown together by Divine—a smart strategy on his part—they hadn't achieved anything close to understanding or peace, much less love or loyalty. How could Divine be so sure when Tiger himself was not?

"Young Klesko," Divine said with a confident smile. "I make bets like this every day. It's how I win."

The sound of the helicopter's rotor changed slightly, and the aircraft began to dip toward the ground below.

The light of dusk was fading when they reached the hilltop overlooking the arms factory. Tiger followed Rachel, and Divine followed him, the man easily matching their pace despite the thirty-plus years he had on them. The overlook was exactly as Tiger and Rachel had left it days earlier—the factory was empty and dark, the perimeter fence strong and intact.

Divine had sent his other two gunmen to establish watch posts on the opposite hilltop. Tiger looked across the valley but was unable to spot them. Each of the men had taken a sniper rifle with a powerful nightscope, so Tiger knew for certain that he would have crosshairs trained on him every moment he was in the open.

"Settle in," Divine said. They spread camouflage tarps on the ground and lay down, arranging brush around them for cover. "Now we wait."

Two vehicles appeared at the mouth of the valley and motored to the factory gate. A security team of eight spilled out of the first vehicle—a cargo van—and Tiger could see that they were much like the team he and Rachel had spotted before. None looked older than fifteen or sixteen. They were various sizes and of different ethnicities, the only common factors being that they were all armed and looked supremely vigilant, scanning the area around the factory with their riflescopes and walking the perimeter fence in teams to be sure the area was secure.

One of the young men unlocked the factory gate to allow the second vehicle inside—an SUV with a trailer attached. The SUV entered the factory grounds and drove around to the other side, out of view. It wasn't long before Tiger learned what the trailer contained. Just ten minutes after its arrival, the sound of an engine came from somewhere on the grounds and at least two hundred lights—inside and outside the factory—came on. A *generator*, Tiger realized. The old factory had power again.

Over the next hour, four or five more trucks arrived, each of them backing up to the factory's loading dock and delivering at least a hundred crates of various sizes. Within another couple of hours, the contents of those crates became clear: the old arms factory—unused in decades—began to pulse with loud music and flashing lights of every color. The factory had become an enormous nightclub of some kind.

The music was something Tiger was only vaguely familiar with, an electronic sound with a tempo faster than his own heartbeat. The volume was insanely high, and if he concentrated he could actually feel the vibration of it thumping through the ground, all the way up at his watch post. The music echoed back and forth in the valley, and Tiger realized the genius of choosing a location like this one for a loud, massive party—the same valley geography that had made an arms factory less of a danger to the surrounding community also provided cover from curious neighbors and local police. Few settings could match this one for privacy.

"It's a rave," Rachel said. "I'm sure they have them where you come from."

"Quiet," Divine hissed, and they all went completely still.

Soon Tiger could make out the sound of approaching footsteps, and a sentry from the security team below came walking along the ridge, a silenced assault rifle in his hands. From what Tiger could make out, the kid looked Asian, his long hair tied back in a ponytail. He was wearing jeans and a black, long-sleeved shirt. He walked slowly and deliberately, passing within just ten feet of the brush-covered post where Tiger, Divine, and Rachel lay low, waiting for the threat to pass.

Within a minute, the sentry had walked out of range. Tiger and the others, however, stayed very quiet after that, silently observing as the events in the valley reached their next phase. As the night grew late, vehicles of every kind began to roll into the valley—two or three hundred of them, at least—parking haphazardly on the barren ground that surrounded the factory. From each vehicle at least three or four people, in their teens or early twenties, emerged and made their way to the gate of the factory's perimeter fence.

Through his nightscope, Tiger watched as a four-man security team processed the arrivals, patting them down for weapons and setting their cell phones aside to be returned after. Each "guest" was stamped on the back of the hand. No money was exchanged. The young people were clearly excited, barely able to stand still until they were turned loose onto the factory grounds. A steady stream of them headed straight into the factory, disappearing into the cacophony of lights and music.

"This is one way Sweet keeps good faith with his soldiers," Divine said, a hint of admiration in his voice. "He does this two, three times a year, a different location each time. Free booze and drugs for all the local kids who show up, and all of his security team have their turn to cut loose. That's the situation you'll be walking into. There will be another kind of guest in the mix—dozens of business associates from around the eastern seaboard are in there already, prepared for a meet and greet with Sweet himself."

"At the top of the tower," Tiger added. He remembered from the scouting mission he and Rachel had carried out days before—Sweet's security team had arrived at the site for recon, and had concentrated their sweep on the top floor of the factory's administrative wing, a tower three or four stories higher than the rest of the factory. On her own visit inside, Rachel had spent most of her time on that top floor, also.

"Yes, Sweet will be on the top floor," Rachel said. "His own private party room."

Over the din of the throbbing house music below, another sound intruded upon the valley—the turbine-engine thrum of a sleek, white executive helicopter, swooping in low from the east and setting down quickly in a space that had been cleared inside the factory's perimeter gate. Through their scopes, Tiger and the others watched as security men swarmed the chopper and surrounded one blond man as he climbed out, maintaining a human cocoon around him as he walked quickly to the factory and disappeared inside.

"The son of a bitch himself," Divine said.

"He won't stay for more than an hour, if that," Rachel said.

"Enough fucking around then," Tiger said. With that, he stood up and left their post behind, hiking downhill.

"We'll be watching," Divine called after him.

"I'll see you in hell," Tiger answered.

29.

WALLY PACED THE WAREHOUSE ROOM, UNABLE TO keep still. How much time had passed since Tiger had been taken? Two hours? Three? The day had turned to night, and the warehouse was unnervingly quiet. She knew her sentries were still in place—she could hear the heavy footsteps of one guard patrolling the hallway outside her door, and at least one other was outside her window, moving around on the fire escape landing a floor above.

Wally didn't know for sure what Divine had planned for Tiger, but he had gone to a lot of trouble to bring her there, and she assumed he had done it to gain leverage over her brother. She understood the strategic reason that Divine had brought them together—a closer bond between her and Tiger would motivate her brother to protect her any way he could, even if that meant risking his own life in some way.

The idea sickened Wally. As far as she was concerned, Tiger had already forfeited his childhood so that she could live the life of an advantaged American teen. The cycle had to end, and the only thing she could think to do for her brother would be to free herself from the warehouse and somehow let Tiger know that she'd broken out.

But how? Wally had been looking for an opening—any sliver of an opportunity for her to make a run for it—but she hadn't found a chance. When he had whispered in her ear, Tiger had told her to search behind loose bricks on the south wall of the room. She'd done that, but every potential hiding place within the wall had been empty.

Tiger had been gone less than an hour when Wally had smelled something cooking upstairs in the kitchen. Hamburgers, maybe? She thought they might feed her—maybe a fify-fifty chance at best, but it was the only angle she saw. There was no way to get food to her other than by opening the door, and she would be ready.

So she had waited. And waited. No food. She had eventually pounded on the door, yelling that she was hungry. Nothing.

Time was flying by, and the only option Wally saw was for her to make some kind of kamikaze break for the fire escape, but she was certain there were still two guards waiting out there, both heavily armed. What good would it do Tiger for her to die without any real hope of succeeding? She stepped toward the windows to take yet another look and maybe spot a flaw in their security, but she'd done the same thing every five minutes for hours, with no luck.

And then she heard a voice from above.

"Wally?"

It was Kyle. Wally felt a hot rush of rage at the sound of his voice—if he had suddenly appeared in front of her, Wally doubted she would be able to stop herself from going after him. When she'd been caught, Kyle had stood by passively and watched it all happen, wearing a look that could only be described as satisfaction. Reliving the moment made Wally feel stupid and weak. If she hoped for some kind of revenge, she would have to be smart.

She willed herself to remain calm. She couldn't figure out right away where his voice was coming from, so she stilled herself, listening.

"Kyle?" Her voice was tentative—it was better for him to believe that she was afraid and in a weakened state.

"Hello, Wally."

Now she could tell that his voice was coming down from the fire escape outside. Looking out the window, she thought she could see his feet on the metal grated staircase—he was sitting where the guard had been, on the landing one floor above. A window near the ceiling was broken, and his voice traveled to her through that open space.

"Are you all right?" he asked.

"No," she said. "I'm not."

"Everything's going to be fine," he said. "Just try to roll with it."

The smarmy tone of reassurance in his voice disgusted her. Her own fate was the last thing she cared about at that moment anyway.

"I'm scared, Kyle," she said, keeping the timid tone in her voice.

"Ha! Don't bullshit a bullshitter," he said. "But nice try."

Playing the girl in distress apparently wasn't going to work.

"You don't think I'm capable of fear?"

"Sure. I've seen you scared—but you were even more dangerous then."

Outside Harmony House and up at the lodge, Kyle had had a front-row seat for the Wally show. She couldn't expect him to underestimate her after all that.

"I *am* afraid—for my brother," she said.

"Tiger is a killer," Kyle said. "I understand you have feelings for him, but the fact is, your brother will die the same way he lived—by the gun. It's inevitable. My father chose Tiger for this job because of who he's always been."

As he spoke, Wally thought she could hear something else: the sound of something rubbing against metal. Had he shifted a step lower on the fire escape?

"The plan to get me here—that was yours?"

"Sure," he said, sounding proud. "From day one, it was my job to get you out in the open, preferably somewhere quiet so they could take you easily without hurting you. It seemed like a simple job, at first, but it didn't turn out that way. Your neighborhood was full of cops all the time. It halfway seemed like they were watching out for you especially. So it was my idea to come into the Ursula Society."

"But the story you told me," she said. "That was true, right? About how you found out about your birth mother, when your stepmother died?"

Thinking back on Kyle's "performance"—about the compelling story he'd told to trick her and lure her away—she suspected that it had not been all lies.

"Absolutely! Thank you for getting that!" he said with genuine enthusiasm. "My father and Rachel—my sister, she was here with you before—they had this idea that I should make up a really sympathetic family history, like out of some soap opera or whatever, so I could really get you on the hook. But they were wrong. Nothing is more convincing than the truth."

"No doubt. And the bruises on your face?"

"We needed to convey a sense of urgency," Kyle said, his voice sounding a little tight.

"The beating was your father's idea? I suppose he did that to you himself?"

Kyle didn't answer, and Wally realized she'd made a mistake.

"Well, your performance at the lodge really kicked my ass," she said, imbuing her tone with reluctant admiration. It took all of her self-control to pull it off.

"That was the easy part," he said, sounding more relaxed now. "You got me really hot, Wally. No acting required there."

The thought of it turned Wally's stomach now, but she had to keep on task. She had an idea about where to take the discussion next, but she was worried it would be too much.

"What would she think about all this, do you figure?" she asked, targeting Kyle's weakest point.

"Who are you talking about?"

"Your mother. Your real one, I mean. What was her alias again? Mercy Smith? What would she think about you right now?"

Kyle didn't bother answering.

"I spent a long time looking for my birth mother," Wally went on, "and I don't think a day went by when I didn't look in the mirror and imagine what she would think of me when we finally met face-to-face. You think about that a lot, right? What would your mother see if she looked at you right now?"

"I'm not looking for her," Kyle said, sounding annoyed. "That was just—"

"Part of your story?" Wally said, allowing her voice to carry just a hint of smugness, as if completely confident that she possessed inside knowledge. "No, Kyle. I'm sure that's what you told your father, maybe even your sister. Like you said, don't bullshit a bullshitter—you think about your real mother all the time. You have to wonder—was she someone your father actually cared about or just one of his playthings? I remember your reaction to the photos of your father's women—you were devastated. That's why you took off at that truck stop. You were too weak to handle it—"

"Shut up, Wally," he said, the tension rising in his voice.

"All this time and your mother hasn't shown up," Wally kept the pressure on. "Why do you figure that is? Your father isn't so hard to find, and neither are you. So, where is she? I'm thinking there are only two real possibilities, and I'm sure you've already figured them out. Either your father got rid of her—which we both know he is capable of, don't we?—or she just doesn't give a shit about you. Huh. Which is worse, do you think?"

"You don't know what the fuck you're talking about," he snarled. "She let me go because my father could do so much for me, more than she could."

"Wow. Like you said, Kyle, the truth is more convincing than anything, and I'm not hearing it right now. Do you even halfway believe what you're saying?"

"You think I should listen to anything you say?" Kyle was nearly shouting now. "If you know so much, what happened to your mother? Yeah, I know all about it—about Shelter Island? She died there. I hear it was a bloody mess. And whose fault was that?"

Wally felt another wave of red-hot rage run through her, but she fought it off and kept her mind clear. Kyle's voice had sounded a little closer then, and Wally could just barely make out the sound of him on the move again, easing down the fire escape a step further. She looked up, and she could see his silhouette more fully now—his body from the waist down, three steps below the top of the window.

It was time.

Near Wally's feet was the stack of firewood that she and Tiger had used to keep the woodstove burning, and only three of the short logs were left. She grabbed the largest one and wheeled her body around, hurling the log through the window.

The glass shattered with explosive force, lethal splinters showering down in every direction.

Wally lunged toward the open space in the window and there were Kyle's feet, almost exactly where she thought they'd be. She grabbed hold of Kyle's right leg and pulled with all her strength, bracing herself against the windowsill as she dragged him off the staircase into the room. He screamed in pain as his body slammed to the floor, and the two of them began wrestling for control. With her left arm, Wally wrapped his neck up in a choke hold, but Kyle was an athlete, after all, and he was strong—he started pulling violently at Wally's arms, and she didn't think she could fight him that way for much longer.

Looking at the ground around her, she saw at least a dozen large shards of glass from the shattered window, and one still had a broken chunk of the wooden pane glued to it. Wally grabbed the shard on the wooden side and jammed the sharp end into Kyle's shoulder. He screamed in pain, and blood began gushing from the wound.

"Ahhhh …" Kyle howled. "You fucking bitch!"

Wally shifted the edge to Kyle's throat, pressing just hard enough to break the skin and make him stop moving.

"Stand up!" she commanded, and clambered to her feet while never letting go of the choke hold with her left arm and keeping the razor-sharp glass pressed tight against his neck. Kyle managed to set his feet on the ground and rise up with her. Wally heard a sound on the fire escape outside and she turned quickly—the guard from below was just raising his gun to fire. Wally pressed the glass harder into Kyle's neck, and he screamed.

"I'LL GUT HIM!" Wally howled at the guard like a wild animal, and he froze. Wally hauled Kyle toward the metal door on the opposite wall. It was an awkward crab walk they were doing together—Kyle was much taller than Wally, and when he stood up straight, it raised her feet off the ground, compelling her to spring free. She responded by pressing the shard against him even closer, forcing him to bend low and return her feet to the floor.

When they reached the door, Wally released the glass from his neck for just a moment, stabbing it again into the part of his shoulder that was already wounded and seeping blood down the front of his shirt. Kyle screamed so loud that her ears hurt, and soon the metal door swung open. Alabama stood there in the doorway, his assault rifle raised and pointed directly at her, the wounds on his face still oozing liquid into his bandages.

"Sure, take your shot, asshole," Wally said to him, keeping her voice as even as she could and moving the glass back into tight contact with Kyle's throat. "But be sure not to miss."

She could see Alabama weighing his extreme desire to kill her against the consequences if Kyle were to die in front of him. Wally pushed Kyle through the doorway and hauled him with her down the hallway to the stairs, keeping her back to the wall the entire time and struggling to keep her feet on the ground when Kyle managed to stand up too straight.

Another guard appeared at the stairway landing from

above—it was the dude with the shotgun, but just as he leveled it toward her he caught sight of the glass still pressed under Kyle's chin. The guard held his ground but from the scared expression on his face it was clear he would not risk Kyle's life by taking a shot at Wally.

She kept moving, forcing Kyle onward as they charged down the stairs. Finally, they reached the ground-floor hallway. She could hear footsteps behind them as Alabama and the shotgun guy followed just out of sight, waiting for an opportunity to stop Wally in a way that wouldn't get Kyle killed. Wally ignored them and kept her focus on moving forward.

As she and Kyle moved down the hallway, they passed some ancient gas pipes along the wall—one had an old valve sticking out. Wally slowed down and kicked the valve hard, twice, before the rusty old pipe gave way and she could hear the hissing sound of gas being released into the air. They moved ahead, pushing toward the main doorway. She hoped that the leaking gas would prevent Alabama and any other pursuers from firing their weapons, since a muzzle flash might set off an explosion—or, better yet, that they *would* fire their guns and fry themselves—once she and Kyle were far enough away.

As they emerged into the parking lot, the crack of a gunshot rang out—Wally felt a strange sucking sound to her left and realized that the shot had missed her by mere inches, flashing past her ear. The shot sounded like it had come from up high, probably from one of the guards who had been posted on the fire escape. Wally began spinning Kyle in a circle as they moved, making them a nearly impossible target. The turning motion caused the glass to slide against Kyle's neck, slicing the skin just deep enough that he howled like a wounded animal. Blood trickled out of his neck now and ran down Wally's hand.

All at once, the gunshots stopped.

Wally had a decision to make: there were five vehicles parked in the lot, three nice Cadillac SUVs, one black Humvee, and one big black Mercedes sedan. One of the SUVs—a black one that Wally recognized as Divine's ride—was parked facing outward.

They sidled toward the black SUV.

"OPEN IT!" she commanded, and Kyle obeyed, reaching for the driver's-side door.

Wally slid in, backward, pulling Kyle along with her until he was seated behind the wheel and she was in the front passenger seat.

"WHERE'S THE GUN?!" Wally shouted into his ear, certain that all of Divine's vehicles would have weapons readily at hand. Kyle's right arm flailed out, pointing desperately toward the center console. Wally clicked the console open and came away with a 9mm Glock, fully loaded.

"KEYS!"

Kyle reached for the sun visor, grunting in pain, and pulled down the keys. Another quick jab with the glass and he started the car, putting it in gear and steering toward the closed gate of the compound.

"GO!" she said, keeping the shard pressed against his neck

with her left hand and holding the Glock in her right.

Kyle accelerated toward the gate as Wally lowered the window on her side. Alabama and the shotgun guy were just emerging from the door of the warehouse, both of them with weapons raised. Wally pointed the Glock and focused herself: she squeezed off two shots, aiming not for the men but into the open doorway. The two gunmen sensed what she was doing and dove away from the door, just as one of Wally's shots hit a metal hinge and kicked up a spark, igniting the gas inside the hallway.

The ground floor of the warehouse exploded in a ball of fire that shot straight out the door and engulfed the SUV parked nearest to the explosion. Within seconds, the vehicle exploded in flames and the fire was threatening to spread to every vehicle in the lot. Kyle accelerated, plowing his father's SUV through the closed gate and squealing out onto the street, pulling away. Wally tossed the shard of glass out the window of the moving vehicle and now trained the Glock at Kyle's head.

"Keep going," she commanded.

A mile to the north, Wally forced Kyle to pull over, and she took over behind the wheel. She forced him into a fetal position down in the passenger-side wheel well. He didn't resist, instead cowering into the jammed space with one hand over the open wound in his neck.

"I'll take you to Tiger," Kyle sputtered, the blood still spilling out of him and clashing with his now ghostly pale skin.

"I know you will," she replied.

30.

TIGER MADE IT THROUGH THE SECURITY LINE easily—he was the same age as most of the local kids who were pouring into the old factory, and he didn't have a cell phone or weapon on him.

The inside of the building was a storm of sensory overload. House music blared at deafening levels, and a full light show strobed along with the beat, the brightest flashes burning into Tiger's retinas until he was seeing spots everywhere he looked. A row of smoking tiki torches ran along each side of the huge, open space—their primeval glow framed the throbbing mass of youth that filled the dance floor, many of them half-naked already and stoned out of their minds on whatever party drugs Sweet's men were passing out.

As he moved along the outer edges of what was once the factory floor, Tiger had to step around the entangled bodies of partiers—some of them were obviously local kids, but an equal number were Sweet's young soldiers, who were mingling with the locals and taking what they wanted, however they wanted.

At the end of the floor Tiger found the staircase that led up into the tower section of the factory. There were four young men at the foot of the stairs, each holding an assault rifle and wearing dark sunglasses. How did they see anything in that room with those shades on? Two were dark-skinned black kids, probably African. The other two looked to be Thai or Indonesian. Their tight, muscular physiques were clad in classic American street-thug attire: white tank tops, brand-new oversized jeans, and spotless Timberland boots. Paired with the assault weapons, they were every street cop's nightmare.

When Tiger reached the stairs, one of the African kids held up his hand and spoke in heavily accented English.

"Mista man, we don't know you!" the kid hollered in Tiger's face. "Fuck off and move your ass away from here!"

"No, bitch—fuck you," Tiger answered, unflinching.

All four assault weapons were in Tiger's face immediately, fingers tight on triggers, twitchy nerves unconnected to anything that resembled a moral conscience. These boys had been through hell in their lives, and Sweet had exploited their pain and suffering, turning it to a white-hot rage ready to erupt upon the world. Tiger looked at them and saw only darkness, nothing behind their faces but greater depths of fury.

Is that what others see when they look at me? Tiger couldn't help but think it. Did his soul look as lost as theirs? He saw no sign that these soldiers—these children—were capable of redemption, but how could one person ever know that about another? Tiger realized that he would have no reservations about pulling the trigger on Sweet, provided he could get close enough.

"What's the worst way you've seen your boss kill a man?" he said to the boys, their rifles still in his face. "That's how you'll die if you do me dirt."

His fearlessness gave them pause.

"Who the fuck is you, boy?" one of the Asian kids asked.

"Tell Sweet that Tiger Klesko is here."

"Gentlemen, we're in the presence of *Vory* royalty!" Sweet boasted—a little drunkenly—when he saw Tiger enter the room at the top level of the tower. "Here we have Tiger, son of the notorious Alexei Klesko."

Sweet hadn't changed since Tiger had seen him several years earlier. He was still pale and short and pudgy, his thinning blond hair even wispier. He spoke in the smooth, precise English that seemed second nature to so many Swedes, giving him an entirely civilized veneer. But the man's eyes—a steely, intensely focused blue with a sense of unrest lurking behind them—projected all the authority he needed to command the attention of the room.

The man stepped forward and wrapped his arms around Tiger, but the warm gesture turned into yet another pat down for weapons.

"No offense," Sweet whispered into Tiger's ear when he was done.

Tiger shrugged—just business. Such caution was how a man like Sweet stayed alive.

The top floor of the tower was comprised of one large room with a high ceiling and windows on all four walls. Set off to the side were remnants of what must have been the administrative center of the old factory—broken-down desks and swivel chairs and endless power cables. The sounds of house music rumbled up from far below, and the floor under their feet vibrated from painfully amplified bass rhythms. At least five of Sweet's security crew kept post at the perimeter of the room, armed and ready.

A dozen mid-level crime bosses were also in attendance, just as Divine had predicted. Dressed in sharp suits and on their best behavior, the hoods hovered near Sweet, eager to curry favor with the man whose international connections could instantly raise their profiles and make them very rich—if that's what Sweet chose to do. The big man's warm acceptance of Tiger instantly gave him cachet among the others; he could feel their envious gazes.

Sweet took a step back and looked Tiger up and down. "Still very pretty. Not quite so much of a child as the last time we met. Not even a whisker on your face back then, yes?"

"One grows up quickly."

"Ah," Sweet agreed, with a sense of regret. "And your father?" The expression on Sweet's face told Tiger that the man already knew the answer.

"The Americans have him buried in a hole somewhere," Tiger said, faking anger at the insult of it all.

"They won't be able to hold him," Sweet said.

"No one ever has," Tiger answered, sounding like a loyal and admiring son. "Not for long."

Sweet nodded in agreement. "I'm pleased you've arrived in time for us to meet—I have only a few minutes to spend here before I'm off. And so...what can I do for you, Tiger-son-of-Klesko?"

"I've worn out my welcome in this place," Tiger said simply. "If you can use me, I'm looking for work. And a ride out."

Sweet studied Tiger, thinking, and nodded as if ready to consider the offer.

"We might have something for you," he said. "Let me think on it. I have some business to finish up, first. *Noblesse oblige*. It's what we do."

Sweet patted Tiger on the shoulder and then returned to his other guests, listening patiently to their praise and proposals. Tiger scanned the room and found the bathroom door near the northwest corner of the room. He made his way there, finding that one of the security boys was lurking just behind, shadowing him. Tiger stopped at the door of the bathroom and turned to the kid.

"What? You want to come in and hold it for me?" Tiger said.

The kid backed off, and Tiger entered the bathroom, closing the door behind him. As soon as he was alone, he exhaled heavily, releasing the tension he had fought back in the room with Sweet. Tiger hated any kind of pretending—he was always better at the shooting part.

He looked up and saw that the bathroom had a paneled ceiling—all sagging and yellow and water-damaged—but the panels closest to the wall were more or less intact. He stood on the toilet lid and reached up, pushing the corner panel up and sliding it out of the way. He felt around in the empty space above, his fingers finally making contact with two items, which he pulled down and set on the sink: a small 9mm Browning with an eleven-shot clip and a cell phone.

He picked up and checked the Browning's mag and slide, making sure it was in working order. He chambered the first round. The cell phone was the folding kind, and when Tiger opened it he found a small note taped to the screen. It read: **Text to speed dial #1 when in position**. Tiger opened the texting app and typed, **In.** His thumb hovered over the "send" button, but he paused.

He considered his options. There were two ways Wally would survive the night: if she somehow managed to escape the Ranch, or if Tiger carried out the hit and Divine kept his word to let her go free. Tiger had faith in Wally's resourcefulness, but the odds were steep against her escaping on her own. The second possibility was equally unlikely—he couldn't trust that Divine would keep Wally safe—but that scenario was the only one Tiger had any control over. If he went ahead and killed Sweet, his action might at least give Wally more time to break free.

Tiger checked the gun a second time, making sure every part of the mechanism was working smoothly. He slid the weapon inside his waistband, just near his right hip, where he could draw it quickly. Sweet's security boys would gun Tiger down almost immediately, but not soon enough to stop him. In that final moment, Tiger would have held the value of someone else's life—Wally's—above his own. If that didn't prove how different he was from his father, nothing else would.

Tiger opened the door and stepped back into the big room.

31.

WALLY STEERED THE ESCALADE OFF THE INTERSTATE and onto a two-lane county road, following Kyle's directions. She passed by a large suburban housing development, but after that the road turned dark and rural—mostly farmland to either side of the road, as far as she could tell.

"How long before the turnoff?" she asked.

Kyle was still curled up in the passenger's-side wheel well, mostly quiet except for his pained, labored breathing.

"Kyle," she repeated, keeping her eyes on the road ahead of her and impatient with his weakness, "how long before the turnoff?"

"I don't know," he said, in a weak and pathetic voice that made Wally cringe, disgusted all over again that she had allowed herself to be made a fool of by someone so unworthy. "A mile, maybe three . . . I'd have to see it for myself."

"Fine. Sit up in your seat."

Kyle slid up and onto the passenger seat, unfolding himself slowly until he was seated upright. The bloody marks on his neck had mostly dried, but the wounds still looked angry and raw, ready to bleed again at any time. He stared out through the windshield, the SUV's headlights stretching far ahead on the country road. After about two minutes of driving, he pointed to a blue reflector on the right side of the road, marking a paved service road that ran northeast off the county road.

"There," Kyle said. "Up that way."

Wally steered the Escalade onto the service road, which was well-paved but completely dark, surrounded by dense woods on either side. Wally was on edge now, anticipating the location that Kyle had eventually described to her on the way: a large, abandoned factory space that was being used as a site for a massive rave. There would be a tower to one side of the factory, where Tiger would be headed. The entire facility would be well defended by the security team of a man named Sweet—who was also Tiger's target.

Within just a minute of driving, the sky ahead began to glow a little, reflecting bright lights from somewhere below. Wally rolled down the windows of the Escalade and could hear house music—thumping bass and piercing electronica—a bit faint for the moment but growing in volume as they rolled closer.

"It's already happening," Wally said, more to herself than Kyle.

She had barely gotten her words out when Kyle suddenly reached for his door handle and pulled it, swinging the door outward and hurling himself out onto the dark shoulder of the road.

"*Kyle!*" Wally shouted, pounding her fists on the steering wheel. She was outraged with herself at being caught off guard.

Wally immediately skidded the car to a stop and jumped out, but Kyle was nowhere to be found. The SUV had been traveling at just over thirty miles per hour when he had jumped, but it still would have been a hard, painful landing. How far could he have made it in just a few seconds? The shoulder of the road was dense with brush and she had no flashlight, so Wally stood still and listened for a few moments, waiting for Kyle to reveal his location. There were no sounds at all coming from the brush, and no sign of movement.

Kyle was disciplined enough to keep himself completely still.

Shit. Wally wanted badly to go in after him—feeling her way through the darkness on her hands and knees, if that's what it took—but realized that if she ventured out into the dark brush, she would be vulnerable to an attack from Kyle. Reaching Tiger was her priority, and she couldn't risk screwing it up.

"I'll find you, Kyle," Wally warned in a normal tone, knowing he had to be very close. "And you'll never see me coming."

She listened for a moment more, then climbed back into the Escalade and motored on along the service road, all the while trying to set aside her frustration at letting Kyle escape. She passed through another mile or so of dark forest before finally reaching the factory complex.

It was a huge building with one long section about four or five stories high and a higher tower section on the far end—where Tiger would be headed, if Kyle's information could be believed. The compound was surrounded by a very high cyclone fence with razor wire on top. Two or three hundred vehicles of every type were already parked in the surrounding fields, with a few dozen young people—excited and talkative—walking across the ground toward an open gate in the fence. A rainbow of flashing strobes leaked from every opening in the factory, and even outside the building, the house music was almost deafening.

Wally left her gun in the car, sure that it would not make it through the kind of security she was expecting. She casually mixed with the other kids as they approached the gate, trying to act relaxed, but in reality staying hyperalert—she could sense that Tiger was very close now, and already approaching his target.

Wally didn't know all the details about her brother's mission, but everything she had learned about Divine and his organization—his involvement in black-market arms sales, the extreme violence he'd used, and the fact that Alabama had been in the market to purchase very powerful, untraceable explosives—told her that something devastating and huge was about to go off. Wally needed to find Tiger before he was destroyed by whatever Divine had planned, and time was critical. She felt as if a bomb was ticking inside her chest.

The guards at the gate—four of them—were nothing like she expected. They were of various nationalities, and no older than she was. They'd dressed in a hodgepodge of guerrilla military gear, and most of them possessed the distant, impassive look of battle-hardened veterans. All were armed with "choppers"—assault rifles—plus knives and handguns stuffed into their belts.

Wally smiled blankly as she approached the gate, matching her outward mood to that of the gleeful, stoned kids around her.

One of the guards patted Wally down, lingering too long on her curves as his hands ran along her body. He had a strange gleam in his eye, as if imagining the things he would do to her when he had the chance.

"Find anything you like?" she smiled flirtatiously, letting her eyelids droop as if she was heavily stoned. The guard—an Asian kid no older than fourteen but with a look like he had been through the wars—winked at her.

"Maybe I see you inside?" he said.

She and the other kids entered the main building and were immediately swallowed up in a storm of music and light, hundreds of dancing, sexing, tripped-out kids filling the vast space. Wally was impressed—the scene was more depraved than most of the action she'd witnessed in Manhattan clubs.

At the edges of the room were dozens of young bodies wrapped up in each other—half-dressed boys and girls in groups with no gender boundaries, writhing around on the floor. They were lit dimly by rows of tiki torches set to either side of the room, flames flickering to the vibrations of the house music and smoke rising up toward the ceiling in oily, acrid plumes. It was like a level of hell, Wally thought—the kind you'd see in a classic old painting at the Metropolitan Museum, where legions of the damned were being roasted alive in a fiery pit.

Wally soon focused her attention on the north end of the

room, where a staircase led up into the tower section of the old factory. There were four security "men" on guard there, each armed with choppers—military-issue assault rifles.

Wally was willing to bet her life that Tiger would be there. She slowed her pace a little and passed by the foot of the stairs, fixing a playful gaze on one of the guards—an African-looking guy of no more than sixteen—his eyes hidden behind a pair of dark aviator sunglasses and a soldier's red beret perched sideways on his head, the edges of an Afro poking out the sides. Once she was sure the guard had clocked her, she headed for an exit at the east side of the floor.

She didn't need to look back—Wally could sense the boy following her. She reached the doorway and exited back out into the night, headed toward a shadow at the edge of the building. This side of the grounds was empty, save for one young sentry standing post at the southeast corner of the building, about forty feet away.

Wally had just reached the shadowed area when a hand grabbed her by the shoulder and roughly turned her around. The African kid wore a cocksure grin as he set his assault rifle against the cyclone fence and leaned in toward Wally, jamming his tongue into her mouth without skill or nuance, like he was pushing a plunger into a toilet bowl. Wally placed a hand on his chest and pushed him gently away.

With a suggestive smirk, she glanced toward the sentry at the corner of the building. Romeo took the hint and yelled at the sentry to get lost. The sentry complied, disappearing around the corner of the building to give the young lovers some privacy. Romeo turned back to Wally, running his hand up her shirt as he leaned in with his lips parted.

His tongue never made contact this time. Wally brought her elbow up hard and drove it into the kid's throat. His eyes bulged hugely as he absorbed the full force of the blow and struggled to breathe, a surge of adrenaline burning through all the oxygen in his lungs until he went limp and passed out on the ground. Wally grabbed his rifle from its place by the fence.

Now she was armed. *What next?* The firepower of the assault rifle clearly wasn't enough to get her through the tower sentries, so she'd have to be more resourceful. There was an outside staircase leading up to the tower, but it seemed inevitable that there would only be more guards posted there than she could handle.

Wally looked around and spotted a metal shed set off from the main factory building—was there some sort of mechanical sound coming from inside? She thought she could hear something barely discernible beneath the dense bass of the house music that filled the air. The shed was about fifty feet away, near the corner where the sentry had disappeared a few moments before. Wally approached the corner and peered around it, smiling at the sentry, who was now leaning against the outside wall of the factory, his rifle slung across his shoulder as he smoked.

"Hi," Wally said.

The sentry smiled back and tossed his cigarette away, heading toward her. As he rounded the corner, Wally whipped her new assault rifle around, striking the unsuspecting boy on the forehead. He dropped to the ground in a motionless heap. Wally grabbed his rifle and flung it away, then approached the metal shed. As she drew nearer, the ground underneath her vibrated with the rhythm of a motor.

She darted into the shed, finding a large engine inside that was running at a high pitch. A generator, of course. The factory probably hadn't been on the power grid in decades, Wally figured, and lots of power would be needed to light it up for the evening's festivities. She knew nothing about engines, but she reached out anyway and grabbed the round rubber thing on the front of the motor that had two cables coming out of it. She gave the cables a strong pull and the rubber part popped right off the engine, which sputtered for a few seconds before shutting down completely.

The music and lights in the factory immediately went dead, and the echo of the sounds bounced back and forth across the valley for a second or two before giving way to complete silence. Wally could imagine the hundreds of stoned kids all standing completely still on the dance floor, trying to figure out what was happening and wondering if the interruption was real or just in their own heads.

After a moment of quiet, Wally heard a stirring from inside, voices speaking and hooting and booing at the interruption of their fun, while others laughed out loud at the sheer surprise of it all. The dim glow of the flickering tiki torches inside the factory could just be seen through the windows, and Wally realized that it was the light of the torches that was preventing an all-out panic among the partiers.

Chaos, thought Wally. *That's what we need.*

She looked up to the highest part of the main factory roof, where there was a row of glass skylights that stretched the entire length of the building. About half were already broken but many remained intact. Wally shouldered her assault rifle and aimed high, toward the glass.

32.

TIGER STEPPED OUT OF THE BATHROOM AND approached Sweet, who was having a close, personal discussion with one of the local crime bosses. Tiger swept his right hand down by his hip, feeling the butt of the handgun there and reassuring himself again that he would be able to draw it quickly. He had covered half the distance to his target, Sweet, when the room went dark. It appeared the power outage was not restricted to the room they were in—the intense pulse of music from the rave downstairs had gone quiet as well.

Sweet's soldiers were young but they were also well trained—without panicking, they immediately produced at least half a dozen bright flashlights and gathered tightly around Sweet, surrounding him with a human shield that would make a shot at him almost impossible. The room came to life with sounds of radio communication, at least three of the boys holding walkie-talkies that they were now using to get a fix on the security situation. Tiger heard the word *generator* mentioned several times, with voices on the other end of the line saying that they were converging on the generator and would have it back on in just a few seconds.

Tiger stood his ground in the center of the room, with no choice but to hold off on his attack. The calm vigilance of Sweet's team turned to full alert when a barrage of gunfire rang out—four long autobursts from an assault rifle outside the building. The gunfire was followed by the sound of shattering glass and then loud, shrieking screams from the hundreds of partiers below, already half out of their minds with dope and now caught up in full panic.

"GO!!!" one of Sweet's security boys shouted. "EVERYONE MOVE!"

Tiger could only watch as the team hustled Sweet to the door and out of the room like a cadre of veteran Secret Service agents, following a key principle: *when in doubt, get the package out*. Tiger hadn't even come close to taking a shot. What would Divine be thinking at that moment? That Tiger had somehow tried to cross him?

If so, Wally was as good as dead.

Shit!

The local bosses stayed close to Sweet and raced away also, with one security man staying until everyone was out. The kid—hyperalert and twitchy—motioned for Tiger to exit in front of him, and Tiger hurried to the door as if obeying the command. At the last second, he pulled up short and crouched low, delivering a surprise punch to the kid's solar plexus. The kid dropped to the floor, out cold.

Tiger snatched away his assault rifle and flashlight.

What next? Sweet was probably halfway out of the factory already, on his way to his waiting helicopter. Should Tiger hurry after him and try to take a shot? He'd never be able to get close enough. Unless...if someone were able to disable Sweet's helicopter, the target would be grounded, and Tiger would be back in play. Tiger had to do something to let Divine know that he was still in the hunt and trying to fulfill his part of the deal.

He pulled the cell phone out of his pocket, realizing that he had never actually completed the first text he'd been instructed to send—the one confirming that he was in position and ready to carry out the hit. Now he erased the first message and entered a new one as quickly as he could: **Target on the move. Take out helicopter and I will find a way to finish**. Tiger was about to press the "send" button but paused. Something was bothering him—the same feeling that had stopped him from sending his first text message earlier.

The confirmation text didn't really make sense—it was an extra moving part in the operation that served no real purpose. Why would Divine need to know his position? From his spot on the nearby hilltop he would know right away whether or not Tiger had taken his shot on Sweet.

And then Tiger understood. In a moment of revelation, he remembered his first trip to the factory site with Rachel, how she had trekked down to the factory without him, a daypack slung over her shoulder. When she had returned to him on the hilltop, her pack was gone—she'd left it behind, somewhere inside the factory.

Tiger began sweeping the room with his flashlight, and it only took a moment to find the spot—the same location he would have chosen himself. The far wall of the room had a section that had been patched over several times, so one more piece of scrap board on the plaster would never be noticed. Tiger moved to the spot and used all his strength to pull away the board, which had been secured with four or five rusty old nails. In the empty spot behind it sat Rachel's backpack.

Very carefully, Tiger pulled the pack out and set it on the floor. He unzipped the pack and found what he already knew would be there: somewhere between fifteen and twenty pounds of plastic explosives, with a cell phone attached to a detonator.

Of course. Once Tiger had been seen entering the tower, anything that happened after that could be blamed on him. He'd been told to confirm his arrival on the top floor with a text message, and sending it would have blown the entire factory tower off the map, probably killing hundreds of local party kids at the same time. Tiger would be dead, unable to tell his own version of the story.

Tiger shut off the power on the bomb's cell phone and zipped the pack up, tossing it over his shoulder—if Sweet had been slowed down on the way to his helicopter, the plastic explosives might be a weapon Tiger could use against him. Divine had schemed to blow Tiger up along with Sweet, but that didn't change the mission: if Tiger couldn't take out Sweet, Wally would pay the price.

With the bomb on his back and the assault rifle in his hands, Tiger charged out of the room. Racing down the tower's staircase, he arrived at the ground floor and was greeted by absolute chaos. Hundreds of drugged-up, half-naked teenagers were screaming at the top of their lungs and fighting each other to get out of the building in a primal frenzy of self-preservation. The crazed throng had knocked down several of the tiki torches as they rushed across the floor, the flames hitting the dry, old factory floor and setting it on fire, causing even more panic than the bursts of gunfire that had set off the stampede in the first place.

Tiger fought his way through the crowd and saw that a window on the east wall had been smashed, teenagers diving through it desperately and cutting themselves on the glass edges in the process. Tiger headed in the direction of the noise and launched himself out the window, nicking his face on the glass.

He raced toward the area inside the south fence where Sweet's helicopter was waiting. Before he could get anywhere near that spot, he heard the high-pitched turbine engines begin to whine and the rotors whirring to life. Within seconds he saw the sleek aircraft lifting off, fifty yards in front of him. Tiger shouldered his assault rifle and took aim, but as he checked the ground ahead he saw dozens of the local party kids racing away, moving across the area directly beneath the chopper.

If he got lucky and actually shot down the helicopter, dozens of those kids would die as it crashed to the ground in flames. Tiger hesitated, his finger tight on the trigger of his weapon.

Until that moment, he had assumed that he would do absolutely anything to save his sister. But that wasn't turning out to be true. He imagined Wally in his position, gun poised and ready to unleash hell—and he knew in his heart that she would never do that, not for anyone.

Maybe he and his sister were more alike than Tiger had realized. He tried to shake off his hesitation, finding Sweet's helicopter in his sights again and tightening his finger on the trigger of his rifle. He willed himself to pull it back the last millimeter and save Wally from Divine's wrath.

But he couldn't do it. Tiger lowered his weapon and buried his face in his hands, howling in agony. One chance to save his sister, and he couldn't bring himself to do it. Did he even know who he was anymore? Tiger was left with only one option: another helicopter would be taking off soon, and he would need to stop it. He took off, racing across the factory grounds as fast as he could.

33.

WALLY STOOD NEAR THE PERIMETER FENCE AND watched as anarchy unfolded in front of her. Partiers ran in every direction, most heading for the gate they had used to enter the compound. She saw a pack of Sweet's security team hustle to a helicopter on the far side of the complex, and she felt sure that Sweet himself was in the middle of that pack, still alive and making his escape with seven or eight of his most trusted soldiers. The rest of his "men" gathered in groups and headed for the half dozen or so heavy vehicles that they had parked inside the compound fence.

Wally had succeeded in breaking up the rave, and she hoped she'd also prevented Tiger from making a suicidal assassination attempt on Sweet. Everything she had seen of her brother in action told her that if he had taken his shot, Sweet would not still be alive.

Now she had to find him. What would Tiger do next, now that his opportunity to kill Sweet had passed? He would find a way to get back to the Ranch and free Wally—Tiger had no reason to know that she had escaped. How would he reach the Ranch? In the fastest way possible. Wally imagined him "borrowing" one of the cars parked outside the complex and racing the forty miles or so east.

She heard a massive crashing sound and saw that Sweet's remaining soldiers were escaping the site by plowing their vehicles straight into the cyclone fence, tearing it out of the ground and pulling it along with them as they raced away. Hundreds of kids saw the opening and headed in that direction also, away from the jammed gate on the other side of the grounds. As Wally watched the mass exodus, she caught sight of a figure moving quickly across the complex, sprinting through the horde of escaping teenagers and toward the opening in the fence, his long, dark hair flying free.

"TIGER!!!" Wally shouted as loud as she could, but with all the action going on, there was no chance of her voice reaching him. As he approached the fence, he headed north at full speed—the opposite direction from the service road that everyone else would be using. Where was he headed? Wally raced after him, hoping he couldn't keep up his pace. She would never be able to catch up otherwise.

As she moved through the mass of fleeing teenagers, Wally only made it ten or twenty yards when one of the kids running beside her—a young girl wearing only cutoff shorts and a lacy black bra—suddenly spun around and fell to the dirt without a sound, a bullet hole in the side of her head. Wally instinctively ducked but continued running after Tiger, all the while trying to deduce where the bullet had come from.

The girl's wound had been large, but Wally hadn't heard a gunshot—it had to have been a sniper shot taken at long range—and it wasn't hard to figure out who was doing the shooting. Now that his plan to kill Sweet had failed, Divine would want to erase all evidence of his plot, and that evidence included both Wally and Tiger. She hoped Tiger, far ahead of her still, would realize the danger and try to keep out of harm's way.

Wally had dumped the assault rifle she'd used to shoot out the factory windows, but she still had the sentry's automatic handgun in her belt. She pulled it out now and held it low to her side as she kept running, keeping her head on a swivel in case any of Divine's men came to get her at close range.

More shots came—Wally sensed one bullet missing her by inches, and it struck a guy near her in the leg. He fell down screaming in fear and pain, gripping his gushing wound. Wally's mind raced—it made her sick that others were taking the bullets meant for her. She ran on, hoping to separate herself from the pack of kids. She'd lost sight of Tiger but persevered in the same direction.

She spotted a black Jeep Cherokee ahead, the last in the line of Sweet's vehicles that had torn through the fence. Progress off the grounds was stalled by the mass of other cars trying to get out of the valley, so the Cherokee was moving slowly. Wally caught up with the car, running alongside as she hunched down to use the vehicle as a shield from more sniper shots. She traveled a hundred yards that way until she noticed another vehicle coming straight at them, moving toward the factory at high speed.

It was a Humvee—just fifty yards away now—charging straight for her. The tanklike vehicle's paint was charred and bubbled on one side, looking like it had just been set on fire—which it had been when Wally had ignited the gas fire at the Ranch. When the Humvee was just twenty yards away, she was able to see through the windshield and recognized the face behind the wheel.

Alabama wore a crazed look, and Kyle sat beside him, bloody and battered after his violent escape from the moving Escalade. Kyle looked as focused and angry as Alabama.

Wally jumped out of the way at the last second, and the Humvee blasted at full force into the Cherokee, demolishing the vehicle and all of Sweet's security men inside. There was nothing for her to do but keep running. The service road she was running on curved away, but she was sure Tiger had been heading toward the hill at the south side of the valley. She peeled away from the road and ran in that direction.

A quick glance behind her revealed that the Humvee had separated from the destroyed Cherokee and was still tailing her. Wally continued on, her lungs burning as she reached the trees and climbed the steep hill out of the valley. She could hear the Humvee behind her still, its progress slowed by the dense forest in its path—there were crashing and ripping sounds as Alabama kept speeding forward, swerving to avoid trees when he could and plowing through those that he could not.

Finally there came the sound of a massive crash, and the engine noises from the Humvee stopped cold—probably sucked into a ditch or stopped behind trees that were too close together for the vehicle to pass through. Wally kept running even as auto-blasts of gunfire came from behind, strafing the woods and ripping into tree trunks all around her. Alabama and Kyle were giving chase on foot now and blazing away with their weapons as they ran. Wally fired her handgun in their direction, hoping to slow them down.

She kept climbing, desperately exhausted now, and came within twenty feet of the top of the hill, where the trees disappeared and there was a very steep slope of loose rock, still damp and muddy from the rain the previous night. Wally stuck her gun under her belt and climbed up the cliff on all fours, struggling to gain purchase on the slope as the loose rocks dug into her hands. She could hear Alabama and Kyle ascending the slope too, gasping for breath as they came up close behind her.

Wally reached the top of the slope and tried to climb back up onto her feet, but a hand reached out and tripped her. She tumbled to the ground and turned, looking up to see that it was Kyle, his gun pointed directly at her. The chase had opened the wounds in his shoulder and neck again, and the blood seeped down his arm and the front of his shirt. His face appeared even more ghostly than it had been when they raced away from the Ranch together.

"You said you'd find me, Wally..." Kyle said, gasping for breath and barely able to stand, yet still able to relish the moment. "But I found you."

Wally was about to reach for the gun that was lodged under her belt, but it had slipped out when she'd fallen to the ground and she couldn't find it. It didn't matter. A huge hand grabbed Kyle from behind, powerful fingers digging into his wounded shoulder and sending him tumbling back down the cliff. It was Alabama. He was unwilling to let Kyle deprive him of his rightful kill. Alabama was a disgusting sight by now, the bandages on his facial burns dangling off him to reveal oozing, infected sores underneath.

"Hello again, bitch," he said, still struggling for breath.

"Hello, asshole," she said, a fatalistic calm overcoming her.

"I'm tired," Alabama said.

"Yeah, well ... you look like hell."

He managed a grunt of a laugh.

"It's a damn waste," he said, "putting down a creature like you. No one ever beat me even once, and you did twice. A damn waste, I say."

He raised his gun and pointed it at her chest, but before he could pull the trigger there came a shot from below, and Alabama's chest exploded as a bullet blasted clear through him. He stood eerily still, then, looked down at the open wound for a moment as if baffled. He turned around slowly, facing the downward slope.

"You spoiled piece of shit," he gurgled.

More shots rang out, ripping into him, but Alabama ignored them, leaping off the edge of the slope and disappearing from view. Wally climbed back to her feet and peered over the edge, where she saw Alabama battling Kyle hand to hand, going at it with everything they had left. She scanned the ground and finally found her gun in the dirt. She raised it up, but she was so drained of energy that she could barely hold it steady.

Looking down at the two men struggling, Wally was overcome by a feeling that things were just as they were meant to be, that she had no part in what was taking place between them. The burden of taking another life was something she could do without this time. Wally turned and staggered away, heading in a direction that she hoped would lead to Tiger.

34.

TIGER HEARD GUNSHOTS RIPPING THROUGH THE trees behind him, but he couldn't let himself get distracted. Divine's route back to his helicopter was short, and he might be flying away at any moment. Tiger pushed himself, his muscles still burning after charging up the steep hillside. He finally emerged from the trees, open field stretching before him.

The helicopter sat at the far end of the field, a hundred yards away or more. The running lights were on and he could just barely hear the distinct clicking sound, one he associated with the start-up sequence of the turbine engine. Once the engines engaged, Divine could take off at any time. In a full sprint now, Tiger approached the chopper from behind, sticking to its blind spot and moving out to the side only when he came within reach of its back rotor. He could see the glow of the control-panel lights through the heavily tinted windows and knew he would have to make his move before the turbines were on and the rotor began to engage.

Tiger set aside his assault rifle and pulled out the Browning—the gun he was meant to use on Sweet. In one fluid motion, he flipped open the right side door of the chopper and jumped in, his gun raised.

But there was no one to aim at. Tiger was alone in the cabin of the chopper. He looked outside and saw two figures approaching it slowly, guns raised in his direction. As they moved in close, the running lights lit up their faces: Divine, of course, and the pilot, each covering one side of the helicopter.

"Ease on out here, kid," Divine said.

Tiger felt like an idiot, lured in so easily, like a reckless amateur. He had let his concern for his sister cloud his judgment, and now he had doomed them both. Once he stepped outside, he'd be dead, and Wally would soon follow, no doubt. Nothing had gone according to plan, and it was time for Divine to clean house.

"Let's go," Divine barked. "No way around it—there's reckoning to be done."

Moving carefully in order to give every sign that he was following Divine's directions, Tiger tossed his weapon out the door of the chopper, then slid the backpack off his shoulder. He eased out of the cabin and spread his arms wide in surrender, crouching down and ducking his head to clear the low doorway. Then he sprang outward and plowed shoulder-first into Divine.

Divine managed to squeeze off a shot, but it flew high. His gun fell to the ground as the two men struggled. Tiger was shocked at the strength of the older man as they wrestled for control, but he used Divine's weight against him and flipped the man facedown in the dirt, landing on top of him with both knees and delivering a blow to the back of Divine's head.

There wasn't time to congratulate himself on gaining the

advantage. Tiger heard steps behind him as the pilot rushed over from the opposite side of the helicopter. He dove away from Divine and reached to recover his handgun, grabbing the weapon and spinning around just as the pilot was raising his own. Tiger squeezed off a shot and the pilot fell, grasping at the gushing wound to his abdomen. Tiger kicked away the man's gun and turned back to Divine, surprised to find that the old man had somehow staggered back onto his feet and had his gun in hand again.

Tiger and Divine stood facing each other, both their guns raised in a standoff. Tiger was winded from the fight and Divine looked unsteady, but the grim determination on their faces told the story: neither man would give ground, ever.

"Put it down," came Rachel's voice from behind Tiger.

"No, you put it down," ordered Wally.

The four of them—Wally and Tiger, Divine and Rachel—faced each other, guns drawn. Tiger kept his eyes on Divine and Rachel, but was unable to hide the surprise and relief he felt at Wally's appearance before him.

"You're here," he said.

She shrugged. "Obviously."

Tiger thought for a moment, running the night's scenario through in his mind.

"The generator?" he asked.

Wally nodded.

"Good idea," Tiger said.

Wally almost laughed, wondering what exactly she would have to do to get more from Tiger. Some small measure of acknowledgment that they were brother and sister, that they were important to each other. This wasn't the time for that anyway, she supposed. For now it was enough that they were together and alive.

"It's over," Divine barked, irate and frustrated that there was nothing he could do to change the situation.

Tiger nodded curtly. "Just go."

"What the hell is this?" came another voice.

It was Kyle. He staggered toward the foursome, his gun held high but his body beaten and bloody. He had obviously survived the hand-to-hand combat with Alabama, just barely. As he moved in among the group, he kept his gun trained squarely on Wally. Tiger now held *his* gun on Kyle but never stopped clocking the movements of Rachel or Divine. Not that it mattered where all the guns were pointed, anymore—if any shooting started now, no one would walk away.

"I'm going to kill her," Kyle said.

Wally looked Kyle up and down, not bothering to disguise her contempt. She wondered if she had made a mistake in refusing to take him out as he fought with Alabama.

"No, you're not," she informed him. "You're lucky to be standing."

"Don't you—"

"Stop with your bullshit!" Rachel barked at her brother. "We give you one job off the Ranch—one goddamn job—and you fuck it up. Be careful, or you might lose your seat in the chopper."

Kyle was outraged. He looked to his father for support, but the old man said nothing.

"Go," Tiger said.

Divine gestured toward the helicopter, urging his children to climb aboard. Before she got into the cabin, Rachel looked back at Tiger.

"We have unfinished business," she threatened.

Tiger shook his head.

Kyle was beside himself at how the confrontation was being diffused. His gun was still raised and pointed at Wally, as if he would rather die there than be forced to walk away. As a final gesture of defiance, he stepped to Wally and traced the muzzle of his gun down her cheek, smirking through his crusted, bloody mouth.

"I got you, though," he said. "Didn't I? Got the best of you, girl. Like a fish on a hook."

Wally pressed her own weapon into Kyle's gut, tempted to take him out no matter what the cost, but she managed to control herself.

"You're just not worth it," she said. "But you already know that, don't you?"

"Now!" Divine commanded from the doorway of the

chopper, and Kyle turned away, climbing aboard with his father and sister. Wally and Tiger stepped back from the rotors and watched as Divine piloted the chopper himself, pulling up off the ground and leaving a swirling cloud of dust in their wake.

35.

THE BLINKING LIGHTS OF THE HELICOPTER SOON disappeared among the stars.

Wally mostly felt numb. Somewhere inside she was happy and relieved that she had saved Tiger, but there were other feelings at war: shame at how she had been taken in by Kyle, for one. He hadn't been wrong when he described her as a "fish on a hook," and the humiliation of it burned.

"What am I supposed to feel?" she asked nobody in particular.

Tiger took a moment, struggling with the question. Introspection wasn't his thing.

"That's the problem with Americans," he said. "It's never enough just to be alive."

"Oh, really?"

Tiger nodded.

"So they get to walk away, and you're okay with that?" she asked, facing him now and starting to feel angry at the Zen vibe he was putting out.

"Yes."

"How can we let it end like this? Not to mention, they'll be coming for us, again. They'll never feel safe with us out in the world—with everything we know about what they tried to do. That's okay with you?"

"Everything will be fine," Tiger said calmly, infuriating her further.

"How, exactly?"

Tiger thought for a moment. "What would you say to them?"

"To who? Divine? Kyle?"

"Yes. Right now."

Wally thought about it.

"I'd tell them, *don't bother looking for us*," she said. "*We'll find you.*"

"Okay," Tiger nodded, pulling a cell phone out of his pocket and passing it to her.

Wally stared at the phone, confused. "What?"

"Type it," Tiger said.

It seemed like a pathetic exercise—a waste of her righteous rage—but Tiger seemed completely serious. Wally took the phone and typed the message into the texting app.

Don't bother looking for us. We'll find you.

Tiger looked over her shoulder at the message, and nodded in approval.

"Good," he said. "Simple is good."

She was about to press the "send" button, but Tiger grabbed the phone back.

"No, that's for me," he said. "You have enough to haunt you."

What the hell was that supposed to mean?

Tiger looked to the sky, in the direction Divine's helicopter had just taken, and pressed the "send" button purposefully.

Two seconds later, a white-hot ball of fire ignited the sky to the east. It was a massive explosion that would be seen for fifty miles in every direction. Five seconds after that, the sound of it reached them, a massive concussion that moved in an invisible wave through Wally's entire body and made her shiver from the base of her neck.

Suddenly she felt lighter than she had in weeks, even months.

The distant roar of the explosion dissipated and was replaced with the sound of sirens—hundreds of them, it seemed—converging on the area and growing louder by the second.

"They're playing our song," Wally said.

The last time the two of them had parted—on Shelter Island—it had been to the accompaniment of a similar chorus. Federal agents and local law enforcement had been moving in, and there was nothing for Tiger to do but run.

"There are businesses in that direction," he said, pointing to some streetlights a mile or so to the east. "A store is open twenty-four hours. Can you get home from there?"

"Yeah," Wally told him, feeling a fresh wave of dread in the pit of her stomach. They were parting again, and she wasn't ready for it.

"You go first, this time," he said.

Their eyes met for a moment, but then Tiger looked away. Whatever connection Wally needed to feel between them was not there yet. Maybe it never would be. She turned and headed alone across the open field, making it only twenty paces before she turned and faced her brother again.

"I love you, Tiger," she said.

He looked straight at her and didn't avert his eyes this time. But he didn't answer her either. Wally would have to be patient with him. And she would be.

"Don't worry," she said. "Saying it gets easier."

Wally turned again and walked away without looking back even once.

Wally sat on the curb outside the convenience store for nearly an hour. When Atley Greer finally pulled up in his unmarked police unit, she climbed in and Greer drove away, headed for the turnpike. They drove in silence for a while, Greer sneaking sideways looks at her as they reached the pike and headed east toward Manhattan.

"Busy night out here," Greer finally said. "An old warehouse in Bayonne burned down. Huge explosions from a cache of weapons inside. And then an old arms factory near here went up too. Some kind of rave out in the sticks. They're still counting bodies."

"It's New Jersey," Wally shrugged. "These people are savages."

36.

GREER DROVE WALLY HOME, CROSSING INTO Manhattan through the Holland Tunnel before taking the Williamsburg Bridge over the East River. The sun was just beginning to rise, striking the tallest buildings but leaving the streets of the city mostly in the shade, the cool of the night lingering as the early-morning commuters made their way to work. Wally realized that she didn't even know what day it was.

"Friday," Greer told her when she asked. For the entire drive he had been observing Wally out of the corner of his eye, trying not to be obvious. He was doing it again.

"Please stop hovering," she said. "Don't be a helicopter cop. I'm fine."

"I can tell you're hurt," he said.

"Aches and pains."

"You have a doctor?"

"Yes."

"You'll go in first thing?"

"Oh my God..."

"Promise, or I'll take you to an ER right now."

"Fine. I promise."

"Was that so hard?"

"Whatever, cop."

Wally took off her jacket and peeked into the bedroom, where Jake and Ella were sound asleep in her bed. The sight of them peaceful and safe filled her with such a powerful sense of gratitude that she could barely stand it. She stripped off her filthy clothes and got into the shower, washing away all the grime and cleaning up the various cuts and scrapes she had accumulated over the previous two days. She pulled on her yoga pants and a T-shirt and climbed into her bed, spooning with them.

"Wally?" Ella said, sleepily. "Welcome home."

"Go back to sleep," Wally said.

"'Night."

Wally slept deeply. When she finally woke, she was alone in the bed. Her cell phone was charging on the night table, and it read two o'clock in the afternoon. She rolled slowly from between the sheets, feeling pain and tightness spread over her entire body. She rose onto her feet and stretched, then shuffled out into the main room. Ella and Jake were on the couch watching reality TV and inhaling a stack of sliced peanut-butter-and-banana sandwiches.

"Hey, sleepy," Ella said brightly.

"How'd it go?" Jake asked, also not moving from the couch.

Wally was confused. "How did *what* go?"

"The new lead," said Jake, looking at Wally curiously—as if maybe she'd gone mental. "The one from your text?"

Jake tossed Wally his cell phone, and she scrolled through its messages, still clueless. And there it was, a text from her number to Jake and Ella, sent two days earlier:

Had to take off. Got a fresh lead, in Jersey. May be gone for a few days, don't worry. Please stay... W.

The message had come in at nine in the morning the previous Wednesday. By that time Wally—and her cell phone—had already been grabbed up by Archer Divine and his men. He had used a fake text to control Jake and Ella, just as he had used a semi-fake text from Kyle to reel her in two days earlier.

Wally realized the phony text had achieved two purposes for Divine. First, it pretty much eliminated the possibility that Jake and Ella would worry about her disappearance and involve outside authorities, at least for a few days. The second purpose was more insidious: by asking Jake and Ella to stay put in Wally's apartment, Divine would always know where they were. If he had run into problems controlling Wally, he could have used threats against Jake and Ella as leverage over her, just as he had used Wally as leverage over Tiger.

Pretty smart for a dead man.

"So, the new lead?" Ella asked. She switched off the TV, and both she and Jake focused on Wally. "Did you find what you were looking for?"

Good question. Had she? She'd found Tiger, but he was gone again. She'd found Kyle, but he was gone forever. Part of her wanted to tell it all now, to share the dark memory of it with her best friends. But she wasn't ready.

"Can I answer that later?"

"No problem," Ella said, rising from the couch. "There's something else, anyway. Don't move."

Ella went to the door of the apartment—still in her pajamas—opened it, and stepped outside. Confused, Wally glanced at Jake for an explanation.

"It'll be fine," Jake told her with a grin, refusing to say more.

In less than a minute, the sounds of several pairs of feet could be heard approaching from the hallway, and Ella finally entered, bringing January and Bea with her. The two of them looked very nervous—and sad. Wally felt a surge of anger at the sight of them.

"You—" Wally began, taking a step toward them, but Ella stepped in between them.

"Hold it a second," Ella said, cutting her off. "Hear them out."

From the expression on Ella's face, it was obvious that she herself—enraged and vengeful just a few days before—had changed her thinking somehow.

"Hear *what*?"

"Wally," January began, looking and sounding ashamed and full of regret, "we are SO sorry—"

"Tell me why you would do that! You kept track of me for some *stranger!* If you knew what I've been through over the past few days—"

"Wait," Ella cut in. "Wally, what happened? You said everything was good…"

"I lied."

"We can see why it looks like we did that," Bea interjected, "like we were spying on you or something. But it was just a club thing."

"A club thing? What does that even mean?"

"This guy approached us at a club downtown," January said, "about a month ago. Big guy, Southern accent. Said his name was Norton."

"Norton Freud Queely, to be accurate," Jake added. "Remember him?"

World's most memorable name, thought Wally. Who could forget? It was the man Wally had known as Alabama, RIH (*Rest in Hell*).

"He said his job was club promotions," Bea said. "He offered us ten dollars a head for every one of our girlfriends we could bring to any club he was repping. You know how we're scraping by, Wally. We don't earn shit at the coffee bar and we have all these bills—"

"*And* an addiction to expensive clothing," January added, clearly hoping to lighten things up.

"We're trying to save money for school," Bea said. "So this

was a great chance for us. We would have just told you that we were getting paid, but it was kind of embarrassing—like maybe we were using our friends for profit. Which I guess we were."

"You got ten dollars a head for *any* of your friends?" Wally asked.

"He never mentioned you at all," January said. "But thinking about it in hindsight, if he'd been watching you or whatever, he'd know that you would be someone we would definitely bring out with us because we'd become such good friends." January's voice trailed off as she began to tear up. "Which we really are, Wally. You're not like . . . I mean, you're different from our other friends."

"And you're our neighbor," Bea added, holding back tears. "Having you upstairs has been really cool. It sounds like we really screwed up, and the idea that we helped this guy hurt you makes us sick. If you can't forgive us, we'll understand, but we hope you will."

Bea was too emotional to say any more, and Wally suddenly felt the impulse to comfort the two of them instead of the other way around. She looked to Ella and Jake, who had been on the warpath against these girls, and they nodded, obviously convinced. Wally took a deep breath and exhaled, willing herself to let it all go. She had a good example in Ella and Jake, who had forgiven Wally unconditionally for the chaos she had created in their lives just last year.

"I'll get over it," Wally said.

"Group hug," Ella said, and the four girls came together, wrapping each other up tight.

Tears were spilling hard now from January and Bea. Wally could feel herself getting choked up too. Jake got up off the couch to join them, a sneaky look crossing his face as he tried to squeeze in between January and Bea.

"Don't even think it," Ella warned him off.

37.

SUNDAY WAS RECOVERY TIME. WALLY, JAKE, AND ELLA shuffled around the apartment like zombies—they took a series of naps, interspersed with a lot of snacking and some Scrabble, plus Jake and Ella took a few trips outside the apartment to do shopping and run errands. For Wally, the time was mostly spent trying not to think about the fact that her best friends would be leaving the next day for Neversink Farm. After months living alone, she'd grown used to having them around, and she dreaded the inevitable loneliness that would follow.

Two things happened that afternoon to lift her spirits. At around three o'clock a courier knocked on the door and handed over a small rectangular box with her name on it. Inside, she found five hundred professionally made business cards. The Ursula Society insignia was embossed on the top of the cards, with all the important contact information running along the bottom. In the middle, the cards read "Wallis Stoneman—Case Agent." A note in Lewis Jordan's formal handwriting was attached: *Don't get cocky. You still have a few thousand case files to digitize.*

It made Wally feel good, and helped her realize that what she really needed to do was get back to work at the Ursula Society first thing Monday morning.

The second good surprise came after yet another dinner of delivery pizza, demanded by Jake and Ella as their "last supper." Wally sat down to check all her online accounts and found an e-mail from someone named Steven Mores. The message read: **It was nice to catch up with you. I'll be in touch, or you can reach me at this email address.**

Who had she recently caught up with? She searched her memory, but couldn't figure it out. She starting writing a response e-mail designed to sniff out the personal information of Steven Mores, but then she saw it: Steven Mores. S. Mores. S'mores.

Tiger was reaching out to her anonymously in case her accounts were being monitored by the authorities, who would still be searching for him. Did his choice of an e-mail handle count as a joke from her stoic brother? *Wow*, Wally thought. *First time for everything.*

Wally wrote back: **It was nice seeing you again, as well, Mr. Mores. It had been far too long. I hope we're able to meet again soon. Be sure to reach me at this address the next time you're in the area. Highest regards, Wallis Stoneman.**

Connection made. The moment filled Wally with a sense of optimism that she hadn't felt in a while. She went back to the couch and snuggled up next to Jake and Ella. At some point, she drifted off to sleep.

Early the next morning, Wally heard Jake and Ella hustling

quietly around the apartment and whispering to each other. Still dog-tired, she wrapped herself more tightly in her blanket and continued sleeping. In a half-waking dream, she saw herself asleep on the couch, Jake and Ella leaning carefully over her and each giving her a kiss on the cheek. When she finally woke, her friends were gone. It was no surprise, really—Jake and Ella hated goodbyes as much as she did.

Wally got up and made coffee and a bagel for herself, trying not to think about how much she already missed her friends, or about the empty pit in her stomach that their departure had left her to cope with. It was a bright and sunny morning outside, and she decided to eat on her rooftop deck. She picked up Tevin's terrarium and carried it out with her, figuring the snapper could use some fresh air.

That's when Wally realized something was different on the roof. It took her a moment to figure it out, but she finally noticed that the dozen or so bags of planting soil she had bought were gone. The planter boxes that lined the edge of the roof—empty before—were now full of the soil, and each box now featured colorful paper markers—seed envelopes—fastened to little wooden stakes, identifying the species planted there and giving watering instructions.

Wally thought back to the "errands" that Ella and Jake had run the day before, and along with her frequent naps that would have given her friends time to do their secret gardening. She herself had struggled to choose what sort of seeds to plant in her rooftop garden, so she was interested to see what Ella and Jake had chosen for her. The markers told her that the plants alternated between vegetables and flowers, all the way around the roof. Vegetables and flowers, a measured combination of the practical and the aesthetic. She could live with that. Attached to one of the wooden stakes was a note in Ella's handwriting.

We already miss you, Wally, the note read. *Take care of these, and we'll be back before long to make a salad. Love, Jake and Ella.*

Wally sat back down with the turtle and placed a few bits of bagel on the little island in the center of his terrarium.

"I guess it's just the two of us now," she said. The snapper responded by staring up at her blankly. *Maybe I should get a cat or something*, Wally thought. And at that moment came a loud knocking at her apartment door.

Wally left the turtle behind and walked to the door.

"Who is it?" she called, her voice wary.

"Wallis? This is Special Agent Bill Horst. We met some months ago."

Bill Horst... he was Greer's friend in the FBI. Horst was the agent who had "debriefed" Wally after the events at Shelter Island. He had been a nice enough person at that time, but before she opened the door, Wally reminded herself that almost every law enforcement agency in the country had her brother Tiger on their fugitive list, so she would have to be careful about what she said.

When Wally opened the door, she quickly found out that

Horst was not alone. He entered the apartment first: a stocky blond man of forty-five in a standard gray G-man suit. He was followed by five other agents of various descriptions, including an intense-looking female agent dressed in a black tactical suit with body armor and carrying a long sniper rifle. As Horst guided Wally away from the open door, the other feds scattered throughout her apartment. One agent sat down at Wally's laptop and began working the keyboard.

"Hey!" Wally objected. "You can't—"

But Horst gently held Wally back and handed her a piece of paper. A quick glance told her that it was a federal search warrant.

"It's a warrant," he said, "but try to relax, Wallis. We're not here for you."

Shit. They were already coming for Tiger? Wally wondered what information they had heard about the violence in New Jersey. She saw that one of the agents was now connecting some devices to her landline phone jack, while the sniper was now just outside on the rooftop deck, standing tall in a rigid shooting position as she scanned the neighboring rooftops through her powerful riflescope.

"Who are you after?" she asked, dreading the answer.

Horst reached into a valise and pulled out a photograph. It was a mug shot of a middle-aged man in an orange prison jumpsuit, unshaven and with the appearance of a caged psychopath—which he was. Though his condition was not good, he stared defiantly into the camera with a monomaniacal intensity that Wally had experienced firsthand.

Ochee chornya. Dark eyes. Like hers.

"Can you confirm the identity of this man?" Horst asked.

"That's Alexei Klesko, my father."

"Have you had any contact with this man in the past two weeks?"

Contact with Klesko? Not possible. The man had survived the gunshot wounds he'd sustained on Shelter Island, four months earlier, but the word was that because he had intimate knowledge of the black-market weapons trade in Eastern Europe and other regions, he had been kept in federal custody and moved to a secret detention facility overseas for "questioning." They called it "Extraordinary Rendition," and it was generally considered to be a dark abyss from which few prisoners ever returned.

"You're looking for him in the wrong place," Wally said, trying not to betray the sense of uneasiness she was beginning to feel. "Your spook buddies have him in a hole somewhere."

"Yeah, well..." Horst hesitated. "Two weeks ago, Klesko was taken out of custody and brought into the field. He was to be our bona fides for a deal in the Sudan, the details of which I can't share."

Shit. Wally knew Klesko and had no doubt where this story was headed.

"In the course of the operation," Horst went on, looking more than a little embarrassed, "Klesko escaped from our custody."

Of course he did. Wally's blood began to race.

"The most positive thing we have going for us is good intel about where he's headed," Horst continued. "We'll be ready—and in full force—when he pokes his head up."

"And that destination would be?"

"Here. At this point, we're not entirely sure why—"

"What do you mean, here?"

Horst paused and looked Wally straight in the eye.

"I mean here, Wallis. Klesko is coming for you."

ACKNOWLEDGMENTS

My most sincere thanks to Ben Schrank, Anne Heltzel, Caroline Donofrio, Jessica Shoffel, and all the folks at Razorbill/Penguin. Kari Stuart, Robert Lazar, and the ICM team have been in my corner all along, for which I will always be grateful. My sources of personal support—spiritual, psychological and otherwise—are legion, including Peter Maduro, Hailyn Chen, Leslie Rainer, Arlen Heginbotham, Sandy Kroopf, Lisa Bromwell, Jon and Margot Healey, David Sanger, Elizabeth McQueen, Kevin and Dagmar Gorman, Dave and Tracy Story, Kate Story, Fiona Story, Naomi Miller-Altuner, Kezia Miller, Bill Martin, Peyton Reed, Mark and Katie Cowen, Rick Hays, Chris Meyer, Susannah Grant, Roxanna Badin, Jodie Burke, Vera Blasi, Geoffrey Sturr, Marischa Slusarski, Ricardo Mestres, Brian Tudor, Andy Day, Lisa Rosen, Diana Mason, Nan Donlin, Nina Frank, Steven Rapkin, and, of course, the Shaw Girls.